WHEN THE GAMES HAD ENDED,
HER ONLY CHANCE HAD JUST BEGAN.

WHEN THE GAMES HAD ENDED,
HER ONLY CHANCE HAD JUST BEGAN.

A ROMANCE NOVEL BY

PATTI WITTER

iUniverse, Inc.
Bloomington

WHEN THE GAMES HAD ENDED,
HER ONLY CHANCE HAD JUST BEGAN.

iUniverse books may be ordered through booksellers or by contacting:

iUniverse
1663 Liberty Drive
Bloomington, IN 47403
www.iuniverse.com
1-800-Authors (1-800-288-4677)

ISBN: 978-1-4620-6028-3 (sc)
ISBN: 978-1-4620-6029-0 (ebk)

Printed in the United States of America

iUniverse rev. date: 11/28/2011

I wrote this novel in 1994, in 1997, I lengthen it to what I feel is the perfect romance novel, with hot, steamy, love scenes.

I would very much like to dedicate to the disables men, women, and children that was abused, sterilized, sedated, and killed by the Nazis, then and now. With Mexico supplying the fuel, the Nazis shot, gassed, poisoned, starved to death, and gave the lethal injection to 250,000 to 300,000 hundreds-thousands physical and mental disables, and the mental ill.

To bred a better white race, I don't believe it, it was just like when any dictator, king, or queen takes over a country, they steal from the poor to be rich, and they would kill on a whim.

Saddam Hussein knew, if you force pregnant women to breathe tear gas, that their babies will be born with disabilities. How long have they known about it?

After the Nazis killed the disables, they cut the bodies up, and sent parts to labs. I just can't see the Nazis doing this for the good of man kind, I just can't. Either, it was done for money, or it was done to find out what cause the disabilities to cause more people to have them. Because, it was too much work for the Nazis to do, if there wasn't something in for them.

From what I have read, they believe that Nazism began in America, and I believe that, too. I had have a Nazis cult and their allies after me, before I was even born with Cerebral Palsy, or it was cause by accident at birth. So, when I tell you it would had been too much work, if there wasn't something in for them, you can believe me.

You will notice that I call them Nazis, and not Germans. I like to think that Germany was just the first country that Nazis took over, and the reason for that is, my mother's mother was full German, born in the German's territory of Texas in 1895. Elizabeth Boenig married Henry Howell, I don't know if Grandpa Henry was German or not.

I know that the rumor probably is that they was Nazis, but I believe it was the Nazis and their allies that killed two of their four children.

It was one day at the breakfast table, when everyone had left, but Mama, Granny Howell, and me. What started it was when Granny told Mama, how much I look like Lorine. She told Mama that she and Henry had hope that her and the other children was too young to remember what had happen to their little girl, but she guess that Bud (my daddy)or someone else have tell you. And my mama nodded.

But, Granny told her all about what had happen, Lorine had caught them going through her mother's and father's things, she told them. And Granny said her and Grandpa went to talk to a attorney in Gonzales, Texas, she said that she felt like the only thing that they did, was to get the little girl raped, and beaten to death by a black man.

Granny said that it took a lot of talking to stop Grandpa from killing the black man right then and there, but they finally got him on the way to the law. But, a man talked to Grandpa before he made it to the law, the man told Grandpa not to put Granny through a trial, that they would make right. Granny said when Grandpa got back home, he ran all of the black people off of the place.

We have pictures of Lorine in what looks like a Halloween school play, probably token days before she was killed in November 1930, she was twelve years old.

Years later, my mama was looking out the window of the attorney's office in Gonzales, where she worked to see a white man arguing with a black man, and the white man pull out a gun and shot the black man.

Granny said that she guess it was a good thing that Bud knew, too. Or my mama would have reported it to the law, and it might have get trace back to Henry. She told my mama that she wished she would have let Grandpa kill that black man that day, then maybe they wouldn't lost their little boy, James.

Granny didn't call his name, but my mama did later. All Granny said was that boy of his, went up to James, and told him that he was glad that happen to Lorine, that she got what she deserve for lying those people.

2

Just recently, I started hearing that they told James, that it was his fault, because he let the black man hid in what he thought was a game of hide and seek, he would had 4 been years old, when it happen.

Granny and Mama both said that it broke little James's heart, he die of pneumonia, he was six years old in 1932. But, they never mention anything about what I have heard recently, either those people wanted to hurt that little boy, really bad, and lied. Or Granny and Mama didn't know about it.

Mama said that they thought that someone was poisoning him, but they couldn't figure how they was doing it, or how they was getting to him.

My mama said that my Granny used to write beautiful stories, Granny told mama, that she used to have more time before the other children came along, not because Lorine was her favorite. Granny said that man's son was coming here as law, so he could stop any help, if any one of us try get to, like Henry did. Granny said that they needed to watch out for me, but she didn't know if it would do any good as bad as he was.

Mama didn't remember what happen to Lorine until one night she started yelling that was a black man hiding in the room, Daddy said, he look everywhere, and he couldn't find a black man anywhere. My daddy had a sense of humor, and they didn't tell us what really had happen.

My daddy's family was from England. The first Witter was a doctor, that they found in Texas was killed by the Indians after making a house call. My daddy, Chester Lowell "Bud" Witter's grandfather and grand uncle went on a cattle drive up the Chisholm Trail, and there seems to be a problem over who really discover the Chisholm Trail.

Now, this is just something that I just pick up on, John Chisholm had children by a black slave, and his wife wanted him to give the honor of finding the trail to some other fellow.

3

The one, who is suppose to have discover the trail is a part Indian fellow, and that is probably why the Mexican Nazis had been after me, too. It goes back that far, at least that far.

I was in my first year of High School, in art class, my teacher was a Mexican coach, and he gave a assignment to write ads. And I did noticed that cheer leader's cheers started sounding my ad, and they got a Mexican cheer leader, but it wasn't like they had broke into my home, but that came later, or me finding out about it would come, later. And I feel sorry for them all, at the time.

I don't know if the man's son had came here as law that year or not, but it was close. And he was here, when my mama and Granny die, a few months apart. Before she die, my mama told me, he was here, and her and my granny wasn't going to be able to be here for me, that it had already started happening to me, and he was here to cover it up for them. My mama and granny die in 1979.

I didn't remember what my mama had told me, but I had this feeling like I needed to leave here, but I really didn't know why. I didn't really feel good, so I went with my daddy to feed cattle and horses, and at that time he haul wood, too.

I heard songs with the sound of my ad, but what could I do? I should have done something, because they stole two of my stories that I wrote as a kid. About that time, I was offer fifty thousand dollars for my pet mare, Four Cricketts, and I turned it down. I just couldn't understand selling her, after we had have her for so long, after what she had been thorough. Sale her?

One Christmas day in the '60s, this man came to my daddy, and told him, how his prize cutting mare had been caught in a fence, he was afraid that her leg was broken, but if my daddy could save her, she was my daddy. Daddy gave her to me, and let me ride her the next Christmas.

On April 23, 1982, Four Cricketts had Cricketts Rose, a beautiful filly, and I was told she was worth seventy-five thousand dollars. In

July of 1982, we lost Four Cricketts to a cut in her stomach's lining, a rupture.

I was bouncing off of walls, and Cricketts Rose was bouncing off of the fences. If I would have knew that someone had viciously killed Four Cricketts, I don't know what I would have done, but I did know that something wasn't right somewhere. She was two months old, and she wanted her mama, she didn't know anything about Nazis being in with the Mexicans, she didn't know anything about John Chisholm, and why he had done it, she just wanted her mama.

In the spring of 1985, I started writing my first novel entitled "A FIGHTING CHANCE" with a pencil and note book, by that time, we had Red in with Cricketts Rose. Red was a calm nature, gelding, and Cricketts Rose adored him, as anyone with good sense would. The novel was about them, and for them.

For my birthday, September 16, 1985, my sister brought me a electric typewriter, and boy, I was in business, or I thought that I was.

In either October or November of 1985, we find out why I didn't feel, or at least, we thought it was low-blood pressure, the doctor gave me medicine, and I started feeling better.

Writing was perfect for me, I could spend time with the horses, go with Daddy, by then it was horses, cattle, and tending to oil wells, both for his self, and for pay. And I could write, even if it didn't ever sale, it was mine. It was my hope to support myself and the horses, to give them the life that they deserves. And it didn't cost much to try.

Don't get me wrong, they was loved, adored, and spoil. But, they wanted the fine things in life. And I wanted to gave it to them.

And one of the things, that I did wrong, was at twenty-nine year old, I wrote a TV and movie star a love letter, and I thought he was just awesome. I remember thinking, it was so harmless, it would end up in a trash bin, somewhere in L.A., California, and the worst thing that could happen was, he could take me up on the offer, and I was prepare for the worst. I have my daddy's sense of humor.

In December of 1987, I got my first computer, up until then, I have been working on my novel, and wrote a few short stories. I started writing songs, and turned a idea for a short story into a episode for his TV show. I don't know it at the time, but the people with the show go back to the Nazis, or the last name does.

The network change a few things about the episode, and made a series out of it, and the songs were stolen. Since then, I have heard that the black and the Mexican people laughed at people, who bought horses from my daddy, telling them that they could steal all they wanted. And the deals that they knock my daddy out of.

I can remember, when I was little, my daddy coming in after a day of working in peanuts or baling hay, and he would eat, used his breathing medicine, going to bed, and getting up the next morning, and go, again.

So, I could heard them saying that about my work, and the Nazis people eat that kind of stuff up. I knew that they were stealing it from here, why I didn't do something about it? Like what? Go to the law? I honestly don't think it would have done any good, move?

My daddy used to tell people, that barn was a hundred years old, because his father told him, this house that we still live in, my daddy built it his self in 1948, and the red two story barn, I just can't remember when he built it. Move?

All I could by myself, was to stay in Austin five days a week for job training, and write at night. If it was just something going on around here, then that would solve it.

But, before I could get it done, I got this awful feeling that I was going to lose Cricketts Rose and Red, and I couldn't think how to get them away here fast enough. I just couldn't think.

In May of 1991, Red started looking like we were starving him to death, we had every test done the veterinarian wanted to do, he couldn't find anything, or at least not that he told us about. We lost Red.

In June of 1991, we lost my daddy's little, Shorty dog. We have had Shorty ever since '77, when my daddy was driving on a gravel road, and thought he heard something, so when he stopped at a stop sign, he open the door, and two little black dogs jump in, hop on the seat, and looked at him like they were ready to go.

In August of 1991, we found Cricketts Rose with what we call founder, by September of 1991, she much better. On the night of September 28, I went to check on her, and found her crawling around on her two front knees, she was frantic, and I was, too. She die the next day of what the veterinarian said was a heart attack. I never did figure out why she couldn't get up.

I went on with the job training, staying in Austin, Monday through Friday and coming home on the weekend. The only thing the job training did was to take away my low-blood pressure medicine, with some claims that the doctor never heard of. I change job program.

And in the late '90's, they found a ring of thieves stealing from the disables at the job training place, but in California. Four white, sisters run the ring. It was on a TV news program.

My apartment's manger was from California, and they had a Mexican handy man. The Bad ending law man had a wife working in the Austin's law, but I did try.

I think that they thought I really believe the romance fiction I wrote, and if the cult could take away any man that I like, they could get away with everything that had been stolen. And you wouldn't believe who some of the men turn out to be, but it is how they got to be who they are, I am sure. I do believe in the romantic fiction that I wrote, and hope to write, again, but I had a feeling that whoever was after was so bad, that all of that was gone for me.

Anyway, I kind of knew if I said everything to one of them, there would be something about me or my Cerebral Palsy that would make them back up, but even I didn't know it was all with a criminal intention, until the stealing had began.

I don't know how they abuse gay people, but I do know how they abuse people like me, they call people like me gay as a part of their sterilize. They used hidden cameras and bugs to get me to move out, because they wanted to crushed me. Just recently, one Nazis woman got this Nazis man that they thought I would like to meet, to take her on a trip to Australia, so they could do a Kimberly and Chance love scene. They just knew it was going to crush me, but I already knew he wouldn't be anything, but a royal pain.

I must admit I did cried for years, to have so many cruel and mean people after you, you would cry, and cry, and cry, but you have got to go on. And they are sadistic, they loved it when they can make you cried. I think it is the only way that they can enjoy sex, if they are hurting someone else.

I did get a job working for the state of Texas in January of 1995, I drove forty-two miles one way, and then I would do some driving after I got to work, and then forty-two miles back. Not bad, for someone that didn't drive five miles into town for chocolate bars, but once or twice a month. Or at least, I didn't think so.

By then, I had a apartment in town, I know it wouldn't do any good, it was just easy to get up and leave the apartment for work, instead of the country. But, in October of '95, I started living in a mobile home beside my daddy and my sister. I called it a big, bedroom, which is what it was.

I resign my job after seventeen months, the job was something I had to try, but I wasn't sure how long I could do it, that is one reason I never wanted to spend money on college. I didn't leave my home, because I wanted to, I want to get away from the hidden cameras, and listen wires.

Three hundred and fifty dollars was what the private eye wanted to come check the house in 1990, and why I didn't bring him home that day, I don't remember, in less, I just didn't have the money. If I could ever caught them by myself, that was it.

But, I was on SSI, and that was probably my whole month's check right there. So, in '96, I decided if I have to fight it, I would rather be here.

And I also figured out that they had been stealing my daddy's horses and cattle. I think he knew, but he couldn't figure out how, or maybe he had. I figure it out, and I also figure out that they trying to get my daddy into trouble, that way, nobody would feel bad for him, and turn them in.

They tried to get my daddy for animal abuse, and the best I could figure out, they were stealing the feed after we would leave the places, and poison the animals. Daddy got the feed bills.

They tried to used me to get my daddy in trouble. It was in '92, while I was in job training, they reported him for molesting me, which wasn't true. But, before I lost Cricketts Rose, I was going to fight with all my might.

And I did, there was just one little teensy weensy problem, I didn't know what in the hell, I was needed to be fighting. The only thing I could see was my two brothers was moving a trailer home in on the back side. We went around and around and around about that. I think they thought that I would so mad at him, that I would have lie to get back at him. It was one of the cheers leader's mother that reported him.

But, I wasn't. I just had to find another to make a living, and I just couldn't do in time to save Cricketts Rose. But, I was going to find out what and who had happen to her.

My daddy thought that they would go after his dogs, every time someone would put one out on our road, and it found it way here, my daddy thought it had found home. He told me, he just didn't want one of them to get hurt, and laid somewhere suffering until it die. But, he never thought that they would came after me, that is what he told my sister.

After I had resigned my job, I made a deal with my daddy, I would work with one or two horses at time to sale, he would get part of the money, and the rest would go for feed. My daddy had a lot of horses, and I knew it wasn't going to help a lot, but I was thinking it was a start.

And I tried writing, again, the stealing was even worst, but I wrote a few short stories, I rewrote this novel, and put all of "A FIGHTING CHANCE" on computer.

In '98, we lost one of my brother to a heart attack, he was fifty year old. By that time, I realized it wasn't my brothers that I was mad at, and fighting with, it was the cult behind them. We was getting along better than we had in years.

In '99, I had the connection between what was happen to my animals, and who was stealing my work. I lost Jake, Cricketts Rose's half brother, a beautiful stallion with a big, beautiful heart. They took more time with Jake, he grew weaker over time, and poorer.

I had them, but I had sold my pickup, as soon after I resign my job as I as I could to stop the payments that I couldn't afford, any more. Which meant I had borrow a pickup, which meant the only law, I could get to was the one that hated me, so much. I couldn't remember what mama and granny had talked about, but I knew that Bad ending law man hated me.

And it did about as much good as I thought it would, the only way I could live with it, is I told myself, he couldn't stand there and say that he didn't know anything about it. And I think that is why he was voted out of his job.

I tried lawyers, and I regretted that I gave one or two of them more time, and the one that I did, said that they wasn't interested in handling it for me, but later I knew why, his name was connect to one of the TV project that come from my work.

10

So, after that I really couldn't afford looking for any more lawyers, I starting mailing a report to the Federal law outside of Texas. I wrote it as a racist, and I will tell you why. Because, they started a rumor that my daddy was a racist, and the best I could tell, they thought I started because one of a character in one of my novel was a little bit racist, and what made me so mad, because the only way that anyone could have known about it is if they were the ones that was stealing my work.

And to think that they was going to hurt my daddy with it. I had to do something, it was just another way to hurt my daddy. And I always thought that law abiding people have rights, especially when they don't steal, and abused my animals, or me. Oh, I think those people should have all the rights in the world.

At first, I waited a few months to hear something, and when I didn't. I figure they were bad enough to be picking it out of the mail.

My daddy die on February 1, 2002. A heart attack, he was 80 years old.

We had to let daddy's dogs go to the humane department, they could only take a few at time. We couldn't afford to keep them all, but we did kept the five that daddy was keeping with him before he die. Bubba, B.B., L.B., Pretty & Smart, and Pretty & Sweet.

The horses that could have pay off the debts, the price fall down so far, because they wanted to stop the sale of horse meat. My mama and daddy used to butcher hogs for the meat. Believe me, the hogs didn't suffer, I know that they didn't, because mama and daddy wouldn't done it, if the hogs would had suffer.

So, here I was, couldn't get the law to stop the cult from causing my animals to suffer, but the law could stop us from getting a decent price for the horses. Something just isn't right, it just not.

I keep adding to the report, and mailing it out. While I was writing the report, I starting remembering stuff, like the time, my daddy was in town, I had the lights out in the front room, when the dogs went to charging toward the road. So, I peep out the window, and sure enough, there was a Mexican woman up at the cattle guard, she looked awful like my granny, at the time, I thought it was the dogs that made her turned back, and me being me, thought the poor Mexican woman need help of some kind. I called my sister at work, she called the law to have someone to check on her, see if something was wrong.

I went to laughing as I remember it, there isn't a bit of telling what that Mexican woman was coming down to do to us. Awhile after that, I am guessing that it was her grandson came down here, park out front, walk around back, got a chicken, and left. I told my daddy, but he didn't do anything. But, when a saddle turned up gone, he called the law, the law caught some black boys stealing off of another place, and the law found the saddle.

See, that is the law used to work, back in the early '80's. Then there was the day, we look down at the pens, and there was three Mexican men looking at the horses. They told daddy, that they were looking for a house with pens, daddy took them where he thought they wanted to go.

I wouldn't try that today, though, they would pull out a gun and shoot you. I think they walked up from the rail road. Today, I think they are running a service like that through our pasture. And why couldn't I remember all of this before I lost Cricketts Rose, Red, and Shorty. I honestly don't know.

But, I can tell you it is awful feeling to lose something like Cricketts Rose and Red, who would want to hurt them, they loved life itself, so beautiful, and so loved.

I see in the news, about all of the teen ages killing themselves. I was lucky, I wasn't abused in High School, or at least not to my face. But, there was this child like Mexican girl in one class that wouldn't leave me alone, but the lady teacher saw what was going, and moved her. There was one girl from my art class, that killed herself. I don't know anything about her, or what happen to her, but now I wonder if she didn't get abuse that was meant for me.

In 2008, I finally found out what happen to Cricketts Rose from a man, who don't even know me, and will say nothing about this again. With that understood, he said that when I plugged in the lights for the barn, there were two of them, they had broken her two front ankles, that is why she never got back up, they left before I could get down there, he said that they finally got it out of the Bad ending law man and his girlfriend. He talked about another horse we had, when my daddy found her, when she was two weeks old with her back leg cut through the bone below her knee, dangling down by a thin piece of skin, he said to remember how little it was swell. And he was right, he also said that they was after her next.

The Bad ending law man's girl friend has a kidnapper and rapist, "it wasn't a Smart thing to do" with her last name, and a 1930's author with her last name, but I guess that's gone with the wind. And the last name has a Mexican connection that goes back to a '60s or '70s western TV show.

In 2008, I lost Lollipop, she lived for ten years with her broke leg. Don't ask me how, but she did. She had heart. I have a lot of regrets about Lollipop, but the biggest is, I didn't hugged her enough.

January of 2007, they killed B.B. with what I am guessing killed a lot of pets that year, but I didn't had the money or a way to get her to a veterinarian, she die in the living room by the fire place. The night that my daddy die, I slept in a chair in the house, and when I woke up the next morning B.B. was laying across my lap, sound asleep.

By the end of 2007, we sold my mama's Home Place, it was the only thing we could do. I self published the short stories in a book entitled "HAPPILY EVER AFTERS, TEXAS STYLE", and put my daddy's horses on my mama's Home Place on the cover, in 2010.

They didn't want it sold anywhere in town, or in book stores, so they got all of that stopped, and a ad that I wanted to run, the fax wasn't answer, not even with a hell no.

I was offer to do two book signings, and I really do appreciate them, but I am a writer, not a PR person, now my daddy, Red, and Shorty could have handle the PR stuff without a problem, but I was thinking about mailing out sign book marks or book covers, that was in '80's.

In 2008, Pretty & Sweet die in the pickup on way to a veterinarian, he did a autopsy on her, it was cancer like my mama had die from in '79.

In 2009, I lost Frankie, a Quarter Horse mare that been with me, Cricketts Rose, and Red since January of '86. She was a half sister to a million race horse, and more importantly, my best bud.

I sent my last report to the Federal law in 2006, I found it under the seat of the minivan park out front in 2007, whether it came back in the mail or someone hand put it there, I don't know. I sent it to a branch of the government in 2007, and that was the last time I sent it, no need to, I doubt whether it left Texas.

In the internet news, I read where they were butchering horses alive for five hundred dollars in Florida. Now, do you want to tell me how these people wouldn't hurt my animals? Do you really want to?

Over the news, one July's night in 2009, came a story about a place few miles down my road, across the county line, some people went out to their automobile, and found a Mexican man without clothes on, asleep in the automobile, they called the law, the law comes, remember it was across the county line. Come to find out, the Mexican man was a illegal alien, who escape from a mobile home, where he and more illegal aliens were being held hostage by two Mexican men with guns. The two were coyotes, people who bring illegal aliens across border for money, but these were holding them for more money, there were three women that they were afraid that these women were being repeated raped.

One of the coyotes name looked like he had kept his mother's maiden name in his last name, it is the last of a CIA agent, or if not a agent, connections to the CIA in New York. I have read how the CIA break people.

14

The same name worked with the married last name of little Mrs. Nazis Australia trip, herself on a TV project stole from my work. And she wanted to take my brother on the trip with them, to get the Witter name connect to them. The people who brought her up, their last name is on the Nazis Party list, with a lot more in the report.

The Bad ending law man's last name was kick out of a music orchestra after being caught in a Nazis conspiracy, and the Bad ending law man has kids, some of them has his name on their birth certificate, and they were brought up just like he was, which is not good for me.

The Bad ending law man has one son, who has a little black boy ready to say that I look like a whore to him. When it gets over ninety degrees in the summer, I wear tube tops and blue jeans, even driving down the road.

Now, you can call me a racist, but they all look Nazis to me. I haven't talk to my two sisters or my brother, about me writing this part of the book to be published, it wasn't their work, animals, or life.

I almost forgot what I think causes they to think that they could pounce on me like that besides the Nazis Bad ending law man, my mama had a brother that Granny had already told her, that he was never right after that happen to their little girl, granny and grandpa had hoped the Army would help him, but Granny thought it had made him worse. Because, after grandpa was found under a tree in the pasture, he was walking, looking for a cow, my daddy said it look like he sit down to rest, but he had a heart attack and die in 1960. I was two years old.

For a while after that granny live with my mama's brother, and his wife in San Antonio, right up until he started beating on her, then my granny called my mama, then she and one of my brothers pull out to get her, and they did. Mama and Granny show my daddy the bruises that my mama's brother had put on my granny. My daddy took them to a attorney the next day, like Granny wanted to do, but the attorney wasn't like my daddy, the attorney wouldn't draw up the papers to put the land in my mama's name. The more I think about it, the more I am sure that he was a Nazis, himself.

And why they didn't just go to another attorney, I don't know, but this was in the middle '60s. My mama's brother's wife was found dead in their apartment in Austin, she was black and blue all over. My mama's uncle told my daddy that some rich friends of my mama's brother had brought my mama's brother out of it.

Now, I don't know whether it was the rich woman Federal judge that end up with one of the places, or the rich, retire Army man, who end up with the other place that my daddy finished paying off for Granny, I don't know.

But, it was a few days before Mother's Day in 1979, and I was in living room, drinking a cola drink, watching TV, when my mama came to the door, and told me that my granny needed paper with lines. My granny had arthritis in her hands, she hadn't written anything for awhile, but she did that day, for my mama. The Monday morning after Mother's Day, my mama told me that the EMS was going to pick Granny up and she was going in the hospital. My mama didn't had a way to go with her, but the doctor was going to be there. And Granny die the next month.

After years, Mama and Daddy had another attorney draw up the papers to put the land in my mama's name, and in 1988, my mama's brother took us to court, got a jury to throw out the papers, and we went back to a will that my mama's brother force Granny to sign, and there was nothing that we could do.

And I know what you are thinking, my granny couldn't sign her name, and my mama did for her to get her on Medicare, and after thirty-one years, I would tell it, or if Granny had changed her mind, I would tell it, now. But, on Cricketts Rose's grave, I swear that my granny did sign her name. The only thing now, is I have a pretty good idea how we were set up.

When Granny told my mama about her son beating her, she said it was almost he blame her for what happen to the little girl. I have a idea that Bad ending law man knew my mama's brother.

If you hear about my granny being abused, I think that they are right, but not by my mama. They found a Mexican man in Mexico, "they called him, the stew maker", who uses poison to get rid of dead bodies, but my granny wasn't dead. That's right, but she was away from my mama for a month in a place that been sue so much. And the Mexican man last name is the same as a Mexican woman, who thinks she is a movie star because she can blackmail her way in to movies with men like the one who connected my work to the animals. I would whisper her name, but you know.

After we lost in court, I guess that they thought that they could do just anything to me, you know, like John Chisholm. As matter of fact, this Mexican clan that is after me, has Indians in Mexico with their last name, who was on trial for killing a San Antonia newspaper's reporter, another one, who raped and murder a twenty-four years old school in San Antonio, and another one who killed a disabled man, and was caught at the bank trying to get the man's money out, and another one who thinks she is a movie star, and another is a "former" member of a Mexican Nazis group, and another one gave Jed Bush a medal in the Army, and one was a TV cook caught trying to hire a homeless man to kill his wife, and a black rap singer with same last name, you can read a ebook with ebook reader with their name on it, they caught one in a burglar ring in Florida, they caught a trailer truck in Mexico hauling illegal aliens, and you can cruise in a new Chevrolet with their name on it.

Hey, ain't that where the Nazis worked, and the black President bail out?

And I will bet that, the Bad ending law man helped this Mexican family get the place where they are now, by using some black people "GOODTIMES".

This family of Mexicans is probably the ones, who hire the black man to raped and beat Lorine to death. Because, of that Bad ending law has them convince that they are suppose to get what's mine.

Well, at least now, we know what kind of people the law will help. Mexican whores that can do 55 men a day, and I am sure those law men check and made sure that was true, even if it took 55 law men to do it.

One of the witness that testify against the Mexican people that bought her over here, was a ringer for the Mexican family that is after me, because she got up there and talk about how she is now enjoying all of the liberties. Get it? They are the ones that are here to take them away from everyone, else, then they sit there and talk about how they enjoy them, and how the law had help them. It is a joke to them, the way that they can fool people in to helping them, while they get to block anyone else from getting help.

And wouldn't you know the law that headed this department for these "special ladies?" has the same last name as a Texas ranch. And I am sure that the black president will legalized them and will find them jobs for their very "special talent". Hollywood always has.

I am sure that the Mexican family that is after me, is trying to take over the whores business, and they are using the law to take out the other people in the business. On the internet news, I read that one woman with their last name was listed on Craig's List as a "Escort" that was in New York with her rapper boyfriend, when she disappear.

As far as the royals goes, maybe the Queen had to watch my mama to learn how to act like a lady, of course, my mama has been dead for awhile, she is forgetting how to act. In early '90, she freaked when a retarded woman hugged her. I guess they meant the one doing the hugging.

I didn't know about Mr. Royal Pain and little Mrs. Australia trip back then, but now I think it might have been her trying to get in good with his kin.

I have read where the author of Peter Pan used to entertain the queen when she was a child, and in the news, they have found a 75 years old trunk owned by a woman with the author last name, in the trunk was two dead babies remains, a Peter Pan book, and I think a picture of herself.

Now, after my granny and grandpa had buried their two children, they put a few things of each child in small trunks, one for each child.

Two of the queen's sons have married women with last names that I went to school with. I guess when you are born and rear to think you are better than everyone else, you are just going need those Nazis gals.

The Duchess of York pimp meetings with her ex-husband for either a quarter or a half of a million, and two percent of the deal, if one was made. Wonder what she would do to her children, and for how much?

Frankie started having trouble around the time a man named Smith from England won the 2007 Belmont Stakes horse race, the horse look like Frankie. But, why hurt Frankie? She was just a sweet, loving horse. But, it is what the Nazis do.

The name Smith had something to do with Cricketts Rose's death, too, and the black President of America goes back to the name Smith.

On the internet news, they was talking about how the royal family take money to be somewhere, I can only image how much, then pay a look alike to lie and pretend to them. I just wonder where Mr. Royal Pain was suppose to be, when he was here sleeping with other men wives.

Now, I bet you are wondering why I hadn't got to a attorney. Well, I have tried. The end of 2007, I started trying, again, one day when I was in Austin, I got so sure that there wasn't one in Texas that could or would help, that I went to the airport to check on flights to other cities. But, I had a bad feeling about being there, I had a Mexican cab driver, and a black woman, who worked at the airport told him, this was the one they wanted to be left alone, now. The next thing I knew, Mrs. Nazis Australia's trip had went to work there.

And after ten years of Lollipop being alive, and well, when the song came out in 2008, Lollipop die. I knew it was coming, but I didn't know how to stop them from killing her, paying a guard that they could pay more? A camera to watch her, I didn't think I have a safe place for the data go.

So, while the song play on, winning awards, and while little Mrs. Nazis Australia's trip and Mr. Royal Pain was on their trip, Lollipop laid dying from what I think was a infection cause by the poison that they eat a deep hole in her hip with. Or they could had cut the hole.

The black man, who sings the song, had been in jail. I think it was the New York city's police got mad because the song mention little Mrs. Nazis Australia's trip first name. And there is a romance writer, that her father was high up in the New York city's police. Air planes, New York City, and 9/11.

I did talk to a attorney, that is in training for another Madoff deal, and he didn't need much more, if any more training. Believe or not, there are connections between the Madoff deal, and what is happening to me, my work, and my animals. If I read it right, it all started with two attorneys, one with the same last name as the coach from High School, maybe not the exact spelling, and one of the men caught in Texas, has the same last name as a country music singer that stole one of the stories that I wrote as child, he even use my first name in the song. All of this is really a Madoff deal.

My daddy had told me, that when we sold my mama home place, and we would have to sale it, because he wouldn't gave us any other choice. I am sure, my daddy meant the Bad ending, and my daddy was right. Abraham Zumwitt was on the deed, and no, I didn't buy a Lincoln, I used that money for a way to a attorney.

Mr. Obama wants to gave these people a "A DREAM ACT", they did get the name right, I have got to admit, they dreams of living like us is a act. Mr. Obama thinks if they smuggle their kids over here, with the rapists, and murders, just go ahead make them legal. Gave them the right vote, and God only knows what or who they will vote in or out. They like abusing people or animals, it gives they a sense of power. And Mr. Obama wants them to be able to join the Army, but who will they be fighting for?

In Mexico, a gang killed 72 people that was coming to America, these people was killed because they wouldn't agree to kill other people, the report said it wasn't clear whether they meant here or in Mexico. But, you can look how the number of them is growing and growing to know which.

The Dream Act. They killed my dream, she die one September night in 1991, a beautiful, Quarter Horse, that never knew why anyone would want to hurt her so much.

Was it the Bad ending Nazis law man, that couldn't stand someone like me own a filly like that. I have heard that while they had her down, he let people who have sex with animals, raped her. They do that in Mexico, too, let people out of prison to kill people. They have a name for people who have sex with animals, and I do, too. I can't tell you what I call it, but it isn't good.

I know that I was on SSI, and couldn't have Cricketts Rose in my name, but I put in the report, I have a bill of sale putting her back in my name, all we had to was to put the date on it, and pay SSI back for that month, and anything else.

I had been told that there a girl, that her parents named her to sound like my name. They already got the old-fashion bath tub, like the one in Grandpa and Granny Howell's house, in the room with Lorine's and James's trunks, and a old barn. The first time I meet them, they had a Mexican boy with the same last name as a romance writer, and the same last name as a Mexican man that was arrest for murder, and one of the family is married to black man, or that is what I been told. I just wonder if he is maybe kin to the black man that raped and beat my aunt to death. It's a cult thing, they steal from someone, and someone else is suppose to came along and make it up to them, but the Nazis got it, now, they just keep stealing and stealing, and give it to the ones, who gave them sexual favors, and pretend like they just got the wrong one.

I read in the news, that they caught a twelve years old boy in Mexico, who was a hit man for one of the gangs, he told them, that he didn't kill the rivals, he killed the innocence ones. They caught him on a plane with his sister, who was a gang leader's girl, and if I remember right, they was headed for America.

I had read in the news about a town in Mexico, where the boys can tell how much money they going to make, by how many sisters they have to pimp.

And while I was made to feel bad about being on SSI and Medicare, I listen to how many Mexican women get pregnant, and running across the border to have the baby, and how much it cost.

And while they used illegal information to make my life so miserable that I would want to kill myself, they worried about not being able go out and enjoy themselves, because the law might be force to do their job, and find out if they are legal or not.

It was in the news about how a group of people was making the mental disable fight each other for the amusement of the staff of a government run home in Texas. One of the ones doing it has the same last name as a Mexican woman who works in my dentist's office. One of the higher ups had the last name as the Bad ending law man's girlfriend.

The best that I can figured out, the politicians love the Mexican prostitutes, and who can get more on the politicians then prostitutes?

No wonder we can't get anything done about them. We can't stop the Mexican prostitutes, they are used to keep the men happy, and while no one is looking, they can steal and kill.

I knew that's how the law around here, works that way, but the whole government is working that way, too.

I notice, it is easier for them to pick on poor people, who can't afford to protect themselves, and when they lose animals, it will look like it is their own fault, and not the cult. When equipment doesn't work, the poor person didn't take good enough care of it, and not the cult messing with it. Anything that they can do to make it harder for a poor person, they will do, they did it against my daddy and us. You see, my grandma Witter wanted to do for daddy that my granny Howell did for my mama. And she did, but my daddy's sisters, and a nephew wanted to go to court about it I wrote my aunt a nasty letter about calling my mama's brother in on us. I can't spell good on my good days, much less, when I am mad and hurt, but any ways, I just found out today, it cause they to hire someone to stay with her, which wasn't a bad thing, any ways, with her calling men who used to beat their mothers.

So, I wasn't too surprise to see my aunts at the grave yard, one day, with one of the cult member, who been trying to hurt me, so bad, that I would kill myself, with them, make up to look like a black woman, who, I guess, is the one that they hire, twenty something years ago.

Believe me, I do know how it sounds, but it was in the news, how they caught a young man made up like a older man at a airport, a group hire to kill a man in another country using the same tactics as the people after me. Plus, they make most of the money in show business.

And the other aunt has a Mexican married to her grandson. Enough said.

I have heard about a nineteen year old girl, who was arrested for a open container, drugs, and a baby in her automobile, she got off with calling it a illegal search, the next time, they arrested her, they added, money laundering. Now, I don't what they call it, when she got out of that, but I call it, having something on someone.

When I notice what was going on, one of my sister wanted me to move a portable building in by Cricketts Rose's, Red's, and Frankie's barn, and I do wish I would had, and I wish I would have locked my work up, but they would had stole in the mail. But, I wish that I would have stay and kept writing, just locked it up. I have heard they can pick a lock faster than most of us can used a key.

But, I was sure that I had to get Cricketts Rose away from here to save her, and I couldn't do it. I have heard that they says sometimes that is the only way they can steal things is to kill it.

I thought if I could had just protect myself, the animals, and my writing better, I could had got help to catch and stop them, then I could stay at home and write. I wouldn't think that anyone would help catch and stop them now, though. These people are a cult, the cult that not only was with Hitler and the Nazis, these people are the ones that started it. The Nazis of all the Nationalizes play with each other, it was never about race. That was just a front, I truly believed.

How do I know that these are the same ones, because while I looking at the news reports and articles on the internet, I came across a picture of a Russia man who was called mental ill, his face was what I call changing. I am not sure how they do it, maybe with dope, or poison, but they sure can do it. They caused his problem, and then probably killed him for having it.

They can't wait to I have a hump back, and my eyes are covered with cataracts, and no doubt, they can causes it, too. The hump back, I think it cause or help along with depressants. Sometimes, I can catch myself, but I can only imaged it is all of the times, that I don't catch myself that will be what get me, though.

We lost L.B. in November of 2010, he came to Daddy just a couple months before Daddy die, he was putting round bales of hay in the back. L.B. had a paralyzed back leg, a pot belly, and he was just a couple months old, but when he sat down behind a chair in the living room, one day, and went to howling and barking with Bubba and B.B., he was just about the cutest thing you ever saw. It was his heart, he retrain fluid. Because, I didn't get the heart worm medicine, even if I knew how important it was, I don't know if I could had afford it. Even though, Shorty lived to 14 with them, and they was already talking how L.B. was going to be next, I still wished I would have gotten the pills.

Even if I couldn't afford it every month, maybe three times a year would had help. Why didn't I get it for them after I had sold land? Believe me, I have thought a lot about it, and I do mean a lot. It is the same mistake I made with Frankie, I was waiting for to get some help to get her to a veterinarian. L.B. was afraid of people, he would find a place to hide when someone was even just on the place. He survived rattle snake bites, and while he was afraid of most people, he sit down in front of me, so I could hugged him around the neck.

L.B. spent his last day with the veterinarian, so they could keep him comfortable.

And while the black President is telling us, we can't afford the border fence, I am trying to put up cameras to help protect the animals. Will I ever be able to them to work? And before they hurt the next one, all I can do is try. Maybe, before this novel is published or before the next one, I will know. I have one camera up, now, that is suppose to record even the computer isn't on. Cross your fingers.

As far as the bad ending law man, and his cult of bitches goes, they are still taking their mental and emotional punches at me. They seems to thinks if they can get someone to said something mean, and hurtful about me, or take part in their Nazis games against me, they can get away with every law that they have broken, and every cruel, abusive thing that they had ever done. Now, why, I don't know. Maybe, it is the money that goes in the police, the District Attorneys, and Judges pockets.

But, I did pick up on that, while I was working on the report, it was like the black man taking punches on my little Aunt Lorine, if I would kill myself, they could say that they had beaten me to death and nobody could do anything about it.

The punches that I know about it is . . .

The Bowl of Cherries fellow that used to work for my daddy, he is a few years older than me, he was good-looking, seems very nice, and he knew how to act. We rode my daddy horses together, I have pick up on that he started a rumor that I was with child, and he was definitely not the father. And I definitely want you to know if there was the chance that I was with child, there was no way it was his. I was having trouble bloating, it was during my High school years, and I would wear stuff that didn't really fit, pouching jeans that I don't remember where they came from. Clothes cost too much for us to be picky, or at least not to wear around home.

Another one of the Bowl of Cherries fellow's punches were, he felt sorry for me, that is why he was nice to me. Well, the disables get that a lot, it's a easy punch. But, not true in this case, it was because he knew of, if not in on these people stealing horses and cattle from my daddy, and he knew about my little Aunt Lorine.

He was friends with the sons of some people that my parents knew, too. The name would put holes in your ears. But, any ways, these sons had a wild riding bunch, that rode in the town's parade every year, Bowl of Cherries wanted to ride with them, he was riding my brother's grey stallion, and me on Red, awhile after the parade had started, this girl that I went to High School with, and her brother was riding with them, he had been in jail the night before, I don't know what for, I just hear them laughing about how he got out that morning just in time for the parade. I didn't party with them, me and Red just rode with them. Red loved a parade, and I loved to ride, still do.

This girl, she didn't have warts, jump on the back with Bowl of Cherries, she had a funny looking cigarette with her, and they pass it around, not to me, you will have to understand, and not to the Bad ending law man that was bringing up the end of the parade.

She didn't have warts told Bowl of Cherries not to worry about the Bad ending law man, he had put her up to it, something about horse stealing, he being kin to the sons of the people we was riding with. And all I was thinking what would happen if they impounded the horses? They couldn't get me and Red.

But, now I know, who and what she didn't have warts was talking about, the kin went back to the Chisholm trail days, they called him Shangri, I found him in the trail drivers books. Now, get this, he was all for the part Indian, he also had kin in a town or a county, where a western writer took a pen name from. They tried to gave him the, he always rode a good horse, but it was my dad's grand uncle that started the Quarter Horses.

There is a picture of my dad's grand uncle, and he was my great, grand uncle sating on a horse that look like it was one of Cricketts's great, grand something. In this book, the people that went up the trail wrote about what happen, I remember one was about how they had save a black man from drowning. My daddy used to say that his grand uncle used to worked black cowboys, now if he meant slaves, he didn't say. But, he did say, that his grand uncle had two little boys that drown, Daddy said his grand uncle rode out from here, and the next time they hear of him, he had bought a ranch in LaSalle county in South Texas, where a famous writer was from. My great, grand uncle also rode with The Wild Bill Hitchcock Wild West Show.

And they said that Shangri got that nick name from doing business with China, but it also what they call using dope on other people. That sounds about right.

Anyways, I rode three times with Bowl of Cherries and this bunch of riders in a two years time. The next parade was in another town, and I really regret that I choose to ride on the back of Bowl of Cherries for two reasons, it look like I was taking her place, and the second is, while I rode double all of my life, but most of the time, I got the saddle. So, I didn't know how to ride behind the cantle of the saddle, and when we got back to the ranch, we run and gallop, and had a good time, but the inside of my legs got bruised up. And for these kind of people, that was probably enough to set tongues to wagging.

The next year, we rode in the town's parade, I was on Red, and the only difference was there was a Mexican girl, who was taking care of the son's mother, because she was dying of cancer. The Mexican girl look like she was a member of the family that is after me.

The Bowl of Cherries fellow also work for a country music band at night, there was able Mexican man that played the drums, and I am sure that Bowl of Cherries had a lot more girlfriends than I met, and he had one with that day. He went to work on off shores oil rigs, and as far as I know, he has been married twice, both women had the same last as people in the country music business, but I didn't make the connection until after Cricketts Rose was dead. So, I guess that it was a good thing I couldn't reach Bowl of Cherries, when I was trying to get Cricketts Rose out of here before something could happen to her.

Because, one night, when I was staying in Austin, I went to a baseball game, and I was at my door, when this girl with hair like mine, and a black, western blouse on, just like mine. It had to be kin of Bowl of Cherries wife, because the black blouse goes back to the wild riding bunch, and he might be still married to the second one. I honestly don't know.

She didn't have warts disappeared in the '80's, and in the late '90's, my daddy told me, that they had found a body buried in a oil field, and they thought it was her. I didn't think to find out if it was her, or not. And I don't know if that was the murder that I was investigate as being involve in, or not. But, I will tell you, all I know about it, I was told that last anyone saw her, she was in a car full of black people.

They thought me and Bowl of Cherries look like something from the TV show "THE FACTS OF LIFE". He also made fun of me spending a week in a Rehabilitation hospital for jobs opportunities. But, I still don't know if he got the Rehab that he needed.

You should know they take their punch, then I take mine.

Made in Shade with a glass of cider fellow didn't want to be seen dancing in town with me, and I thought he would be doing the jail house rock with the rest of them. But, he danced his last dance, and die a couple a years ago.

One fellow didn't want his picture took with me, one made fun of the way my arm shakes, they made fun my limp.

The Blew It fellow, hoped I would get my teeth fix before I started hanging around, hoping for a date, that was one that I had done business and had a crush on for 17 years, I, now take my business somewhere else. That is one worry off of his mind, and I had already heard in either '92 or '93 that this was the one, who was going to play nice until I was too old to meet some nice, man and had a child. The man, who was doing the talking, was wondering what his wife was going to say when the Blew It did it, and now I am, too.

I was fifty years old, when I heard what he had said from a about 17 years old dancing around behind the counter. The only reason that I think he made it that long, is because we didn't do that much business together.

The people, you tried to do business with are targets for them. They always think the fellows deserves someone better me. And that's fine, but like I said in the report, it don't gave them the right to steal from me.

Mr. Royal Pain thought that I have been too abused to enjoy anything he could do for me. He got it all wrong, I am not abuser like he is, so I wouldn't enjoy what he does.

Mrs. Nazis Australia's trip called me retard, that is a easy one, but that's the only thing she could do.

And the Bad Ending law man is one punch after another, and these people seems to enjoy telling me about, but this one, about not wanting to have to watched me waddy up to any of their men in town, they got a cowboy poet with his girlfriend's last name. I hate to have to tell him, but I never spend much time in town.

I saw this Bad Ending law man when we were children, he was at a arena with another boy, the other boy grown up to have a hell of career, with stuff stole from me, I knew that it was, because he kept a Mexican with him on a Dailey job basic, he said that it hurt his eyes to look at me. Someone should teach him to turn his head, most learn how when they are baby, but some do have learning problems, and this poor man sound like one.

This is how I know that the cult set up their own children to be used in the cult later on.

And another one of the Bad ending's law man punches, is something about, he just couldn't let me do the other guys like I had done him, so he has to go around protecting them from me. And as bad as I hate to admit it, he is right, I expect them to do what is right, do their job, not to used dope on other people, not to steal, rob, or cheat. If he didn't protect from me, they wouldn't be any use to the cult.

The TV and movies star came to Texas with his then wife, they had a baby in Austin, while they was here, he later married a girl with a name that sound like she is from Texas. Ain't that sweet? But, he did go into rehab, his ex-wife married a Mexican actor, who wants to dances like Bowl of Cherries. But, I kind of knew something, when the TV and movie star came back to TV with a producer with the same last name as one of my daddy rodeo producer buddy, and a writer with a name like that sound like the Mexican family, that is stealing from me, just not spell the same.

One Mexican man compare me going looking at riding horses to a retard person, but that's alright, I bought one on line. And I have been told that the veterinarians thought what I did with the animals look like something like a retard person could do. Well, it's a relief that I don't do what I do for the veterinarians. We can all breathe easier.

But, I did lose one of my kitties, Little Mr. Innocent, and after tests after tests, they could only guess at what killed him.

I have got to get the cameras up.

And I had have about two to make a reacted to my Cerebral Palsy's hand, my right hand mostly. One remark was, they didn't have to worry me running my Cerebral Palsy's hands thorough the Blew It fellow's hair, and that's a fact.

Sound like my name's father had a reaction to shaking my Cerebral Palsy hand. And when I was looking thorough the Nazis stuff on the internet, I did noticed a poster on how ugly Cerebral Palsy person hands was. That's one of things I don't understand, but maybe I just didn't go into it enough. Some of the reports or articles was about how the Nazis lied to the disable's families, and some said that the Nazis waged war on the disabled people like me. They had posters against us, and stuff like that.

Hitler and the Nazis called the disables, now this was in almost every news report and article I read, we were "useless eaters", "life unworthy of life", and "freaks". What do I have to say to that? Right back at you, Nazis, along with mass murders, robbers, kidnappers, rapists, abusers, and just not good people.

Hitler had Doctors that would do whatever he wanted. I really think that is what happen to my blood pressure medicine, if I understand it right, the cult wanted to slow me down, so they could get in my place, or ahead of me. And it is just such of embarrassment to the Bad ending law man, if I did better than his cult whores. I am just guessing, but he probably keeps his head hanging low, or he really should.

And did you know the disabled should be kept feeling bad about themselves, or is so someone else can feel good about themselves. They always want to give my stuff to someone else.

And with the Mexicans, the black people, and the other nationalists using dope, illness, lies, stealing my stuff, and whatever they had to do to hold me down to let Nazis go on. And don't never think they wouldn't do that kind of stuff, as easily as the Mexican cartels uses machine guns. The Mexican cartels are people that stole horses and stuff from my dad and me, and now, they have the Nazis are in with them.

It was said that they used to put me to sleep like they do dogs and cats, now. And that is true, it is also true that my mama and granny used to break the chicken's necks, like they did, when the Nazis were caught and hung. A lot more Nazis men were hung, than women, I only hope this time it will be more even number. Because, those bitches breed.

This is something they have on me, Cerebral Palsy is cause by brain damaged. Yea, but what is their excused for having brain damaged and not having Cerebral Palsy?

And do I think my mama and daddy would have still have me if they would only knew I would turn out? Do you think they mean the Cerebral Palsy, or just in general?

Don't feel bad for those people, because nobody made these people steal from me, nobody made them kill my animals, and nobody made them abused me like they do, to get away with everything they had stole. No Hitler, no army to force them to do it. It was done out of greed by mean and cruel people, and they did it as a cult.

And they didn't know that some people wanted to keep the disables around like pets. And I don't know why we are suppose to legalized a bunch of people, just because they beat the law for so many years.

And it is people like me that is to blame for so many of them, and I don't remember my job with border patrol, or my vote giving them anything.

I have also heard that the Bad ending law man used to tell them that his parents had authorized them to uses so much dope on my mama that I couldn't be nothing, but retard. And if you will look at the cover of my novel "HAPPILY EVER AFTERS, TEXAS STYLE", you can tell what they did to my mama.

And I have also heard, that my mare Frankie was worth a quarter of a million, and to be honest, I have no earthly idea about how much she was worth. She was Frankie, she was worth millions to me.

I have heard, that the Bad ending law man and the Mexicans are telling people not to do things for me, because I will never "put out" for them, and I must say that is the truth. I have always been hard to close to, and the cult did what they was suppose to do, made it impossible, now.

And they say that there is just times when they had to used all of that illegal stuff to get anything on people like me.

I have heard that they was telling the kids in my High school what they was going to do to my mama and granny, so they could go ahead and steal all they wanted to.

Negro means black in Spanish, why do we think it is a bad word? Is it because we connect it with slaves, and why was the word used so much with slaves?

I have heard that there was a black man, that was laughing about how Mr. Royal Pain had done me, about that time the earth quake in Haiti, and I got to thinking, maybe that is what earthquakes are, Satan laughing, and these people have really been keeping him laughing, lately. And one time, he may even show us how they are making us sick, causing cancer, and whatever.

Nazis isn't always white, now you have to understand that.

I finally did get a PI out, and I was right, he couldn't find any bugs, but what I had up. Now, it could be that they gotten the bugs out, or they used theirs close to mine, or this man that look a whole lot like someone I knew a long time ago, wasn't a PI. Was it a Nazis game? Like I was always afraid it would be.

I don't know, if you would have sent those reports out year after year, with the only answers you would get, was when it got sent to a State DA, and not a Federal DA. I even had heard that when I agree to let the law uses what in the report to catch these people, I was giving them my short stories, novels, songs, and whatever. I wrote in this report, and that is all I meant. I might not had put it just like that, but I know that I sure didn't give them my copyrights.

Why would I take a chance on being sue, first they will have to buy the book, which I can't see that happening, and second they will have show themselves in court. Would it be worth losing what is left of what my daddy and mama worked so hard for? You didn't watched Cricketts Rose die, I did.

And why hadn't they kill me, yet? I hear "we can still steal from you", a lot, or is it because they aren't ready to show themselves, yet? But, I saw on the internet news, where the reporters found two Mexican men, who stole children's Social Security Numbers, and made bank loans, and things like that. The reporter said, that it will those people years to straighten it all out, and the Mexican men was working at their jobs.

And in this town, one man beat his Mexican girlfriend to death, and that's another reason that I am publishing this, so when something does

33

happen to me, there will be a chance that someone will know who was behind it.

It has finally happen, I accidentally hurt one of my own animal, Bubba isn't just a dog, you will have to understand, he is a member of the family. The only one around here with any sense, and he will tell you that himself, if he thought you would understand. My sister took him to a veterinarian, he will be fine.

They also got me, where I don't clean up every night, like my Dad didn't, which couldn't been good for his breathing problems. But, we didn't have hot water when I was a kid. My Daddy built this house himself with help in '48, and when the hot water heater went out, they didn't have money to replace it, so Mama heat our water on the stove for dish washing and bathing. And when one of kids got big enough to pack hot water, then they could bathe whenever they want to, but of course, to my mama, I was never that big enough.

It was after she had die, that I would pack pitchers of hot water from the kitchen to the tub in the bathroom. But, my Daddy made a oil deal in the early '80's and we got a new hot water heater, a used washer and dryer. We were in high cotton!

This is something they have on me, in either '71 or '73, we were in a very bad dry spell, so the Government either paid part or all of digging water wells, only for the livestock, not households. The thing is, we used tank water for the house.

Now days, what is the Government worried about? How to legalized a bunch of Mexicans whores. And the men that uses them.

Don't feel bad for these people, they are Narcos, they feel powerful when they can get someone hurt. They are for abuse in any form. I believe what they do to themselves, is nothing to what they will do to people like me, with the Nazis in with them.

My grandpa Witter used to share crop this place, that my Daddy bought, and my grandpa Witter pick crops all the way to California. Not once, did I hear about him killing somebody pets to get his pride back.

My grandpa Witter married my grandma Maggie May Harris-Witter when she was fourteen and he was twenty-four year old, and I am really very happy he did, or they wouldn't had my daddy, and he wouldn't had meet my mama, and they wouldn't had me.

But, I think it got Grandpa Witter the nick name, The Ole Man, and he called Grandma Witter, Mama. And we have heard many times, how Daddy met our mama.

They uses to tell my daddy, that I was that little Lorine girl came back to haunt them, and they didn't like me to ride a horse, because even with Cerebral Palsy, I could still sat a horse like that damn uncle of Bud's (my daddy's).

And I really wished I knew how to get the permission to used my great-grand uncle's picture, and they made a hit song out of what he wrote for The Texas Trail Drivers. I used to love that song when I was a kid, and I play it, again, this year, when we lost Dillon.

I am going to self published this novel, and more, or I hope to, and I just wanted you know, because I don't know how much editing I will be able to afford. So, I am kind of apologizing in advance. And don't think I should just try to mail out to publishers, because this novel has already came back though the mail without postage, it was in'98.

My daddy did a lot of things to make a living, he worked in a grocery store, in the oil field, on road crew, combine crops, sold wood, raised peanuts, hay, peas, corn, hogs, cattle, geese, turkeys, mules, donkeys, horses, and when he wasn't busy or too tire, he would draw me pictures. I wrote a story when I was about the age, Daddy was drawing me pictures, I hope to put them together, one day, for a children story entitled "PATTI LOU AND CISCO".

Even though, I knew at a early age that I would never dated or married, I never thought I would have to take a gun in one hand and a bull whip in the other hand, and fight them off of everything else. But, I think my daddy and mama did.

Patti Witter

P.S. If you ever have a crush on someone, and whether they gave you false hope or not, it still hurts to see them with someone else, I think this might help, think of Frankenstein and his bride, and Hitler married his long time mistress Eva Braun on April 29, 1945, the year that the Nazis was finally put out of power. I went to High School with a girl with that last name, and now she is going with my "ex" brother-in-law, and I would have never thought I would be so happy to call him my ex brother-in-law.

This is my daddy's crop of peanuts, I don't know what they told him
when they took away his peanuts acreage.

GRANNY & GRANDPA HOWELL (I CAN'T REMEMBER GRANDPA)

MAMA (IRIS WITTER)

Henry C. and Elizabeth Howell. We think the C in my grandpa's name
stands for Clay, you know like the black boxer.

The news reports said, that the Nazis starting killing the disables, because of a poor farmer had a severely disabled son, he wanted to put his son to death. This is Lorine and Jack.

Ernest Lowell Witter and Maggie May Harris-Witter. I know what you are thinking, he was a dirty old, man, but he wasn't. They just went together like hot biscuits and butter, even in their 70's and 80's.

Lorine is the tallest and the only witch.

This is little James Howell. We have a picture of James, he looks a couple years older maybe, with his head hanging down. I figured that it was the day that the Bad ending boy was mean to him. Can you image what kind of people would be mean to this little boy?

Now, imaged a cult of that kind of people after this little girl. Or both of them. Yea, this is me, Patti Witter and one of my sister, I won't mention names, but the red headed one.

This is me and Daddy with Four Cricketts. They killed her
granddaughter in the latest killing spree.

This my grandpa Witter, me, Daddy, and Four Cricketts.

Nellie was gave to me during my High School years, she was a great horse, came off the King Ranch, then a trick rider's horse. We got her when she was eighteen year old, and she was still much of a horse. We had one of her grand-daughters, she was not only the spitting image of her grandmother, she moved and acted so much like her. We lost her in their latest killing spree.

China was also a great riding horse, she was also Dillon's mother. We lost her to a very rare disease.

Now, I didn't get to ride Babe too much, and I will tell you why, too. While I was at school one day, Daddy and the Bowl of Cherries fellow was doing something with the horses, and my mama look out the door at exact same time that Babe had a reaction to something that cause her to rear up, and from then on Mama had that same reaction to me riding Babe. But, she turn out to be good horse, Mama just didn't live long enough to see Babe pull Daddy and his wagon down the street in a parade with no reaction.

This is Red and Sammy, Sammy like to prance.

Now, Prince was a charming fellow, Daddy got him, after we lost our little, black Shetland pony, Midnight, he was a great pony, too. Daddy would let me ride, while he was at the barn. Daddy started telling me that my brother's mother-in-law was either 1/8 or ¼ Indian about the time we lost Midnight.

Now, Cisco was here before I got here, but I had heard about how when Daddy got him, he would rear up every time anyone would get on him, and he said how he and the man working for Daddy got him to stop. I just can't remember how. He was ready for me, when I got here. Cisco was a great horse.

Now, Red was adored and loved, and just not by me and Cricketts Rose, but by anyone who met him. He worked cattle, rodeos, pulled wagons trail rides, and he loved parades. And my two brothers used to get on App, he was a grey stallion, and put a three or four year old me on Red, and here we went fallowing cattle trails. Red would fallowing along just perfectly. I can't remember it, but Red was raise on a bottle, Mama said, he would come to the back door for his bottle.

I had gotten to ride some great horses, and one great mule, that I either can't find or don't have a picture of. There was Midnight, App, Thunder, Sugar, Shorty (the horse), then there were some I could only ride in the lot, J.B., George's Girl, and Silver Blue, and then there were some that I could only ride with someone else, mostly my daddy, there was Bill and Sammy when I was a kid.

One time, my daddy let me ride with him, while he moved cattle from one place to another. This was when I was a little, kid, there wasn't, but maybe, two or three cars on the road, and with mama in the station wagon, and my dad's two uncles, Elmer "Buster" and Alan "Cap" Harris in a pickup blocking all the side roads. And with me and Daddy riding behind them, we had our own cattle drive.

And I am betting that is the day that they thought that I rode too much like that damn uncle of Bud's. It could had been my great, grand uncle Webb came from Heaven to ride with us, I bet he laughed every time we went by mama, and she wanted to know, if I was tire, and did I want to get off?

Well, of course not, but my mama worried about that kind of stuff. I wrote about it for school one time, and made A+.

I got to flag relay, (it's kind like barrel racing, but with buckets of sand on top of the barrel, you put a flag in and take one out, take it to the next bucket) with my brother and App, but when Mama saw us, she didn't think it was a good idea.

And that is what they called my daddy putting me in danger. Those horses was so train, I was as safe as I was sitting in my mama's lap, while she read horse stories. I thought I was living some great horse stories, and to me, I was.

Every time the government talk about legalizing millions of illegal aliens, they put me, my animals, and our way of life in danger. Don't let the color of their skin fool you, they are Nazis.

And they was some great horses that I didn't get to ride, they was daddy's daft horse, Flax, he love to take baths, Little Blue, I can't remember whether I got to ride him or not, Lucifer, look like the angel before he sent away from Heaven, Apple Grey that was never train to ride, Short Cakes, you had to be able to get on her quick, but everyone loved Short Cakes. They killed her in the latest killing spree.

Then there was this cow horse of my daddy, I remember she was a perfect Quarter Horse, they called her, Crazy. As my daddy used to tell people, if you working cattle in the pasture, and she went after a cow, you had two choices, you could hang on thorough mesquites, under trees limbs, and over cactus, or you could just came off, and let her go get the cow. Daddy always talked like the ladder was the best choice. Once they put her after a cow, that was it.

Both my daddy and Grandpa Henry had Joe Bailey's mares, he was a racing stallion, who lived close to Grandpa and Granny Howell.

Now, this Frankie, named after the Elvis Presley's movie "FRANKIE AND JOHNNIE". Daddy was keeping her for a friend, out in a cattle pasture, until I got worried about her, and thought that she should be here with Baby and Red. And after the first day of letting them together in January of 1986, when Baby went out from under their barn to tell Frankie just what was what, but Frankie wasn't so sure, Baby whinny for Red, one time, and here, he came to her. He gave Frankie a good talking to, and from then on, it was Baby, Red, and Frankie. I guess that the friend that they got along pretty good together, because he gave her to me, after he got the okay from my daddy, that was in '86 or '87. He also told us that there were another part owner.

This is Frankie, me, and Jake.

I always felt like there was something that Frankie's veterinarian wasn't telling me, but the guilt of not getting him to her sooner was so much, I couldn't be sure, even though, the first time we talk to him about her, he was talking about putting her down. Now, I found a children author by the name of Mrs. Patti Blew It. Do you think he knew something?

Now, Jake's veterinarian had the same last name as the author's wife last name from my great-grand uncle Webb Witter's county. And I was told, that he bought a place close to granny and grandpa Howell's.

The cult seems to think that Cricketts Rose's veterinarian kill her for them, and the only thing that I can think of is he knew what had happen and I didn't. He came from Gonzales, Texas.

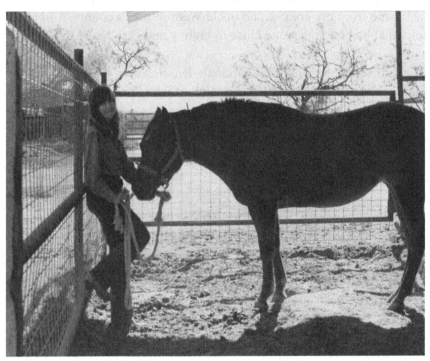

This is the picture, I sent to the TV and movie star. I would had thought this was what ruin my writing career, but for that to had happen it would had gotten a lot of attention. I know now that the cult was already watching me to steal anything and everything. I heard it said, that they would watched the mail room, and steal ideals for other people.

This is Cricketts Rose.

61

I have hear they said that the one of the two who killed Cricketts Rose is the father of a relative, and I thought that he was from the Mexican family that is after me so bad.

I haven't been close to my brother's kids since my mama's death in '79, and their parents divorced in the early '80's. So, I can't tell you, who's father, he is, but I can tell you this, it doesn't make a difference. If anything, it put me and my animals in more danger.

They talk in a code, I think that they teach some people the code to said mean things to them, and nobody else will know, or nobody can hold them to anything. They do it to their victims, and I am a victim, that Bad ending law man made sure of it.

But, anyways, I been hearing them talk about what my nephew and his cousin had plan, and sure enough, when they pull that off, I knew it was coming. My sister have had the cousin to work on our horses pens, and he kept doing jobs for us, and coming by.

And when his girlfriend of sixteen years (I think) left him, and wanted him and his stuff to move off of her grandparents place. Everyone was extremely worry about him, poor fellow, was he going to be okay?

My sister said he could move his stuff in on the front 10 acres of her place, but I notice, he wasn't moving his stuff. And when my brother said he might want to leave his son, and him 15 acres, it didn't seem to move him much, if anything he wanted to laugh.

But, my sister said that sometimes, when she talked to him on the phone, she thought he had been crying, and the reason he haven't moved yet, is because this time when he moved, he wanted a place that would be his. My sister told him that was his. Now, Ladies and Gentlemen, dry your eyes, blow your noses, and put away your hankies, because that boy done got what he wanted, a $50,000.00 piece of land.

There just one little problem, it isn't the place they thought it was, he brought in a girl that I went to school went, induce her like she was a guy friend's wife, she has that first name, and Harris like my great, grandma. They was after the place where she, and my daddy's uncles lived, it is also the place where my great, grand uncle Web Witter rode away from, it is the next place.

But, bless this boy's heart, he is so cult, he just can't help, but gave it away in a code that he thought nobody, but cult will understand. He learn how to play the victim from watching me, he laughed the 15 acres, because he had something so mean planed, that I might walk away and he could have the run of the whole place, like the man from England did, and he made fun of the men who used to pretend to like me, I suspect he learn how from watching the women that pretend to like him.

I quit going to England people's place in the beginning of 2009, (I think), they put it up for sale, this year, or that's what I was told. I quit going to my sister's place a few weeks ago. My temper and creeps don't mix. My brother had already told us, that he used to play with little Mrs. Nazis Australia trip, herself.

And this cousin wanted me to know that the man that gave me Frankie, would have rather this little Harris thing to have Frankie, because at less, she wasn't on SSI, and could put Frankie in her name. And I bet she does gets pay for every tricks that she does. I just glad that man didn't try to take Frankie, because I would hated to see the big man cry.

And me, I am going to try to get back on SSI, in less, I can the rest of my part from my parents, and the way they are giving it away, I might can get my part. But, keep buying my books, when I make over so much, I just turn it back to SSI, what they paid.

I need to apologized to Australia, I thought they fought with Hitler and the Nazis, I thought that meant against them, but now I think they meant together. It was on the news how they turned down a family with a teen aged son with Downs Syndrome for the right to move there. They was afraid he would end up on Government support, just wait until the Mexican women get there, having babies, and expect the government to pay for it.

No, Australia wouldn't like me, but that's okay, because I found a Australia writer the same last name as the Bad ending law man's girl friend. And wouldn't you know she writes about a silver stallion, and the movie that I bought and watched, was about a woman, who writes stories on a note pad for her, look like a twelve year old daughter.

She started being published about the time this girl's family started trying to snuggle up to brother, but he had already retire his silver stallion. Me and Bowel of Cherries was riding him.

In October of 2011, the Mexican police arrested a man with the Mexican family last name. He was arrested for being the division head for one of the cartels.

This is Bell, one of my daddy's team of mules. Before Daddy die, she helped him raised a baby calf, and after my daddy had die, I rode Bell. But, before I could get everything work out, I watched Bell fall down dead, we didn't have money for a veterinarian, but me and Daddy had token her mate, Bounty to a veterinarian, when Bounty fall down dead, and the veterinarian told Daddy that it might not had help to gotten there any sooner, it could had been a tumor, or anything. Months later, Daddy went to the veterinarian's funeral, he had die at either forty-one or forty-two years old of cancer in 1990. He was a mule man, too. I made him a pot of stew before he die. Bell and Bounty acted like they had the same thing before their deaths.

This is Little Mr. Innocent. He got his name one day, when he walked from pile to pile knocking stuff off, and then he got comfortable on one pile of stuff, and looked at me with a perfectly innocent face. I have heard that they smother him to death, but I don't know, he was so stiff when I found him.

This is the Del Rio Kitty, he found a hole in my mobile home floor, under the kitchen's sink, that I had no idea was there, and the dogs killed him.

This is My Kitty, she loved the Del Rio Kitty, I used wake up in the
morning with one on one side and on the other waiting for me to get
up. She didn't like other kitties too much, so when I moved back into
the house, I left her in the mobile home. I don't know whether she was
poison or had kidney problems.

Now, this is a picture of L.B., token after a rattlesnake had bitten him, he was a golden color, and this picture don't even came close to showing how sweet he really looked.

B.B. is the one standing up, Pretty & Sweet is the one next to the door.
Bubba and Pretty Smart is in front, they are still living, and we have
one of Daddy's that found home.

The day this picture was took, I had on a pink & blue blouse, and my face was full, and then one day I found this on my computer, but they change anything but Dillon, until May 2011, when he lay down, and we knew he wouldn't be getting back up. But, we hadn't expected to go back to him and find his leg broken into. I thought I have a camera recording, but I went to it to check on it, it wasn't on. He was a buckskin.

This is Lollipop.

My rose brush was killed in the early '90 killing spree.

This is Apple Grey.

Now, this me and Shorty.

You might not think that I was right about how they can change
people's looks, but this is my mama.

This is Granny Howell, we think it was on her wedding day.

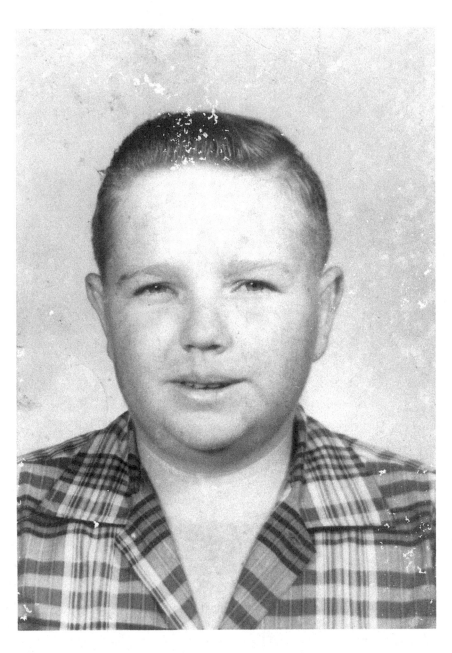

If you think it's age, this is my brother Bob in grade school.

This is Bob, the year that he graduated from High School.

This is Bob in the '70's, when he was in his twenties.

And this is Bob when he was about thirty-two year old.

And this is me, Patti Lou Witter on Hammer in 2010.

Chapter One

THE PHONE RANG TWICE IN her apartment, she put down the Computer's program manual, and listen for the answering machine to pick-up, there wasn't too much more in the apartment besides the answering machine. But, she didn't need much.

Her computer, printer, a shelve full of books that she wanted to read, two full of books that she already read and wanted to keep by her favorite author. Chairs that didn't match, but was gave to her, she had her rocking chair placed in front of her computer, and a bed in the bedroom.

She took a deep breath to braced herself for another crank call, she figured the calls was part of a game, but she couldn't let herself think of it in that way, or she would go mental insane. Maybe, like the ones that was doing it to her.

The machine pick up. "You have reach Kimberly Racks, she can't come to the phone right now, but if you will leave a message at the beep, she will get back to you." It wasn't Kimberly's voice, but it didn't matter, because the message would be the same.

"Kimberly, this is Chance K. Sway. You know me, and I know what is going on. I want to help you, so if you are tire of being the Hometown Joke, come see me. Please, Kimberly, this isn't a game."

She gave the machine a oh sure, look, and listen to the phone number for her to call for appointment.

She knew the name, but she couldn't remember where from, or who is he was. He sounded sad to her.

She got up to replay the message, she was about leave for her father's ranch, any ways. It took her a couple of times to get the phone number down. Now, she had to decided whether she wanted to call or not.

He said that is wasn't a game, but she had a feeling that her life has been a game to other people for a long time. They had been playing with her emotions, and her whole life without her even knowing it. But, the very worst part of it was for a painful period in her life, she had know what was going on, and she had tried to play. Even if it was to catch them to turn over to the law, only to find out the law was bad.

But, Thank God, she never got off of the main part of what she was trying to do, she had stay with what she had to do for herself. And maybe what she had to do for the rest of her life.

She known that no one would ever tell about what had been going on, so there wasn't even a need to think about it, much less, trying to do everything about it. Everyone would tell her that she was mental ill, and she really needed to get help for her problem. Everyone, except this Chance K. Sway, but she was sure that by the time she met with him, he wouldn't know anything about what she was talking about. Of course not, she chuckled at the thought.

But, then again, it wouldn't hurt to met with him, she wouldn't say anything, in less, he did. This man may be the only chance that she had.

She pick up the phone, and dial the number, a woman answer the phone with. "This is Sway and Company, may I help you?"

Kimberly thought to herself, "oh, God I hope so ", but she said very slowly. "Yes, this is Kimberly Racks, and . . . ."

That was as far, as she got, when the woman's voice came back on the line. "Yes, Kimberly, please hold."

Kimberly heard a couple of clicks, than Chance come on the line.

"Kimberly, you should have just pick up while ago."

She noticed that he sounded happier than he did awhile ago, but all she said was. "Maybe, maybe not."

"No, no maybe this time." But, he let it go. "You don't remember me, do you?"

She shook her head for herself, as she said. "No, sir, I can't place you."

"I tell you what, if you can't remember me by the end of the meeting tomorrow, I will tell you how and where you know me from. Fair enough?" He asked.

She had to smile, as she answered him. "Fair enough. When tomorrow? And could you tell me what this is about?" She wondered what he would say.

He took her questions one at a time. "In the morning at nine. And Kimberly, I would rather wait and go into it face to face, if that's alright with you."

She agreed, because she likes talking to people face to face. She listens as he gave her the address, and told her how to get there.

"Just be careful, Kimberly, and I will see you tomorrow." Then he hung up the phone.

When the phone rang again as soon she hung up, it caused her to jump a little, she almost pick it right back up, thinking it was Chance. But, she thought to wait, and sure enough, whoever was calling didn't had everything to say, they just hung up.

She know this was where she was suppose to get so mad that she got on her computer, say things that she will regret, trying to get them to leave her alone.

But, Kimberly know that doing it wouldn't end it for her, only she could end it for her. So, she pickup her purse and her keys, switch her computer off, then she walked out the door.

The Texas weather was warm, the beginning of fall, not too hot even when the sun shining, and the sky was clear blue. It was the kind of day that makes glad you were alive, but she couldn't quit being nervous, not yet, and maybe not ever.

Chapter Two

THE NEXT MORNING, KIMBERLY LEFT her apartment thirty minutes earlier than what she needed to for the drive to Austin, which would take about a hour or so.

She drove into Austin as far as she feel safe doing, then she parked her pick-up at a mall, and she called a cab.

She had thought about a bus, but she didn't know which one would take her there, a cab was the quickest, and the safest way to go.

The cab driver let her out in front of a large building, that looked to her like it could hold many offices. It was one of the nicest part of Austin, or at least that is what Kimberly was thinking, but she didn't know that much about Austin.

The receptionist on the ground floor told Kimberly that Sway and Company was on the top, and the sign on the building told her that Sway and Company probably own the building. Not that really matter to her, but she did like it, to her it has style.

She was told that the elevator would stop facing the President's office, and that is where she needed to go, so that is where she went.

When she stepped into the office, she noticed it had the same appeal as the building, from the wood floor to the shade darker, wood panel on the inside walls, the outside wall was windows. You could look out over the streets.

Kimberly made her way to the woman sitting at the desk at the far end of the office. The "May I help you?" told Kimberly that she was the one who answer the phone yesterday.

She barely got pass her name, when two men came out of the office's door behind the receptionist's desk. They stopped talking when they saw her.

The taller one with black hair, dark, blue eyes came to her saying. "Kimberly, it has been a long time."

She said. "Yes, it had been a long time." She shook his hand, when he gave it to her. Yea, this was Chance, because he was the one that was familiar to her, and it had to been along time, she thought, because if you meet this man in the last ten years, you wouldn't had forgotten him.

"Kimberly, this is Brad Matters." Chance induced her to the other man, who wouldn't quiet as tall as Chance was, he had dark, brown hair, and brown eyes. They was both in their late thirties to forty-something, she thought.

"It's very nice to meet you, Kimberly. I have heard a lot about you." Brad told her with a smile.

She wanted to say, "I just bet you have, but what come out was.

"It's nice to meet you, too."

Kimberly listen as Chance tell Mrs. Felts to hold all the phone calls, and anything else that might come up. Mrs. Felts was the receptionist, or maybe, she was Chance's secretary.

She was in her middle fifties, with grey hair, a business manner to go with her appearance, but a kind heart, you could see it on her face.

As Kimberly watched them talking, she remember exactly where she had known Chance from, and how long it had been since she saw him. She was about to tell him, when he and Brad show her thorough the door that they had came out of.

When she stepped through the door, she immediately like the office. The pictures of cowboys, riding, and rounding up cattle that was hanging the walls was by the best western artists, and so was the sculptures the cowboys running hard and fast.

There was sculpture of a Brahman bull standing on a slope, it was beautiful, you could feel the pride that he had in him. The details in the sculpture, and in the pictures couldn't be better or more beautifully done. She smile to herself, that is why they are the best in their field.

The wooden chairs that her and Brad sat down in, was covered in soft leather. They sat facing Chance, who took the oversized chair behind a large wooden desk. The desk's wood was beautifully finished, it's finished matched the finished on the chairs, the small crouch, the odds and ends tables and the file cabinets in the office. It was western enough for Kimberly to feel comfortable in, but still formal enough for any business. The wall behind Chance's desk was windows, the office was impressively arranged, it made a statement.

When they was settled in, Kimberly was about tell Chance that she had remember him, and how glad she was to see him again.

When he sit up in his chair, placed his arms on the desk, and started saying. "Well, Kimberly, I guess, you know that I wanted to take you dancing in San Antonio, Dallas, and Houston, I wanted to take you places that you would want to go, let you do things that you always wanted to do. but, you wasn't ready, then they wouldn't let me." He made a face of muck regret. "So, in place giving you a real chance to go, I just took another woman. Now, don't you feel sorry for me?"

He stressed the me part, when he asked.

At first, it set her back, the glad feelings that she felt about seeing him left her, but then she realized he was really about tell her what had been going on. The glad surprise feeling that she had was still gone, now she had a hopefully feeling that she wouldn't have to go through it alone, any more. Maybe, he wasn't going to tell her that it was all in her mind, that she had mental problems.

Her light blue, eyes meet his dark blue, eyes, and when she smile, and said. "Oh, yes, you are breaking my heart."

The hatefulness in her voice kindly of threw him, this wasn't the same Kimberly that he had known, but you couldn't expected her to be the same, not after what she had been put through. The Kimberly that was full of life, and love was gone. Why did he feel like it had been took from him?

His eyes search her eyes, her face, there had to be a part of the old Kimberly still in her, the part that kept her going, living, and trying, that kept her getting up every morning, knowing what she would have to face every day.

Wondering what kind of hope she really had for her future, knowing whatever she wanted to tried will be turn into a game. Could he face it?

Chance searched her face one more time, what he saw was the tensed, stressed out feelings, but there was a spark of curiosity on her face, too.

"No, it isn't me that is breaking your heart, it isn't your family, either or everyone else, for that matter. It is you that keeps breaking your heart. Believing that some one out there that was trying to do all these things for you."

He sallow hard, and tried to keep the hatefulness out of his voice. "There isn't everyone that is coming thorough for you. Is there, Brad?" He looked at Brad.

Brad gave her a apologetic look, when she turn to him. "No, there isn't everyone coming thorough for you, except at night when you are asleep, and if they could do that, they could wake you up to go with them. But, you know that, don't you?" Brad asked her.

When she nodded her head, Chance took back over. "We aren't here to play games, we aren't here to make you think that someone is coming thorough for you, if you do that or if you don't do this, we aren't here to tell you that you are mental ill, or that you need help." He smile at her. "We are here to help you."

She wasn't quiet, sure what to say, she wanted to heard him said it out loud, just one time, that she was right about everything. She wanted her peace of mind back, and she knew that this was the man who would gave it to her, although, she didn't why yet. She just known he would.

So, she asked. "You mean that I was right about the tests to find out if I was gay, or a man chasing flirt. I was right about the tap on my computer, on the phones, bugs and cameras planted around, about people coming in my place at night?" She shivered without knowing it.

Chance and Brad nodded theirs head.

"And I was right about the man, who was supposed to had wanted to married me, or whatever, and my family was supposedly keeping us apart?" She asked.

"That is what they wanted you to believe." Chance answer her.

She stood up, and walked to the windows behind Chance to look down at the Colorado River that runs thorough Austin, his office had a beautiful view of it.

Chance turned his chair around to watch her.

She smile at them questioningly, and made a statement. "This man was a set up, a test himself."

"Yes, he was supposed to get your attention, make you think all of this was going on, then tell you it was all in your mind. He was supposed to make you think that he care for you, but he didn't, Kimberly." Chance told her as gentle as he could. "No one could put you through what they did, if they really cared about you."

She sat back down. "I knew that there wasn't something right about him, and I still fell for it." She didn't tell them, but that is what hurt the most. She fell for it, she shook her head sadly.

Chapter Three

"NOW, KIMBERLY, THINK ABOUT WHAT all you had been through before you got there." Chance had turned back around to faced her, he leaned his arms on the desk, again. "How did it made you feel when yours brothers moved back in. Did it make you feel like all the years that you spend there didn't mean a thing to anyone?"

Kimberly looked at him like, man don't that, but she said.

"I know all those years that I spent at home, didn't mean a thing to anyone, but to me, Cricketts Rose, Red, Frankie, and Jake."

She smile when she thought about them. "But, as for as anyone else is concern I could had been anywhere. I can just accepted it better, now."

"And how did it feel where you just knew that if you couldn't get Cricketts Rose and Red out of there, you were going to lose them. You was going to had watched the live go out of them, and you couldn't do anything to help them, no one would help you, or even cared to help you. How did it feel, Kimberly?"

Chance wanted to know things that you couldn't put into words, she looked at him with tears coming into her eyes, but she took a deep breath, as she look to the floor, she wasn't going to cried.

When she looked back to Chance, she shook her head. "I shouldn't had stay at home, I should had gotten a job, I shouldn't had gotten on the disability payments from the government . . . ." Kimberly stopped, because Chance started to say something, but when he didn't she kept going. "if I had a job, I could have gotten what my mama left. And if I could have gotten what my mama left me, I could have gotten them to another place in the country. I shouldn't had counted on my sister to help me get them away from there, when my brothers moved back in." She shook head.

"You shouldn't count on any one." Chance sounded sure of it.

And Kimberly was just as sure, when she nodded her head in agreement, but somewhere along the way, she had left them for another place in time.

She had just graduated from High School, and was well on her way to becoming one of the finest artist in Texas or maybe the world. What she liked best about it, was her work would let her stay at home, while she earn a living for herself. But, then the wreck happen.

She had gotten a job doing the illustrations and the covers for a book, she had caught a ride in to Austin with a friend that worked in Austin every day.

Kimberly and her friend was driving along, when they was hit from behind not once, but twice. The pick-up that they was riding in was sent off of the road, the two cars that had hit them, then collide with each other.

She remember opening her eyes once, and seeing the trunk of one of the cars was opened, there white power looking stuff in there along a case full of money that had came opened, the people from inside the cars was opening the doors as the flames came out from under the cars, then they run.

She realized that she had to get herself and her friend out of there, but when she moved, she pass out. Then the next thing she remember was being pulling out of the passage door of the pick-up. Her friend had been killed instantly, the cars had blow up along the drugs and the money, the people from the cars had run away, unharmed.

And Kimberly was rushed to the nearest hospital, the staff kept saying, how could she still be alive. She didn't think that they knew she could heard them, but she could.

The next day, they told her that she wasn't be able to draw or paint again, she wouldn't had the control of her hands that she needed, her speech would be impaired, she could walked, but with a limp. They had told why, and what had been damaged, but she didn't understand, she didn't tried.

Now, did they say that she could had been killed, or that she should had been killed. But, even then she knew that it could have been worst. The gas from the cars didn't have time to spill, and the pick-up was just barely far enough away not get caught by the flames from the explosion, just barely.

She had always been kind of a loner, she was either caught up a painting that she was doing, or one that she was about to start. She had been told that in her paintings, you could feel the spirit in the wild stallion running free, you could feel the happiness or the sadness of the people in her paintings. You felt like you were living the moment that were captured in time that would now live forever on paper. But, that ability from her forever ever, token by a drug deal that went wrong.

And if she hadn't been painting, she would had been with the horses, she spent a lot of time horseback riding, bouncing on one then running like the wind was chasing her, she had run barrels, worked cattle.

And she had been told many times that she took too many chances with her ability, but she had always said that anything could happen to her at any time, and she had been right. Now, she hardly ever got a chance to ride a horse, much less, bounced on one, that ability was gone, too.

After the accident, Kimberly spent a lot of time with her mother, who was a quiet, gentle, country woman with a kind, loving heart, and the patients of a saint. Her mother tried to tell her that she still could do anything she wanted to, she just had to find her way of doing of it. All this disability meant was that she had find a way around it, that she couldn't changed what had happen to her in any way, shape or form. When people thought her speech impaired meant she was retarded, that was their problem, let they deal it. And Kimberly knew that was the attitude you had to have just to want to survive.

If her mama ever felt like she had less of daughter after the accident, Kimberly never saw it or never felt it in any way. She couldn't be at her friend's funeral, because she was still in the hospital, but she was at her mother's a year later. She had pass away of cancer.

After that, Kimberly had survived, not much more. They had talked to her about going to college. But, the only things that she could do day in and day out that would justify spending that much time and money on, was drawing, painting, or the horse business. Drawing and painting was no longer a possibility for her in any way.

She had started thinking about trying the horse business. She could raised horses, and do some of the ground training. Then the worst probable thing happen, she lost her pet mare. All in that one night, she saw what kind of treatment she would get from her family and other people as well. She couldn't handle it then, and maybe not ever.

After that happen, she had been destroyed, the only hope she had left to make a living for herself was no longer a real possibility for her. But, there was two months old filly that needed her. Or was it the other way around.

When they brought Cricketts Rose home, she was bouncing off of the fences, calling for a mama that would never came to her, again.

Kimberly spent a lot of time with her, she had finally got her calm down, and eating good. When they told Kimberly that Cricketts Rose would be stunted, that she wouldn't grow like she should. Kimberly didn't say anything, but she thought, you just hide and watch.

Cricketts Rose grew from a undeveloped two months filly to one of the most beautiful horse that Kimberly had ever saw. From the pertness of her ears, to the brightness of her eyes, the intelligent way she held her small head, her neck was tick and well form, her chest was wide, her back was straight and strong, her hips was powerful, legs was muscles, her dark chestnut, red coat would shine in the sun light, her mane and trail would fly in the wind when she would run.

And she ran often, because she loved life, she just loved being alive. You could just look at her and tell she full of life. She was Kimberly's baby, maybe her whole life.

"She meant the world to me." Kimberly realized that she said it aloud, she pulled herself together, and sat up straight, but this time she didn't tried to stop the tears from running down her face. "You should have seen Cricketts Rose, Chance. She was beautiful, full of life, high-stung, and very spirited, you would had love her."

Chance gave her a sad smile, then his eyes went to Brad, and they both bow their heads to listen to her.

"She may have been too high-stung, she was far too sensitive. I wouldn't let everyone trained her. I was afraid that they was be too rough on her, but I did what I could in the training department."

Kimberly smile to herself as she remember how proud she was the day that she saddled Cricketts Rose for the first time. Of course, Red had to be saddled first, just show her how it was done.

Red was a twenty-five year old gelding, he was Kimberly and Cricketts Rose best buddy. He had a calm spirit, and a heart that wouldn't quit. He had done it all, worked cattle, trail ride, rodeo, he even pulled wagons, but what he liked best was the parades. His head will come up a little higher, his step become a little spryer, and he would still be just as steady and just as calm. Kimberly and Cricketts Rose had adored him until the day that he had pass away at thirty-two year old, four months before Cricketts Rose did.

When Red and Kimberly had Cricketts Rose saddling without going to pieces on them. Kimberly took a old pair of blue jeans, and a shirt that was too small for her, and stuff them to make a dummy to put on Cricketts Rose.

One day, Kimberly put the dummy in the saddle, then she turned Cricketts Rose lose in their patch. Cricketts Rose buck a few times, then she came running to Kimberly scarce to death, but she wouldn't ever come running to her, again.

Kimberly couldn't mount and ride her, but she did tried her to the fence and sit on her, with Red standing along with them. Kimberly did drive her some, but not as much she should had. Kimberly regret not doing more, and she had her too spoil and barn sour, she regretted that too, but now it was too late.

"I had almost find a way to bred her that wouldn't be too hard on her, it wouldn't put too much stress on her, because I didn't to cause her to hurt in any way. But, it is too late, now, she is gone." Kimberly wipe the tears off of her face, but she didn't stop crying. "I spent most of her life trying to kept her from hurting in any way, and that is all she did for the last few weeks of her life, was hurt. She couldn't stand it. She loved life, and I watched it go out of her at nine years old."

Chapter four

BRAD WAS ABOUT TO SAY something, when Chance motion for him not to. Chance came around to her, he pull her into his arms, he leaned against his desk, and just let her cried for her baby.

When she pulled herself together again, she looked up at him, and said, very, quietly. "I am sorry." Then she sit back in the chair, she took deep breaths to stop crying.

Chance handled her, his handkerchief out of his pocket, then he nodded to Brad.

"Kimberly, what do you think about Cricketts Rose's death?" Brad asked, and even he know how dumb it sounded.

She gave him a blank look, then it dawn on her, what he wanted to know. She looked at the handkerchief, and said. "You mean do I think that she was killed like her mother, because their wasn't worth as much as those people made me think that they was. Because, I was about to bred her, and might find out that they was worth about ten thousands, not the fifty to seventy-five thousands that I was lead to believed." She looked from Chance to Brad, and with a sad calmness that kind of scare her. She kept talking. "But, that wasn't it, they was worth that much, and more. Was it because it was the only way they could take them away from me, and make they hurt. Because, they wanted to get me out where they could tested me out, see how I would behave, see what kind of person was, I was going, they didn't had to take her from me. But, it wasn't how much she was worth, that it what they couldn't let me have her, and her mama. That had to be it." She nodded her head.

"You know who wanted to test you, and what for?" Chance asked softly.

She kind of chuckled. "Yea, I read a book about my condition, but it's okay, I didn't like them very much, either. Before Cricketts Rose was gone, I said things that was mean and hateful, I didn't even believed them. But, I would had said and done anything to get her out of there, before it was too late for her." She smile at Chance. "It kind of serve me right to fall for him. It certainly did make me the hometown joke, didn't it? But, the joke is on them, they just read stuff that I put on my personal computer."

"He is was the one that you agree to married the second time?" Chance already knew the answer, but he needed to hear from her.

She nodded her head. "Wasn't that silly, agreeing to marry someone that was already married?" She didn't wait for answer. "But, he never was married, was he?"

Brad answer her. "No, but he was probably talking about some one's else wife?" He gave her a sympathetic smile.

"I know." She nodded her head. "And don't feel sorry me, I knew about it, before I agreed to marry him. I don't why I thought that I could have live with him after that, I just don't know." She kind of smile up at Chance. "But, it was only on the computer, and that stuff don't count, no one was even on the other end, no one ever talked back."

"That is what we want to talked to you about. We can prove all of this, the tap on the computer, the bugs, the hidden cameras, they coming in at night while you were asleep, the tests that they had those people put you through, the people who was suppose to help you, the way that they made a game out of your life." Chance looked at her so sadly, but he had to tell her the truth for her own good. "It was all just a game to them, but they did believe you were crazy about him. Enough to kill yourself over the way he was doing you, so they get away with they had stole from you."

"I know that, Chance. I figured that why they did all the tests to see if I was like them, flaky, not a very stable person." She grinned when Chance and Brad chuckled. "And they wasn't caught up in the games, they really wanted to hurt me, even kill me." She shook her head. "But, that place that I went to for help to get a job, they set me up, very well, didn't they?"

"Oh, yes. Now, you would have a record of having mental problems." Brad answer her. "And that's what they wanted, so if you found out about what all was going on, you probably couldn't do everything about. They set you up, very well."

"I figured that is why they did it." She kind of smile at how easy it was for they to do that to her, and she had promised herself that she would never be that stupid, ever again.

"You have lost a lot of pride, haven't you, Kimberly?"

Chance asked her, when she nodded, he keep talking. "You know what they said about pride, don't you?"

She shook her head.

"When you swallow it, you either cough back up, or you choke on it, or it just goes out the other end. "He smile when she did. "But, most importantly, when you make more, you take better care of it. And I know you, Kimberly, you got enough pride to walk away from the games, you are smart enough to know that they was going to hurt you every chance that they got. They aren't ever going to let you have anything real, they are that bad."

She kind of smile. "I don't think that I am suppose to ever have anything real, a real relationship with a man. I am not sure why, but I am not suppose to. And I don't want one with another woman. I wasn't sure why they thought it was up to them, but it was all of about stealing and getting away it?" Before Chance or Brad could said everything difference, she asked. "But, y'all can prove this?" She look at them with doubt.

They both laughed, but Chance answer her. "Yes, they didn't plan on us, they didn't plan everyone ever caring enough about you to help you." When he had said, he know how it sounded, and he wanted take it back, but he couldn't. "Kimberly, I didn't meant it like it sounded."

"Why not? When you right, you are right." Kimberly had already figured it out.

Chance looked at Brad for a way to make it sound better, but he didn't get any help there. "We can take them down, Kimberly, we can make them pay, and pay big. We can ruin all of them." Chance said it like doing that would make everything okay, but they know it wouldn't.

"You are talking about going to court?" They nodded.

"You know who killed Cricketts Rose?"

"We will go over the details, when you are ready."

Chance nodded his head.

But, she shook her head. "We aren't going to court, I don't want their money for Cricketts Rose, I do want my money for my work, if we have to ruin them to get it ruin them. But, the law isn't any good now, I tried more than a few times. The women of the law are treating it like it was my work, they was other artists, and going to use it to better their careers. That is who the law is now. So, now I was thinking more about a baseball bat, or," She rubbed her hands together like she was really thinking about doing it. "a lead pipe, maybe."

She figured when she said that, all of the help that they wanted to gave her wouldn't be there, any more.

"But, do you know how much money we would be talking about?" Brad said in amazement.

"I have a pretty good idea." Kimberly thought that shedid.

"But, money can't bring Cricketts Rose and Red back to life, it can't take away the hurt that they cause you, it can't buy back the pride that you loss, and it can't give your life, or your peace of mind back. Can it, Kimberly?"

Chance knew that better than anyone else.

Chapter Five

"NO, MONEY CAN'T DO ALL of that." Kimberly gave them a sad smile, and she shook her head. "They got the attorneys either bought off or scare off, I would be going in to a kangaroo court."

"But, it's yours. After what they did to you." Brad couldn't believed it.

But, Chance did, and he asked. "What do you want, Kimberly?"

She looked into his eyes, as she gave it thought as how to put it. "Can you take away the tap, the cameras, the bugs, and better locks to stop them from coming in to my place at night? Can you?"

"Oh, yea, Kimberly, we can do that, easily."

Chance sounded so sure that she almost believed him, almost. "For how long? And can you get that stuff off of my record at that place?"

This time Chance smile. "We can ruin that place, they will do what we want. And we will keep people out among them, if anything start up, we will have it stop. Anything else, Kimberly?

She nodded her head. "Why did they do it to me? We know that I am not the best looking woman around, not the best built, and not the richest, so why?"

Chance and Brad looked at each other, then Brad answer her. "You were easy prey." It sounded so horrible, that he added. "But, you kind of fascinated them, and you were right about them knowing about your condition, they read books, and that why you were tested."

"No, I didn't, they was just trying to get away with what they had stole from me and my family. And I did do things that I shouldn't have had, exploration how sexy I am or was. "She become embarrass, and didn't want to talk about it. "But, nothing illegal, nothing that they could jailed me for, and that what they was after, right?"

"They read the book and did tests, you got to know them. You do know who was behind all of it, don't you, Kimberly?" Chance smile at her.

"The tests and anything was done by the one that I agree to marry, the second time."

"Can I asked something?" Brad wanted to know.

She took a deep breath, and nodded.

"How do you live like that? Knowing that you are being watched all of time? Knowing that everything that you tried to do will be game to someone else, everything you loved can be gone just like that for a game? How do you live like that?"

Brad asked in amazement.

"I would like to know that, too." Chance said.

She kind of smile at them. "Because, the alternative is a killer. And I am not ready to give up, but it isn't easy."

They nodded their heads as if they could understand.

"What now, Kimberly?" Chance wanted to know.

"A job, so I can make a living for myself, so I won't end up like I was when I lost Red and Cricketts Rose." She smile at Chance. "You don't think that I can get a job or hold one for very long, do you?"

"I don't think that you could have gotten one right after the accident, you didn't have a chance of getting one."

Kimberly nodded that was what he was going to tell her awhile, ago.

"Now, they almost got to, there is a law, that says you have right to have a job that you able to do." He shook his head. "But, now you have been through too much, and you have always been country. I don't think that you would able to take the city and a office job for very long before all of this, and expectantly not now, Kimberly."

She nodded her head, and said. "But, I have to tried.

What else could I do? Just gave up? Go mental insane?

Tried to kill myself, where they could save me, and have a record that I am really mental off? They would love that!

Thanks, but no thanks." Then she thought to asked. "If you know that I have bugs on me, why are we talking about all of this?" She raised her eyebrows.

Chance smile. "Where is your purse, Kimberly?"

She looked down on the floor besides her chair, she hadn't noticed that Brad had put a case down next to it.

"You didn't wear a watch, did you, Kimberly?" Chance had already made sure of it.

"No, it is in my purse." Kimberly looked up at him.

"There is a device built in the case that is cutting them out. They aren't hearing anything right now, Kimberly.

There is nothing there for them, now, Kimberly. I ask you, is that not justice or what?"

She almost couldn't believe him, but she did. "Really, you can do that?"

"Yea, we can do that." Chance smile at her. "We will have them took out before we leave here, or we can let they do now? Whatever you want to do."

Chance made it sound like they was all leaving together, she didn't why he thought that, she must be misunderstanding him.

But, she told him. "You can do it now."

Then she watched Chance pushed a button on the phone, and tell Mrs. Felts to send in a Mr. Cabot. In a few minutes, a man in his middle forties come to get her purse, and the case.

When Mr. Cabot left, Kimberly said. "I guess, in a way, I have been living with him."

This time it was Chance that shiver. "It has always been for his benefit. He has went on living his life, and gave you nothing, never any love or affection."

Brad sat back down, he asked her. "You sure that you don't want the money?"

She smile at him. "No, I want to made my own living."

"And what if you can't, then what, Kimberly?" Chance felt like heel, but he wasn't sure that she could keep a office job for very long, expectantly not now.

She looked him right in the eyes, and told him. "Then I will try something else besides a office job, and if I can't do that, I will tried something, else. And I will keeping trying something else until the day that I can't anymore." She meant every word of it. "And don't worry, Chance. I am not got to kill myself, you know me better than that. Besides, life is too short the way it is."

"I know you better than that?" Chance asked.

"Sounds like a country song to me." Brad said with a chuckle.

Chance gave him a look to be quiet, and he asked her, again. "I know you better than that?"

"Yea, my mama and his mama used to take in launder to make money." She was talking to Brad, but grinning at Chance. "I used to have to play with him. I could out ride him, out shoot him, and out rope him. He was a punk kid."

She shook her head in disgust, but you could tell she didn't mean it. Brad laughed.

Chance was trying not to smile. "Out ride, shoot, and rope me?"

"Yea, punk kid." She smile.

"She has it all wrong, Brad. It was the other was the around." He pretend to defend his honor.

Brad was laughing about any one calling Chance a punk kid.

"Don't believe him, Brad." She told him, she face soften. "How is your mother, Chance?"

The smile left his face. "She was killed in auto accident along my step-father a few years ago."

"I am so sorry, Chance." Kimberly remember his mother as one of the most nicest, kind lady, you ever wanted to meet.

She spent a lot of time with Kimberly's mother after Chance's father pass away. After a few months, his mother had worked for enough money to move to her sister's in California.

"She remarried?" It surprised Kimberly, because she was very much in love with Chance's father, very devoted to him.

Chance nodded his head. "He was a good man, he loved her very much, Kimberly. He had a very hard time trying to convinced her to married him." He smile as he remember. "At first, she was worry about the money he was worth, she didn't want us to feel second best to anything. He finally got her over that, than she was afraid that he was a lady's man." He starting grinning at her. "And you know my mother wouldn't put up with that." He shook his finger at her.

She nodded her head, and said. "She wouldn't had put up with that."

"When he prove to her that he wasn't, they were married, very happy married for many years. They had my little sister, Polly. She is why we find out about you."

"Really, why?" She was curious.

Chance took his time about answering her. "She was in the accident with them. She has the same damages, as you do.

Gave or take a nerve, or two."

Kimberly took a deep breath without realized it, and almost said that she was sorry, but thought better of it.

"How did you know?" She wonder out loud.

"I talked to your mother after your accident, she told me everything. You wouldn't talk to me."

She smile at him. "There wasn't anything to be said."

"I was on my way to see you, when something come up, I couldn't leave." He looked at Brad, then back to her, wondering how much to tell her, and decided to tell her the whole thing. "The reason that I couldn't come to you, was because we was losing too many business deals, and we didn't why or how. It was suggested that we have the office swept for bugs, and sure enough, they found bugs." He swallow hard. "It was my ex-wife to be, that was doing it. She was selling the information to other companies. It took us awhile and a lot of hard work to build up our business again."

Brad was totally amazed that Chance was telling her this, he didn't tell anyone about this. And when he did, he never mention who had done it. She had hurt Chance very badly, she had shook his faith in himself, much less, the people who was around him.

Brad had watched Chance go from a fun loving, easy going man, who could make the right deals at the right time, to a man that made the deals happen. He did most of the work himself, and what he didn't do himself, he would checked to make sure it was done. He had made everything that he and Polly have.

"He did most of the work himself." Brad told her.

"That is why you know about bugs, and that kind of stuff." She understood.

"We learn a lot about that kind of stuff, very quickly."

Chance nodded his head.

"I am sorry, she did you that way, Chance. Very sorry."

She gave him a sad smile, she kind of understood the hurt, and the betrayal, he must had felt. And maybe, he understood hers.

"It's okay, Kimberly, because we learned from ours mistakes, and we go on. There is nothing else we can do, you understand that, don't you?" He had kneel down beside her.

She smile at him. "We can decided how we go on."

He stood up and lean back against the desk. "That is true." He gave it some thought, then he told her. "But, any ways, that is why I didn't come to you. And then we started doing very well, again. The accident happen."

"Why is its Sway and Company? That wasn't your Sept- father's name, too. Was it?" She had to asked.

It was Brad that answer her. "When he built the company back up, his step-father handle it over to him, and the name was change. Not more than two weeks before they was killed."

Chapter Six

"BUT, POLLY WASN'T KILLED?" SHE knew it was stupid question, she already knew the answer. She didn't know what else to say.

"No, it was a miracle. She is a miracle." Chance smile. "Kind of like you, she took it in stride."

Brad was in full agreement with him. "She is a miracle."

"But, what does it had to do with you?" Chance know that she was wondering.

She gave him a apologetic look, when she nodded her head.

"After the accident, I started looking into what could be done for Polly. There's a doctor that has come up with a experimental operation, that can done in Australia. That is where we are moving to now. We have just a few more holdings to sell before we are totally sold out in the states. We will kept stocks in difference companies, but this is one of the last places that we have left to sell. The last in Texas."

He paused to look around the office, and gave a sad smile. "And it is the one that I liked the best."

She had to said. "It is very pretty."

"My step-father had built many years, ago." Chance told her. "But, any ways, when I found out about the operation, I thought of you. We were coming to Texas, and I wanted you to know about the operation. So, me and Brad went down there." He look at Brad. "We had a feeling that something was going on, we listen for awhile, then we started to investigated. We decided to wait to we had enough evidence together, before we talked to you. We got the proof, Kimberly."

"You can prove that I was the Hometown Joke?" She asked.

"Hometown Game." He corrected her.

"What is the difference?" She didn't see any.

"None." He answer her sadly.

"Tell me about the operation?" She wanted to hear about it more than anything.

"It will repaired the damages, take away the limp, the speech impaired, and it might gave you enough control of yours hands for you to draw and paint, again."

"Really?" She was shock.

Chance shook his head. "I said that it might, Kimberly.

Or it might killed you. The doctor would had explained it all to you."

"What do you mean, would have?" She didn't understand.

"Like I said, it is experimental. The doctor is working on a grant from another country, he doesn't want a lot publicity. You understand?"

"You are afraid that is what I would caused him. And it wouldn't be good publicity." She understood now.

"We thought of a way around it, though, you might not like it."

"But, I might do anything, too." She would almost do everything for this operation.

"You would go to work for me in California to help with my sister, a couple of weeks later Kimberly Racks would be killed, and Kimberly Chandlers would moved to Australia with Sway and Company. How could you be killed?" Chance asked, hoping she wouldn't know.

"Fall from a tall building or cliff, or drive off of a cliff and the pickup exploded. I would had to be kill instantly, and it would have to happen very quickly."

Brad caught his breath.

"You have thought about it?" Chance asked her, and he wasn't happy about it.

"You think about a lot of things. Don't you?" She asked as calmly and as innocently as she could. When they nodded their heads, she said. "But, we choose the way the way we go on."

"You just remember that." Chance looked worried.

"Don't worry, Chance, I will." She smile. "Do you believe in recreation?"

"I haven't really thought, Kimberly." Chance smile at her, he looked kind of amused.

She turned to Brad, he said. "Me, either."

"I want to." She nodded her head. "I believe if I go through this life, God will gave another one." She smile. "I always thought that I would came back in Australia, and live on a ranch in the last frontier. If I killed myself, I would go to hell." She shrugged her shoulders. "And I don't want to do that. It will all even out in the end, it just got too."

"You got faith in God?" Brad asked.

"You mean that I am very religion." She shook head. "No, I just believe that there is right way to live and there is a wrong way to live. And it will even out in the end."

She added more to herself. "It just got too."

"And that is what keeps you going?" Chance asked.

"Yes, but just in case I am not right, we better find enjoyment in what we do in this life, and every day of what we have." She know that better now than she had ever did, before.

"You sound wise." Brad said.

And for the first time, since she walked in, she laughed out loud. "You are making fun of me, aren't you?"

Chance started to come to his defense, but Brad come to his own defense. "No, not at all. I like the way you have handle this. You had calmly accepted the fact that you couldn't everything about what is going on, not without help.

And you have accepted that there isn't any one to help you.

But, you have kept going. I admire you a great deal."

She looked at Chance, and said. "Yelp, he is making fun of me."

Chance shook his head. "No, I think that is very sincere about what he is saying. But, you have help now. That is why we are here."

She smile at him, then it dawn on her. "Polly is why y'all can understand me. Because, I haven't had to repeat a single word. I should have noticed it before."

Chance and Brad looked at each other, and said. "Like talking to Polly."

Chance smile at her. "Just don't get excited on us, and we will continued to understand pretty well."

"I will try not to, but we will have to see when you finished telling how Kimberly Racks will be killed, and who is Kimberly Chandlers?" It sounded exciting to her.

"You will moved to ours ranch in California, to work for me. We would be showing Polly what a full, happy life, she can still have in spite of her disability. On the road to ours ranch, there is a curve that if you miss it, you will drop straight down in to the ocean. There isn't any cliffs that your pick-up could landed on, or bump on your way down." He explained it very calmly. "You won't know the roads well at all, you can't swim, even when you kick the windshield out, you can't survived. You will be lost at sea.

Or at least, that is what everyone will think. But, what will really happen is, you will have a wet suit on under your clothes, there will be a tank of air and a mask in the pickup with you. You will have to get the mask on before you hit the water. Me and Brad will be under the cliff waiting for you, when the pickup land on the bottom, we will be there to get you out and back to the ranch, before anyone know what has happen. If we are lucky, we will need to be the ones to report you missing. It will be so sad, but it will be just one of those thing."

Kimberly looked as if she was in shock, but she got out.

"You could do that?"

"Yes, but Kimberly, there are risks, even with us being right there to help. There are risks, that you will have to consider hard, and very careful. If you make it, you will become Kimberly Chandlers, you will go to Australia, you will have the operation, then you will spend the rest of your life as Kimberly Chandlers. You need to think long and hard."

"It would be the end of the games for me either way."

And that's what counted to Kimberly, she could live without games, without bugs, taps, hidden cameras, and without people coming into her place at night. A nice life.

"Yes, but Kimberly, would it be worth risking your life for?" Chance know how he would feel, but it was her life, her choice.

"It would be worth it just to end the games, but to be able to have the operation. You couldn't understand how much that would mean."

"Maybe. But, there are other ways we can help you. We can ruin them."

She interrupted him. "That wouldn't end the games, and you know.

But, that might the only way to kept them from hurting more like me."

"We can get you a job here in Texas." Chance smile at her. "Or I will give you a job, and still take you to Australia with me, with us."

"But, no operation?" She smile at him.

Chance gave it some thought before he answer. "Maybe, after awhile, Kimberly. When they have more backing for it, when there is more confident in it."

"I believe that the only way for me to have a happy life, one that I can truly enjoy, is for Kimberly Racks to be killed. I could relaxed, and maybe just enjoy living.

Especially, if the operation works." It was what she truly believed. "It would probably be my only chance for peace of mind. If I can ever have it again." Maybe, she couldn't, but it worth a try.

"You will be giving up everything."

She started shaking her head. "I will leave Frankie, and Jake to you. I have other horses that I will sale before I leave for California." She moved in the chair. "And I have paintings that needs to sold before I am killed." Then she thought. "Or maybe, I should leave them to you, too?"

Brad started shaking his head. "That would looked too suspiciously. We will have them sold, and you will have the cash with you when you are killed. Your purse and I.D. will be found, but of course, nobody would really think the cash will still be there."

She turned to look at him. "You are good."

"Yea, he is beginning to scare me." Chance gave him a look of leery mistrust.

"I learn it all from him." Brad told her looking totally innocent.

"I was afraid of that." She said it with sincerely that they didn't buy.

Chance kicked at the bottom of her boot. "Hey, who are you going to believed?"

She looked up at him, and said. "I know you."

"And that is a point for me." Brad join in.

"Of course." She said.

"Good thing, Polly isn't here, or y'all would really just rake me over the coals." Chance seems disgusted with them.

Then Brad and Kimberly laughed.

But, Chance seems to be more interested in the paintings. "You have paintings, you did before the accident?"

Chapter Seven

KIMBERLY NODDED HER HEAD. "I have a few left. I couldn't get them sold in time to get Red and Cricketts Rose to another place. Then I didn't want to, they are all that I have left of time when I could paint and draw." She shrugged shoulders. "But, if Kimberly Racks is going to be killed, I would rather have the money. There one that I would like to give to my dad, and one to my sister."

"It would only be the right thing to do?" Chance asked.

She nodded.

"I am looking forward to seeing them. We will help you pack them up to be ship to California, today."

"Today? Why so soon?" She asked.

"We need to do this quickly. Like I said, we are getting ready to leave the states. We will closed the deal on this building, today. And if you really don't want to go to court?" Chance raised his eyebrows.

She shook her head. "I thought you were going to scare them?"

"Not now. Now, we are going to keep they nasty bugs and whatever else out of our way." Chance shrugged his shoulders. "When they figured out what is going on, they will either have to come to us, or leave it alone. I think we can kept it up for two weeks, after Kimberly

Racks is killed it shouldn't take long for them to leave us alone?" He turned to Brad.

"I wouldn't think so." Brad shook his head.

"Who is Kimberly Chandlers?" She asked.

Chance and Brad chuckled.

"She has lost both of parent in auto accident when she was very young. She has no living family, she become a responsible of the state, until she met Polly. Then I put her to work for me. She can talk, but she don't, not since the accident. She walked with braces, but she doesn't leave the apartment. She does computer work for me, in my personal business. No one in the company has ever met her, no one will remember her, but the state will have records that she was under their care."

"She doesn't exist?" She raised her eyebrows.

"Oh, but of course, she does, Kimberly. Me, Brad, and Polly take very good care of her. She never did without anything, she just don't go out in public, because of the disability she ended up with after the accident. She is going to Australia with us to have the operation. Of course, the doctor will have to do his tests, because it has been so long since she had been to a doctor."

"She hates doctors." Brad added.

"Where has she been all this time?" Kimberly looked at them.

"She has been in a apartment in Las Vegas, Nevada."

Chance answer her.

"Las Vegas, Nevada?" She had to asked. "Why?"

Chance chuckled. "Yes, that is where I stay most of time. On a ranch in Nevada, we have main offices in Las Vegas, and in California, but I don't like the earthquakes, I won't stay there for very long, I have had to travel a lot on business, but when we sale out in the states. I can stay in one place for a long time, in a beautiful country, on a beautiful ranch, and not have to worry about business trips.

I will be home. No cities for miles." He seems to be looking forward to it.

"You haven't been in Texas?" She was amazed.

He looked down at her, and smiled. "No, Kimberly, if I would have been Texas, and know about what was going on, I would have gotten to you." He frown at her. "You have to believe me?" He could tell by the look on her face that she didn't.

"Las Vegas." Was all that she could say, she wanted to believe him, but she knew better. Still, on the other hand, how would he know what was going on.

"She is in L.A., now though." Brad said.

"We have either sold, or moved what we wanted to keep on the ranch in Nevada, we had rented the land out. The ranch in California will be sold, there won't be anyone there, when we get there. They will come back to work when the new owner takes over next month." Chance told her. "After you are killed, Brad will take you to the apartment, you will read all about Kimberly Chandlers. Where she was when she meet Polly, stuff like that. You will change your hair, wear braces, so you will automatic walked difference, and wear dark glasses. No one has seen Kimberly Chandlers more once, and that wasn't close. And that was Polly." He smile. "Any questions?"

She chuckled. "Just a few."

"Okay, what do you want to know?"

"I can't move Frankie and Jake to another state without having them tested for certain things, I know it takes days to get the results. And I haven't had any idea what you do to go to another country?"

"That is Brad's job." Chance told her.

Brad took a fake bow, and told her. "I know that I was getting pay for something." Then he grinned at her. "We have special arrangements with a lab, we will have the results in a few hours."

"It will take me a few days to sale my other horses."

"I will buy them by the pound, we will pick them and moved them, before we leave tonight."

"Tonight? We can't get everything pack up and loaded by tonight." She looked at him like he was crazy.

"You don't want to take everything, Kimberly. You may decided that you don't like working for Sway and Company, you don't want too much with you to move back home. Understand?"

"I won't need much, and what I do take will have to be ship back to Texas after I am killed." It finally dawn on her what he was telling her.

"You have got it, but it is just in case you won't like working for us. Get it?"

"I have got it." She nodded her head. "But, maybe we ought to pack everything up and moved it to my Dad's. That way, my family won't be left to do it, when the time comes."

They nodded their heads in agreement that it could be done.

"You will need clothes, yours paintings and drawings, and a few personal items to take with you. Everything else will be boxed up and move to your Dad's until you are sure what you want to do." Chance smile. "What else?"

She was going to kill, what was the most important things that she needed to tend to. "I want off the disability payments, and Medicaid, before I am killed. When my life is over, I want to be supporting myself." She was very determined about it.

"It's a matter of pride." Chance told Brad.

Brad started nodding his head. "I am beginning to understand."

"With what I will be paying you, plus your room and board will be provided, you will be took off. We provide health insurance, too." Chance smile at her. "You will be token off, you can be sure of it."

"Yes, but I want it settled as soon as possible." Then she thought to add. "So, I won't get into trouble, I won't want to do everything wrong."

"Very good." Chance nodded his head with approval.

"I will take care of it." Brad promised her.

"And I will probably need to pay back this month's payment." She was thinking as fast as she could.

"It will be on me, and I will take care of it. Don't worry about it." Brad promised her, again.

"On you?" Chance asked.

Brad nodded his head. "A matter of pride, remember?"

Chance chuckled as he nodded his head in agreement.

"Thank you." She smile at him, then she starting thinking aloud. "Clothes, books, and stuff like that can be replaced. It won't make sense for Kimberly Chandlers to have pictures of Red, Cricketts Rose, Jake, and Frankie, but Chance would want to have them, because he will have Frankie and Jake. You made copies, before you sent back to Texas?"

He nodded his head. "And we will make sure that is known that Kimberly Chandlers love horses and the country, she will have a lot of books about horses, and pictures, too.

She reads a lot about the stuff that she wants to do. Even though, she don't get out to do them."

"We have token a lot of Chance's and Polly's magazines, and books to the apartment." Brad told her.

Kimberly nodded her head. "I will need a will." Before they could said anything, she told them. "I have a picture that I painted of Red, back with he was younger, he was beautiful, and full of pride. Cricketts Rose's mama was in it, too, Jake was in it, when he was a baby. And I want Chance to have it."

"That way, you can have it with you, too." Chance had already figured it out.

Brad just smile, as he started writing on a pad.

Kimberly smile herself. "That's true, but if anything does happen to me, I want you to have it, honestly."

"I am honor." Chance bow his head. "Sway and Company provide all new employee with a will, if they want one. Just tell us, what you want."

She thought for a minute. "I want all of my stuff to go my sister, personal items, and whatever my part of mama left me. I think that we had already had it done, but just to be sure. And the money from the horses." She thought. "What will you do with them?"

"I will make sure that they are resold to someone who will keep them, and break them out, before they are sold, again. They wouldn't go to the meat market, if that is what you are worry about." Chance assured her. "And there will be a life insurance policy that we put on all of our employee. Who will it go to?"

"Life insurance, that will be . . ." She didn't finished what she was going to say.

"This will be one that Sway and Company will off ourselves. We do that from time to time." Chance told her with a smile.

"Who will it go to, Kimberly?" Brad asked.

"When everything is pay off, divided between my Dad and my sister. My pickup should be totally, won't it?" She didn't know about those things.

"We will make should that is cover." Chance told her, then he asked. "You do know that they didn't do all of that stuff because they was afraid of your father?"

She laughed. "He was part of it."

Chance nodded his head, and Brad caught his breath.

Then Brad asked. "Divided it?"

She gave him a sad smile, and said. "They was all in it. Divided it. But, Frankie and Jake will go to Chance Kincaid Sway."

"So, when we get to Australia, Kimberly Chandlers can be put in charge of taking care of them?" Chance smile.

"I would think that would be the thing to do." She sounded sure of it. "But, if anything happen to me or Kimberly Chandlers on the operation table, I would want them to be with you."

Chance nodded his head. "Is there anything else, you want us to do, or anything you want to know?"

She grinned. "How long how y'all been planning this with Kimberly Chandlers? And what would y'all have done with her, if I didn't do this?"

Chance grinned at her. "She only exist on papers through the years, we went back and put her there, she only been seen recently, when Brad moved her to a apartment in L.A., and that wasn't by name. If you have decided not to do this, the paper trail of Kimberly Chandlers would disappear, just as easily as it was put there. Like I said, Kimberly, when we moved one way or other, it has to be quick. You understand?" He wonder if she did.

"Believe me, I understand everything, but why are you doing this for me?" She didn't understand that.

Chance swallowed hard, and looked her in the eye, trying to find the right words to tell her how he felt about her.

Brad was waiting to hear this himself, was Chance's love for Kimberly, was that why they was doing this, or was it because it was just the right thing to do. Brad was waiting just like Kimberly was.

"I care for you more than you realized, and I wasn't about to leave for Australia without seeing you. When we find out what was going on, I decided that we was going to help you in whatever way you wanted us too." He smile at her, then he looked at Brad. "To put in words that you will understand, it is a matter of pride. We wouldn't leave you living this."

Kimberly had tears in her eyes, when she stood up.

Chance put his arms around her, and just held her.

Chapter Eight

BRAD SMILE AS HE WATCHED them, he said to himself. "A matter of pride"

Chance looked down at Kimberly, who had her head laying on his shoulder, and he asked. "Is there everything else?"

She raised her head. "No, I can't think of anything right now."

He gave apoplectic smile. "After we leave here, we won't talk about it again. Me and Brad was here on business, we have been working on this deal for weeks, while we was here I wanted to see where I spent part of my childhood.

While we was there I remember you, wanted to see you, find out you were looking a job, and I had the job for you.

Helping me with my business and showing Polly how much you can do even with a disability. You understand, we won't talk about any of this, you will keep on living and planning like you have your whole life ahead of you." He shook his head. "There will not any talk about a operation for you, just Polly, and Kimberly Chandlers. When we talked about her, she is someone that you will meet with we leave for Australia in a month. I will tell you about her, because you will be helping me with her, too. She is a good friend of Polly, but we won't talk too much about her. For some reason, she won't come to life until after the operation."

"I wouldn't know why." She shook her head sadly.

Chance grinned at her, but in a most serious tone, he said. "This the way it get to be. We won't talk about this again when we leave this room, we can talk about a lot of stuff, but not this. I just happen to know people that want horses to break, good timing. There are reasons, you can't have the operation, medical that can't be explained until they do more tests in Australia, and that is all that will be say. Understand?"

She stepped out of his arms, trying to think if there was anything else that she needed to know. "Frankie and Jake will be leaving with us tonight? Then on to Australia with us? Who will pay for this?"

"It is on me, I have horses of my own, two more isn't going to bother me." Chance told her, then he asked. "Are we ready?"

She looked at them, then she thought. "If we can't talk about this, how will we plan my accident?"

Chance looked at Brad. "Well, that will have changed, we will have to wait to see how soon we can get yours painting sold. We can find a safe place for a couple of hours to plan it, don't you think, Brad?"

"I would think that we could, the day that you get paid for yours paintings, that will be it." Brad was thinking though. "Maybe, we better plan it, now. So, if we can't get together later, she will know what to do."

Chance nodded his head.

"When we paid you the cash money for your paintings, it will be almost night, but you will be so happy, you are to going to take it to the bank that night. While you are changing your clothes, me and Chance will go in to his office at the ranch, his office over look the coast, you can leave his outside door, and get down to the water without being see, no matter how close you are being watched."

"We will crawl on the ground." Chance said.

Brad nodded his head in agreement. "We will have ours sub-gear hidden, we will get in it, and go down the coast to where you will be going off into the water. Your pickup will be park in the garage, Polly will sneak sub-gear into your pickup, just the tank and head gear, you will have a wet suit on under clothes. When you go off the cliff, you get out of your seat belt and get the head gear on. When you land on the bottom, me and Chance will get you out of the pickup, we will take you back to the office the way that we come out, you will crawl through the house into the floor board of my car that will be park in the garage. I will go by the apartment to check Kimberly Chandlers, and that where you will stay for two weeks, until we leave for Australia." He smile at the amazed look on her face. "You will going in to town late, so Chance will decided that we meet you at the shopping center where the bank is. It is right on outside of the city, you will not have any problem getting to it. We decided it a good time to turn your pickup over to Sway and Company, we will arrange a driver to meet us there. Chance and Polly will plan on picking you up at the shopping center, I will go by the apartment, and meet y'all later in the city at a restaurant."

"But, . . ." Chance took over. "when me and Polly get there, you are nowhere around, you aren't in one of the shop, we called the bank to have they check, and you never made it there. Polly will remember that the guard rail around the curve was down, but it has been like that for awhile, because I am going to replaced the old one with newer, safer one. We will wait awhile, then I will get uneasy, and we will go ahead and call the police. If they will not go ahead and start searching in the water below the cliff, I will hire a crew to start, because I will just know that something has happen to you, if you are not the water, you have met with foul play. One way, or other, we are determined to find you.

And when they dive into the water, yours pickup, yours purse with I.D. will be found, and part of clothes that you was wearing will probably be found floating in the water down the coast. But, your body will never be found, and the search will go on for days. I am pretty sure that you will be declare dead before long, if not before we leave for Australia, I will fly back for your Memorial Service whenever it is. The new guard rail will be name after you. We won't ever know what causes you swirl too far to the outside, or what really happen, but you did kick the windshield out, trying to get out, but you couldn't swim, more than likely you couldn't had made it, any ways. You would have probably been in shock. It is very sad, but . . ." He shrugged his shoulders. "it couldn't have been help."

"Just one of those thing." Brad nodded his head in agreement. "But, if there is anything else, Kimberly, we need to know, now."

She tried to think, but she couldn't think of anything, so she shook her head.

But, Brad did. "What would you like on your headstone, Kimberly?" He looked at Chance. "A loving friend, a loving daughter?"

Kimberly went to laughing. "You will put Miss Kimberly Branche Racks. And that is all you will put. Understand?"

"Branche?" Brad said it with a question in his voice.

"And no comments. Can you put on a headstone?" She knew that Kimberly Branche didn't sound quiet right.

Brad looked at Chance, who was standing straight up now, gathering papers and things from the desk, he looked up long enough to nod his head.

"We can do that." Brad smile.

But, Chance looked her up and down, and said. "Miss."

Kimberly didn't comment on it, but she had to asked. "Wasn't they listen in when you called me?"

They both grinned, and said together. "Not that time."

"But, when I replayed it?"

"They will have to talked to me or Brad about it, and how would they know about it? We will waiting for them to come to us, Kimberly." Chance told her.

"It won't be in a nice way." She warned them.

They tried to hide their smiles. "We will tried to be prepared for them." Chance assured her. "All they will want is for us to take part in their game, which is your life. We will figured how to handled them when the time comes, Kimberly. I promised you." He closed his brief case, and asked. "Ready?"

Chapter Nine

KIMBERLY TOOK A DEEP BREATH, and gave these two men that she was putting her life, and the end of her life in theirs hands, a long, hard look. Did she trust them that much. Would she have much of a life, if she didn't trust them. She didn't think so.

Like Chance had said, to these people, her life was no more than a game to amuse themselves with. She had no privacy, no hope for a future, and she know that she wouldn't ever have a man in her life, not one who would share her bed, to hold her like a man should hold a woman. It wasn't meant to be for Kimberly Racks. If there was ever a chance for her to have that, even after the wreak, it was gone now.

Chance came to her, and rubbed his hand up and down her arm, trying to bring her comfort. "If you change your mind, just don't go to the bank, we will know what you mean."

She look up at him, he was tall, lean built, and very good looking. He didn't seem like the type of man who put up games, much less, play them with another person.

"Don't worry about it, it is the only way that I will a chance for the operation, or even just a happy life. I won't back down." She was sure of it. "Ready?" She asked them.

Chance grinned, then look at Brad, who was standing at the door with his hand on the knob. They nodded their heads, and said together. "Ready."

Brad opened the door, and Chance took her by the arm to lead her toward the door, before Chance closed the door behind them. He took one last look around the office, the office of a man that had loved him like his own, a man that had trusted him with his life work, the man who had this building built from the ground up. Chance too, was leaving a life behind. He closed the door.

Kimberly asked. "Now what?"

Chance and Brad chuckled.

"Now, the work begins for us, Kimberly." Chance told her, before he turned to Mrs. Felts. "You can tell the regular secretary that she come back to her desk, now. And if you would, please had the one painting that I show you earlier, and the sculptor of the bull ready for shipment before you leave."

"Of course, Mr. Sway. And I would like to say how sorry I am that Sway and Company are selling out. But, I am sure that you are doing what you feel is best." Mrs. Felts told him with respect that come natural. "Texas will miss you."

He gave her a smile. "That is very nice to hear, Mrs. Felts. And I can't tell how I appreciated you coming in today. I wouldn't know any one that I could have trusted more."

"It was my pleasure." Mrs. Felts told him.

Chance and Brad shook her hand warmly, then Chance turned Mr. Cabot Who had been sitting in the out of office with Mrs. Felts, now he was standing, waiting for his orders. "We will take Kimberly's purse, now." Chance told him.

"Yes, sir, it had been clean out." Mr. Cabot pick it up off of the floor to hand it to Kimberly.

"Kimberly, this Mr. Cabot, he is the best . . ." Chance hesitated for a minute, then he said. "bug man in the business. He will be with us for awhile. Mr. Cabot, this is Kimberly Racks. She just started working for us, today."

"Congratulations, and it is nice to meet you." Mr. Cabot smile at her.

123

"I have called Roy, he is on his way to pick up the horses and had them weighed. I told him, that we would meet him in town, then we will help him load them." Brad had been on the phone, before he rejoin them.

"That is very good." Chance told them as he lead the way to the outer office's door, then on to the elevator. "Me and Kimberly will take you and Mr. Cabot to Kimberly's pickup, so y'all can go on to meet Roy to weighed his truck and trailer. Me and Kimberly will trade in the car for a truck and trailer for Frankie and Jake, and everything else that she might want to take with her. We will help Roy load the horses, I will take blood from Frankie and Jake, and send it to the lab with Roy."

"You can do that?" Kimberly asked him, as they step out of the elevator.

He smiled down at her, as he nodded his head. He take her by the arm, and they lead the way out of the building into a parking lot. All the while, he was telling them what they was going to do, and how.

"While the lab is testing the blood, we will help Kimberly clean out her apartment." His tone suggested that was two meaning, but the other one wasn't said.

But, Mr. Cabot nodded his head like he understood.

Chance helped Kimberly into a long, four door car, while Brad and Mr. Cabot got in the back seat.

"We will unload the stuff that she didn't want to take at her dad's and sister's, then we will load Frankie and Jake, go by the lab on our way to the airport."

They all nodded their heads in agreement.

Kimberly told him where her pickup was park, when they pulled up as close as they could get to her pickup.

Chance told them. "Don't clean out it here, wait until you get out on the highway, then pull on a country road. Do as quickly as you can."

Brad said. "We will, then we will meet you in town at where we need to weigh the truck and trailer."

Chance nodded his head, and Kimberly handed Brad her keys to her pickup, then she watched Brad and Mr. Cabit take cases out of the car's trunk.

When they started the pickup, Chance pulled out of the parking lot.

"We are going to the airport, now, a side enter." He smile at her.

Kimberly watched the shops, the malls, and the fast food places go by, she turned to Chance, and asked very quietly. "Can you tell me what you had been doing? I mean, since you left as a kid?"

He chuckled, and said just as quiet. "Yea, I can tell you that. If you promised not to fall to sleep on me?"

She gave him a oh, sure, look, but said. "I promise not too."

Before he started talking, and he turned into a entrance gate that you a way thorough a high, net wire fence with barb wire at the top.

Chance show a barge to a guard who sitting in a small booth, the guard gave him a wave to go ahead.

"When me and my mother moved to California to live with Aunt Louise. Mother went to work for a Company, after a while she started keeping house for the owner, after awhile she was offer job in Nevada, still keeping house for the owner."

He smile as if he was remember it.

Kimberly noticed he headed away from the main buildings, and was making his way to where there was a huge plane standing still, there was a truck and a long, cover, goose- neck trailer parked beside it.

"Don't forget where I was, and I will finished telling you about my life, later." His tone told her that he was making light of it, but she was very interested.

He stopped the car, they was climbing out, when a man came down out of the plane, smiling at Chance.

"How is going, Gus?" Chance asked him.

"Everything has been very quiet as usually, Mr. Sway."

Gus seem like he was puzzled about something.

"I have a feeling that it is all about to change, though. Just keep your eyes open, and be on your toes, ok?" Chance already knew Gus would, he just wanted him to know important it was, now.

"Of course, sir, you know that I will" Gus assured him, then he nodded his head to Kimberly.

She smile at him, as she watched Chance opened the door of the truck, he was taking out a change of clothes. A pair of old work boots, a pair of blue jeans, and a long, sleeve western shirt.

"I was wondering why you was going to pen horses in a business suit, and three or four hundred dollars pair of boots." She grinned at him like she thought that he had lost his mind.

"That's a dressing room in the trailer." He look at her like how dare she questioned his judgment.

Kimberly ignore the look, and said. "I know."

"I will just be a minute." He told her, as he opened the side door of the trailer.

The dressing room was in the front part of the trailer, it was closed off like a small room of a house. Kimberly knew that some of them had build in showers, carpet on the floor.

But, she hadn't seen the inside of the newest trailers, she didn't what kinds of stuff they had in them, now days.

This one had the dressing room, and room for four horses, hay racks, and hangers for feed buckets, there was rubber mats on the floors, to help keep the horses from slipping down. It was of the nicest one, that Kimberly had seen.

Her and Gus was waiting for Chance, as he come out, after just what seems to be a few minutes.

Chance must have seen the surprise look on her face, because he told her. "It don't take men as long to change their clothes as it does women."

She gave him a dirty look, as Gus chuckled, and nodded his head like he understood completely.

"Don't gave me that look. I will tell you like I tell Polly." Chance put the three piece, western cut, suit and the dress boots in the extended cab of the truck. "You pick out what you want to wear, you take it off the hangers, and put it on, and then you don't worry about if it bring out the color of your eyes, or if it flatter your hair, or your figure." His hands went in the air, and come back down. "You just wear it, and go on with your life."

Gus went to laughing, and Kimberly had no idea why she was getting such a lecture on dressing, but she could only guess that it was a ongoing thing between him and his sister. And for some reason, it made her think more of him.

But, she said. "Well, any ways, I think that the light blue western shirt, you are wearing bring out the color of yours eyes beautifully, and it flattered the color of your hair and bring out your tan." She shook her head, and went.

"And mm, mm, it and those jeans should do flatter your figure."

She was doing her best not to start laughing, but Chance and Gus wasn't.

It had been a long time, since Gus had seen his boss cutting up and teasing with any one, but Polly and Brad. It also surprised him, because Chance and Brad didn't talk like this was going to be happy trip, but maybe it has change since he was told about it.

"Thank you, Kimberly. It makes a fellow feels pretty good about himself to hear things like that, we do try to keep ourselves in shape for you." Chance told her.

"You are welcome, just remind me not to ever asked your advise on what to wear." She rolled her eyes for the added affect.

"Oh, you are like Polly, you looked pretty in anything." Chance smile, as he gentle took her hand and lead around to other side of the truck.

She tried not to smile, but she did. "Does Polly buy that?" She asked him with a side look.

Before he closed the door for her, he told her. "Yea, but when we are in a hurry, Brad has to tell her. Big brother's opinion may not always be right." He shrugged his shoulders like he didn't understand.

But, Kimberly did, although she didn't explained it to him.

He said something Gus, who started laughing, again. Then Chance climb into the truck, gave her a smile. "Ready?"

She nodded her head. "Ready"

He started the truck, and wave at the guard as they pulled back out on the highway, making extra wide turns for the trailer.

When he was line out, again, she asked. "The job in Nevada?"

He grinned. "Yea, I was all for it, I didn't like California. So, mama took the job, and we would be staying a ranch, that was for me, of course."

"Of course." She agreed.

"Mama went from housekeeper, to being his hostess, to being his wife. It wasn't easy for him, he had to convince that he was in it for life, that he wasn't one to take marriage or divorce lightly, but when he did, they was married and they had Polly." He grinned without knowing it.

"When I finished collage, I was going to leave the business, and start up a ranch of my own. But, that is when my ex- wife-to-be decided if she was going to a lot of money out of me, she had better do it then, and she did. "The grin had already left his face. "She wasn't the ranch type, if you know what I mean?"

Kimberly nodded.

"Then I couldn't leave the business, not until we make up for what we had lost, and when we had, he turned it over to me. At the time, it was such of a surprise, that I didn't think. But, it did start me to thinking about what I really wanted to do, and I was about to tell him that I really didn't want to be the head of a business, but they was killed before I did. And after that, when it wasn't business, it was looking for a way to help Polly. And while I was in Australia, I decided that is where I wanted to stay for the rest of my life. I talked it over with Polly, we went over all of our options, and what we are doing now is the best for me and Polly. She gets half of the company's assets, of course. And after the operation, she can decided what she wants to do, if she wants to come back to the states to start up the business, again. It will be possible for her to do it without too many problems."

"Do you think she will?" Kimberly didn't why, but it surprise her.

Chance made a face. "She could if she wanted to, but I think that she would rather get married and stay at home."

He grinned. "That's what I think."

Chapter Ten

BEFORE SHE COULD SAID EVERYTHING, they met the womanize, whore chasing bastard that she agree to married the second time. The man behind all the tests, all the games, and the man behind the first man, who had her believing he wanted to marry her.

She wasn't sure why she fell for the first one. She had always knew that there was people who just wanted to be married, she could only think that is what happen to her, at that time, her whole life was changing, and she had finally wanted to try marriage.

But, now, she was even relieve that he was nothing more than a setup, he was meant to fool her. She had thought that he could handle her disability, since he worked with people with disability, but he couldn't, he just worked with people with disability. She didn't blame him, she blame herself for letting herself get in that bad of shape, so bad of shape that she had fell for it. She realized now that it was just the thought that someone out there who wanted do all that stuff for her, that is why she got so caught up in all of the games.

But, this one that they was meeting with the cute girl sitting right under him, now she fell hard for him. He was the man of her dreams, tall, good-looking, cowboy, and he seems so nice and sweet. And he was the one, who wanted to take her all of those places, let her do all of these things.

At first, when she figured it out that it was him behind all of it, she thought it was so romantic.

But, then she also figured out, that they had lived in the same town for all of those years, and he never said a word. And if he never really married, she could imaged all of the women that he had been with.

Most of them would have to be her, so called, friends from her High-School days, and theirs sisters. She had figured it out, that he is probably caused of the breakups of at least three marriages of people, she had knew. When he started working cows with their fathers. And God only knows how many more.

What got her was, she knew what kind of man, he was, and she still fell for him. And he sat there and told what kind of women he like, when she had thought about it, she could remember him standing at the rodeo one night watching one of those well-endow woman ride barrels. God, it was sicken back then, much less now, that she had fell for him.

She wonder if all men was like that, and she had decided that they was. And here he was now, showing her that it was all just a game, not to count on him, or anyone else for that matter, that everything was a game.

At first, he had a phony driving with all the women either in front or following along behind, then it was the man himself with one sitting right under him. It has caused her to cry for hours at night, and he could hear and see her, he was the one behind the bugs and the hidden cameras, watching dress and undress, listening to her crying and never coming to her.

But really, she needed to thank him for showing her what kind of man, he really was. She owe him a present, too bad she wasn't going to be around long enough to give it to him.

The worst part about it, was it proves that she was flaky herself, it all caused her to take a good, long, hard look at herself. God help her, she wanted to improve herself, she wanted to mature.

"And do you know what the worst thing was about what happen with my ex-wife to be?" Chance asked her.

He startled her, she shook her head. "No?"

"She made me look like a fool, you know what I mean?"

He knew that she did, but she nodded her head any ways.

"She played me for a fool, I will tell you that."

What he was really telling her was that he knew who that was, and they couldn't talk about it.

"She made me doubt myself, because I was the one who let her play me that way. I didn't trust my judgment of people any more, it was very hard for me to build the business back up feeling that way, but maybe it help me, too.

It made me more caution, and that may had helped me to go farther in the business. I wasn't so naive, so I wasn't took in by people who wanted to take advantage of me. Understand?" He gave her a smile.

"I understand." And she did.

"Do you think Polly ought to count on getting married?" He raised his eyebrows.

"I wouldn't think it would be a good idea to." She didn't think this day, and age, that marriage wasn't something that any one should count on.

He nodded his head sadly. "I was afraid of that."

She was so surprised, that she asked. "Don't tell me that you do?"

He smile. "I think that she should have the right to think she could. Right now, she don't think she could because of her disability, and that isn't true, Kimberly. That's why I hire you, remember?"

She nodded her head. "I remember."

"It's just too bad those letters you wrote to me went to someone else. It's a good thing that we come to check on you, before we left for California."

It took her a minute to figured out what he was doing, he was trying to help her save face. Those letters that she wrote to that man who set her up so well, those letters that she wrote thinking that he really care about her, the letters that she wished with all of her heart she hadn't written.

Chance was letting her save face, and she knew that there wouldn't ever be a way to thank him enough. Where did this man came from?

"Yea, I really hate that I got it mess up. Don't you know, it scared him?" She was following his lead.

Chance chuckled. "Yea, I really feel sorry for him."

But, you could tell by his tone that he felt a lot of things for that man, and not one of them was sympathetic.

Kimberly was just so glad, that she hadn't gave the man who was behind it anything real. Thank God, she hadn't been so stupid, again.

Kimberly and Chance met up with Brad, Mr. Cabot, and Roy with his truck and trailer at the scales. From there they went to her father's ranch.

Kimberly listen as Chance told her father and her sister that he was giving her a job with his company in California, then they was going to Australia. They was going to help her pack up what she would need for a couple of months, just until she was sure that she wanted to stay with them.

They was going to help clean out her apartment, so her father and sister wouldn't have to do for her. He knew someone who wanted the horses, it would be less work for them not having to take care of the horses. They was going to help her found a buyer for her paintings, because she had decided that she just had too many to keep. It all sounded very reasonable.

Chance received, a lot of, do you think, he knows what he is doing, looks from Frankie, Jake, and Kimberly with his took the samples, but he seem to know what he was doing.

The horses was loaded, and left with Roy along with Frankie's and Jake's blood samples.

The apartment was clean out, even by Mr. Cabot. The stuff that she wanted to take with her was left on the trailer.

And now, Kimberly, Chance, and Brad was starting to uncover her paintings.

When Brad uncovered one of the paintings, he gave a low whistle. "I was wondering why you didn't took up computer art, but never mind. It is beautiful, Kimberly."

She just smile as they uncovered them one by one.

There was one of a grey hair, woman with a kind baby, face, her green eyes sparkled with life, it was her mother standing with her father.

"That will go to my sister." She smile.

There was one of a team of mules, painted in detail with their harness on, the man behind the plow that they was pulling is her father, with his blue eyes shining in the sun light on a beautiful day. "That one will go to my father."

Then there was one of a gelding, his chestnut red coat was shinning, his head was held high with pride, he had a white blaze down his face, and two back white socking legs.

His eyes told you he was a kind, gentle fellow, but plenty of heart, and he was full of spirit.

And standing with him was a mare, she was a Quarter Horse to a tee. She had a arch neck, low in the front, and high the back, she was built for cutting. And from what Kimberly had been told she did it with the best of them, right up until the time she broke back right knee. That is how Kimberly come to own her.

But, she was still a beautiful mare, she was a dark red, with shade lighted red mane and trail, a slip or two of white on her face. Her eyes said that she was kind, quiet, and wise.

Standing along beside her was a small, baby colt. He was a dark red, with a tin white blaze that ran down his face. He was one of the quietness, gentleness, loving colt you had ever seen. His eyes was full with a gentle curiosity, and a loving playfulness.

Kimberly wipe the tears from her eyes. "This one goes to Chance. It is Red, Cricketts, and Jake."

Brad smile. "That is Jake? He was a tiny baby, wasn't he?"

She nodded her head in agreement.

"It is beautiful, Kimberly. Thank you very much, I can't tell you how much it means to me." His eyes took in all of the details of the painting. "You were pretty good, were you?"

"Pretty good?" Brad repeat in amazement.

Chance gave him a look that said he was just teasing her. "We don't want it to go to her head, do we? Remember, we will be living with her?"

Brad snapped his fingers, and said. "That's right. They are pretty good, Kimberly."

There was a painting of a couple being marrying under a mesquite tree in south Texas, with a dog, horses, a cow, and a calf standing among the couple's two legged friends, and family.

One was of a older ranch style home that was built with only the top of the line materials, it was surrounded by big, oak trees, there was another couple being married, you could almost the music coming from the trees, as the wind would brow thorough them.

Another one was of a old-fashioned rock building that set on the outside of a small town, it has a sign that said the owners was partners in marriage, as well as law.

One was of couples dancing around a camp fire, theirs horses was tried around them, and there was a full moon shinning down on them. From the looks on the couples faces, you knew that they knew exactly what they wanted.

There was one of a girl sitting in a beautiful old- fashion building, that set in the middle of a small town business district. She was watching a tall, lanky cowboy walking down the sidewalk, she was having quiet dreams about a future with him, from the look in her eyes, you just know that they were going to come true.

There was one of a girl and a cowboy standing under a tree, with a moon that wasn't quiet full, and a herd of cattle bedding down the night in the back ground. From the looks that was in the couple's eyes, you could tell that they had just started believing in each other, and you just knew that in the years that fallow they wouldn't do anything to take that look out of each other eyes.

There one of a couple standing on the sand of the Texas Gulf Coast, the water had gentle waves in it, the shy was a beautiful blue, and the sun was shining bright. The couples was surround by officers of different types of law offices, and you could tell the preacher was reading them the laws of love, the ones that they would gladly obey for the rest of their lives.

There was one of a couple riding a beautiful, white stallion, they looked like they was riding for their future together, and the stallion looked so powerful, he could moved like running wind, he would make sure that they spend the rest of their lives together.

There was one of a beautiful a Quarter Horse filly crossing the finish line of The All-American Futurity in Ruidoso Downs, New Mexico, the filly was a full length ahead of the other horses. In the back ground of the painting, there was a couple dancing under a tree on the San Antonio River Walk, there was also a older framed house a short distant from a racing stables with horse walkers, and a race track done in detail, and there was one the filly when she was younger, she look like she was saying, if you give me a fighting chance, and I will win that race.

It was Kimberly's favorite painting, because it was several paintings brought together in one.

Kimberly took a deep breath, when she looked at the other water color paintings, and the difference drawings. She didn't mean to, but she said it out loud.

"It is a good thing that I can't paint any more, or they would ruin them."

Chance took a breath. "You know what they did?"

She nodded her head.

But, Chance had to put his finger to his lips, meaning for her to be quiet.

Brad just shook his head sadly.

Kimberly shook her head sadly, too. She painted from fantasies in her head, the paintings wasn't of real places or people, or even people that she would like to meet. She might take one thing that is real, or maybe something that she wanted to do, then everything else was built around it from her imagination.

They didn't ruin the painting itself, they either ruin what was in the painting, or had another painter take the idea of her painting, and redo it in a difference form.

Kimberly believed that they had burned down at least two houses, that looked like the ones in her paintings, and then there was a time or two that she could had swore that another artist had done her painting over.

At first, she thought she was just being foolish, but after all that she had been through lately, she had decided that she wasn't foolish.

"I was right about that, too?" She just had to know.

They both nodded their heads.

There was tears in her eyes. "It is a good thing that I won't be able to paint, again."

She didn't understand why person would take another person's work, all the love that they put it, and in one way or another ruin it.

Why? Because it was like Brad had said, she was easy prey.

"It is a good thing that I won't ever be able to paint, again." She said it, again, but this time even she was totally convinced it was the truth.

135

Before, they started packing them up for shipment, Chance asked. "Do you have any more ideas for paintings?"

She smile. "I think that I could do two more like the filly winning the All-American Futurity, one would be just as good as maybe even better, and several more like the others." She looked at her hands, then shook her head. "But, I won't ever be able to paint, again."

And Chance couldn't argue with her, no matter, how much, he wanted too.

Chapter Eleven

AS KIMBERLY AND CHANCE LEFT pulling the trailer with Frankie, Jake, her paintings, and what stuff she wanted to have with her, she wonder what would happen to her father and sister when they heard that she had been killed in a accident.

But, she figured they was tough, they would be okay, she was really hoping that somehow they would be better off without her. And if this was the only way that she could have the operation, she would do it. Her father and sister would go with their lives.

She took a side look at Chance, the only thing that worried her was him having to take the responsibly for her being in California. She didn't like that part of it, but surely he had thought it all through, before now.

He caught her looking at him. "Are you sure that you have everything that you want with you?"

She nodded her head.

"Did you get all of your pictures?" He asked with a grin on his face.

He and Brad had given her a hard time about how pictures that she had of Cricketts Rose. They had decided that it was too bad that she didn't think more of her, the rolls and rolls of pictures that had been token of her, just wasn't enough. They had both agree though, she was beautiful. And they didn't even get to see her when she was full of life.

They didn't even know what beautiful was, but Kimberly did. It was something that she wouldn't ever forget.

She also had pictures of Red, Jake, Frankie, and a good many more. She had even had some of when she was little.

She grin at him. "Yea, I think that I have most of them."

He took a breath and repeat. "Most of them."

She chuckled. "Yea, don't forget, I would like to have copies of them made, to send back home. So, they would have a copy of them."

"No, I won't forget, Kimberly." He nodded his head. "I won't forget."

When they pulling up to the plane, Brad and Mr. Cabot was there waiting for them. Brad and Mr. Cabot had left before Chance and Kimberly to go by and pick up the results from the lab.

Frankie and Jake was ready to go anywhere, there was just one problem. How was they going to convinced Frankie and Jake that they really wanted to walk up a long ramp into the damndest looking trailer they had ever seen.

Kimberly was at the back of the trailer helping Chance unload them. "They ain't going to like this." She told him.

"Don't tell that they never flown before?" He asked with a mock look of surprise of his face.

"No, to the best of my knowledge, they had never flown before. We are not jet setters like some people." She smile at him.

"If we can't talk them up there with feed, we will give them something to calm them down, and if that doesn't work, we will try something, and keep trying until we find a way."

He smile at her. "We won't let they get hurt. Do they get upset easy?"

She shrugged her shoulders. "There is a difference between upset and excited? Isn't there?"

"Let me guess, they are known for getting excited?"

She kind of grin. "Well, kind of. Not often, either, but I don't know why, but I do think this will be one of those rare occasion that they will get a tiny bit excited."

"Now, I just know that I am going to regret asking this, but what is the difference between upset and excited?" He asked with a skeptic look on his face.

"Excited is when they perk up and pay attention, upset is when you have to give them time to look things over, and calm down." The expression on her face told him, that she thought everyone should know the difference.

"Now, I know. I guess, that I have been in Nevada or other places too long. I have forgotten what is what, I am sorry." He shook his head like it was truly unforgivable.

Kimberly smile at him teasing her, and Frankie and Jake back out of the trailer excited.

"Which one goes first, Kimberly?" Chance wanted to know.

"I will take Jake first, and you bring Frankie." She looked at Jake, then at the ramp, it had a rail on both sides of it, and mats all the way up it, so the horses wouldn't lose their footed. She didn't know anything about planes, but ones the she had seen had movable stairs going up a side door. This had the moveable ramp going up a wide side door.

"Ready?"

"Are you talking to me or Jake?" Chance asked with a grin.

"Both." She laughed.

"Okay, clear the ramp." Chance told Brad, Mr. Cabot, and Gus, who had been loading the paintings, clothes, and the other stuff that Kimberly wanted with her.

They had brought Frankie's and Jake's feed and hay with them, because changing their feed all at once could cause problems for theirs system.

She grin at Brad. "If we have problems bring feed."

He nodded his head. "Will do."

When she and Jake started up the ramp, she whispered in his ear. "Now, don't embarrass me, Jake. I am going with you, I will be right there with you all the way."

He gave her a look that said, is that really suppose to

Make me feel better.

But, Jake walked up the ramp without a problem, and Frankie was right behind him.

139

Inside the plane, there was portable stalls set up with straw for they to stand on, they was tried up in the stalls.

"I have to change my clothes to get ready for the meeting to closed the deal on the building. They are coming here to sign the papers, so if you need me, just hollow."

But, before he left the plane, he turned around to whisper in her ear. "What did you tell Jake right before you started up with him?"

She smile up at him. "I told him not to embarrass me, that I would be right there with him. And do you know what?"

Chance shook his head.

"He gave me a look that said, is that really suppose to make me feel better. Can you believe that?" She shook her head like she couldn't believe it.

"I just don't understand it, it would make me feel better to know that you would be with me." He told her with a smile, then he going out the door." Hollow, if you need us."

Kimberly nodded her head that she would, as she watched him go off of the plane.

Then she turned back to Frankie and Jake, who were looking the place over with their eyes opened wide, they was smelling of the place where they were tried, but other than that they seem quiet enough. They didn't seem like they was going to get too upset about the whole thing.

Kimberly could understand why it didn't mean much to them that she was there. At first, she stopped spending so much time with them, so when she finally got a job, and went to work, they wouldn't miss her, and she wouldn't miss them so much.

But, now she was afraid that she had neglected them, because of some damn old game. It was a part of the games, that if she fed them, that the game was over. Believing that kind of stuff was bad enough, but if she had ever caused these two beautiful, loving horses any pain, because a game, it made her sick to think that she might had.

She could only hope that Frankie and Jake could forgive her, and with time maybe she could win their confident and their loved, again.

Even if she wouldn't be around long to win their trust, again, she was leaving them with Chance. He would made sure that they had everything that they needed, she was sure of it. She didn't know why she felt that he would, but she did.

She rubbed her face softly against theirs, and told them that everything was going to be okay, it was just a funny looking trailer. She told them where they was going.

They watched a limousine put up to the plane, Chance and Brad got in, when the driver opened the door for them.

Kimberly put up a brush from a tack box setting besides the stalls, and started brushing Frankie and Jake off.

By the time, Chance and Brad climb out of the automobile, Frankie and Jake was standing quietly, but still with wide eyes.

"Well, what do they think of it?" Chance wanted to know when he and Brad come back up the ramp into the plane.

"It is the damndest looking trailer that they ever seen." She felt sure that was what Frankie and Jake was thinking.

Chance and Brad chuckled.

Chance looked around the plane, and said. "Yea, I have to agree with them, it is the damndest looking trailer that I ever seen, too. Before, you leave, let me check and make sure that I have all the stuff we need." He told Brad, before he went over to the tack box, he went through it, picking up medicine bottles, reading on the labels, then put them back.

"We have everything that I think we will need." He nodded his head to Brad, then he looked at Kimberly. "I forgot to asked you, was there every one you wanted to see before we left?"

If look could kill, Chance was sure that he wouldn't be alive right now.

Kimberly thought that he must had lost his mind. "You are joking, aren't you?"

"No, but I might as well had been. Right?"

She nodded her head in agreement.

"Then I guess that we are ready to leave now, Brad."

Chance said, but he raised his eyebrows at Kimberly.

She look at Frankie and Jake, who were standing quietly listen as though, they understood every word, and that made her grin as she said. "We ready."

"Kimberly, I will used your pickup tonight and part of tomorrow, then before I catch a flight to California, I will leave it with the transport company, and it should be in California in about three days. Is that

141

okay?" Brad asked, before he went on to tell her what he was going to do.

"That will be okay, just be sure to take care of it. I wouldn't want everything to happen to it." Her eyes had a sparkle of humor in them that only Chance and Brad would understand.

And they did, but they didn't said anything, just grinned.

"I will take very good care of it, I promised. I have some business to take care of for Sway and Company, then I will take care getting you off of the disability payments, and I will call the office either tonight or tomorrow, when the details of your will, it should be ready when you sign some other papers for Sway and Company." Brad started to shake her hand.

But, she told him that they were dirty.

"Well, any ways, it will be a pleasure to work with you." Then he turned Chance, and said. "I will take care of everything, and see you tomorrow. "But, before he went out the door, he turned back to Chance. "Tell Polly . . ."

Then he caught sight of Kimberly, and changed his mind. "Never mind, I will call her myself."

Chapter Twelve

KIMBERLY AND CHANCE WATCHED HIM walked down the ramp, then the ramp was moved away from the plane. Right before Chance closed the plane's door, Brad and Mr. Cabot gave them a wave.

And Kimberly said, goodbye to Texas for the last time. She used to love Texas, what she thought it stood for, and what it was, but now all of that has change, it made her sad.

Chance closed the door, and told her. "You take a seat, and I will show you how to buckle up. Then I will tell Gus that we are ready for takeoff."

When he came back to her, he took a seat beside her, and buckle up, he gave her a smile and said. "We will start moving any minute now."

And they were up in the air before Kimberly knew it.

After they had told Frankie and Jake that everything was going smoothly, they received looks that said, What in world was that looks from Frankie and Jake.

They sat back down, Kimberly looked up at him.

"Can you tell about Australia?" She wanted to hear about it.

He smile. "It is beautiful, Kimberly. It means to me now, what Texas used to mean. You can ride for days and never seen another person."

Chance told her all about his ranch, or a station in Australia, how many acres there was, how many heads of cattle he could run on it, how people that will be working on it, and what kind of horse operation he was going to have for extra income.

When he was finished, she told him. "It will take you all day every day, just to keep it going."

He had a kind of a dreamily look in his eyes when he turned to look at her, and grinned. "Yea, I know. My only regret is that I couldn't started on it sooner. But, I am going to enjoy what time I have left. I don't know how long that I can push myself like I want to, I will just had to wait and see."

Kimberly understood what he was saying, they wasn't getting any younger, she was in her middle thirties, and Chance was two or three years older than she was.

"I wasn't cut out for board rooms, business meetings, and offices. But, I did learn how to run a business successfully. I think."

Kimberly took a look at the man that he had became. "I would think so."

They landed at the L A airport, before Kimberly thought they would.

Chance open the door, and they watched a ramp being brought up to the plane. On the ground, there was a truck and a goose-neck waiting for them.

"What do you think? They will be overly anxious to get to the ground?" He already knew the answer, he just wanted to know if she was thinking on the some lines that he was.

"Oh, yea, I am pretty sure that they will be anxious to get to the ground." She know that they would be excited.

"Well, we will see, won't we?" Chance grinned.

Kimberly took a good hold of Jake's lead rope, telling him all the time, it was going to be okay. They went down the ramp at a quicker pace than they went up, but still without a problem. Frankie was right behind them.

There was lights and noise all around them, but they went in the trailer without a problem, when they was loaded, Kimberly let out a breath.

And Chance chuckled at her. "Were you worried?"

"Yea, they aren't used to all of this. But, they did good, didn't they?" Kimberly was pride of them.

"Yes, they did good." He bow his head to them.

Kimberly was laughing, when a girl came up behind Chance to put her arm around his waist.

She was a few inches over five foot like Kimberly, but she had blonde, medium length, curly, hair, while Kimberly had long, light brown, hair, she had dark, blue eyes like Chance had, while Kimberly had light blue eyes. And Kimberly was about ten years older than she was.

Chance grinned down at her, as he put his arm around her shoulders. "How you doing, Sis?"

"I am okay. How about you, big Brother?"

When she starting talking, Kimberly could tell that she had a speech impairment like herself, but to Kimberly, Polly sounded cleared.

"I am okay, too. I want you to meet Kimberly Racks.

Kimberly Racks, this is my little sister, Paulet Louise Sinclear. She answer to Polly, but if she give you problems, called her Paulet Louise Sinclear, and she will almost always straight up." Chance told Kimberly with a wink.

Polly gave him a dirty look, as she pulled away from him, she gave her hand to Kimberly. "It is nice to meet you, Kimberly."

Kimberly accepted her hand with a smile. "And it is nice to meet you, too."

Chance shook his head. "Kimberly, don't say things you will live to regret." He tried not to, but he did smile.

Polly looked up at him. "If she puts up with you, I will be a piece of cake."

Kimberly laughed, and told him. "She has a point, you know?"

He narrow his eyes at Kimberly, then he turned to the trailer. "At least, Frankie and Jake will be on my side.

Ain't that right?" He was talking to Frankie and Jake, who gave him, oh, sure, looks.

Polly went over to the trailer to meet Frankie and Jake.

Kimberly couldn't get over it, she had heard that there was other people like her, but looking at Polly was like looking at herself ten years ago. Not in appearance, but in their disability.

Gus was already unloading the stuff from the plane onto the front part of the trailer, again. All, but the paintings, and Chance had to promised Polly that he or Brad will bring her out to look at them before them was sold. She could see his painting when they got to the ranch.

Gus told Kimberly, that he would be looking forward to seeing her again, at her blank look, he explained that he would be flying them to Australia.

Kimberly told him, that she had just forgotten about it, and that she would see him there. She didn't looked at Chance and Polly.

When everything was loaded, and Polly was in the extended cab of the truck, and before Chance started the motor, he looked at Kimberly with a serious face, and said. "Now, Kimberly, tell Polly how to dress."

Kimberly turned around in the seat, grinned at Chance, but talked to Polly. "You take so much time as you need, try on as many outfits as you need to, to make sure that it bring out the color of your eyes, flatter your hair and figure. You know, like Chance does."

Chance gave her a muck look of shock, and Polly gave her a high five, and roll with laughter, when she asked. "You noticed that, too?"

Kimberly nodded.

"And he has the nerve to complain about how long it takes me to get ready." Polly sounded astound by it.

Kimberly rolled her eyes. "Men."

"Now, can I help it, if I think that she looked pretty in the first thing she put on?" Chance asked Kimberly without cracking a smile, but there was one in his eyes.

"And you know what, Kimberly? He actually thinks that I am going to believe that." Polly told her before Kimberly could answer Chance.

"Of course, you are suppose to believe it, because it is the truth." Chance told her.

"And you know what is worst, when he is in a hurry for a meeting or whatever, he gets Brad to tell me that load of crap, too. Can you believe that?" Polly had a muck look of disbelieving on her face.

Before Kimberly could said anything, Chance said. "I don't have Brad tell you anything, he just gets tired of waiting for you, too. But, I am sure that he believed it, too." He assured her with a grin.

Polly gave him a oh, sure, look, and said. "Yea, I just bet that he does."

Chapter Thirteen

KIMBERLY KEPT QUIET, AS CHANCE and Polly discuss her overly obsessive with clothes, jewelry, and how well they went together.

Kimberly could tell by Polly's designer jeans, her blouse, her jewelry, and her hair, that she was well into that kind of thing.

But, when they talking business, she was well informed in that, too. While, Kimberly didn't understand what all they was talking about, she understood enough to know that Chance wasn't patronizing his little sister, he value her opinion.

And thought enough of her to kept her informed.

They talked about what was the better investments, what had the greatest risks, and what they want to try.

Kimberly just listen to them, and she watched as they left Los Angles behind. Before she knew it they was well out of the city, and they turned off on a smaller road, following the coast.

They came to a stop at a small stables, there was two horses with their heads over their stall's doors. They whinny at the sound of the trailer pulling up.

Chance pulled to a stop. "Welcome to California, Kimberly." He smile at her.

She smile back at him, but she was kind of in shock. The stables was one of the nicest that she had ever seen, it was well lighted. She could only guess that the lights was left on for their arrival.

But, it was small, it looked like it could stable four horses with a feed room and a track room.

Then it dawn on her, this was California. This is what they called a ranch.

She had a real smile on face, but Chance proudly took it off of her face, when he informed her.

"This is the private stable, it goes with the house."

He pointed to a huge home setting on a cliff overlooking the stable on one side, and the ocean on one. "It is used for pleasure riding horses. The stables and the working cattle barns, and pens are further up. I will show it to you later on. Okay?"

She nodded her head, before they started climbing out of the truck.

"We decided to put them down here, so you could look out the window of your bedroom, and see them. We thought that you would like that." Polly grinned, as she added. "Well, Chance thought that you would."

Kimberly gave him a grin, as he starting opening the trailer gates to back out Frankie and Jake. "I will like that much."

He shook his head, as he handed her Jake's lead rope. "I don't know why, but I kind of thought you would. But, don't asked me why."

When Kimberly lead Jake by the other two horses, he wanted to be introduced to them. But, she told him that it was late, and they could talked across the hallway that runs between the rows of stalls. That seems to satisfied him.

When he and Frankie was settle in the stalls, they was fed hay, but not their grain. They would let them calm down for awhile, before they are fed their grain, it would be better for them.

Frankie and Jake took a look around their stalls, stiff it, thoroughly. The stalls were twelve by twelve foot cover under the roof of the stables, there was a door leading to the outside in the rear of the stalls. The doors leaded to a small run outside of the stalls, each stall had a run.

Kimberly decided it might be a good idea to go ahead and let out to check out their runs. And they did make the most of it, they ran from one end to the other.

Jake was a dark, chestnut red, stallion, with a tin white blaze running down his face, his eyes said that he was usually calm nature, gentle, kind, loving, and wise. He was long and lean with powerful shoulders, hips, and a well shape neck.

Frankie was a light, sorrel red, with a wide, white blaze running down her face, her eyes said that she was sweet, gentle, loving, and kind of curiosity. She was as tall as Jake, and she had a wide chest, and high hips.

They had calm down, and standing with their heads hanging over the stall's doors, watching the waves in the water. The stables was a safe distance from the ocean, the waves that was coming and going looked calm, cool, and just about right to play in.

Kimberly, Chance, and Polly had been quietly watching them, along with the other two horses. Who shook their heads like they wonder what was wrong with those two.

"Wonder what Frankie and Jake think of the ocean?" Chance asked Kimberly.

She gave some thought, then said. "It is the damndest tank of water that they ever seen."

Chance roar with laughter.

A full moon was coming up farther into the sky, as they left the stables. They had unloaded the rest of the hay, and a few sacks of sweet feed, grain. They left the lights on, so they could came back to fed them.

They had went up the cliff to stop in front of a huge home. In the distance you could see stables, barns, and cattle pens.

The home was beautiful inside and outside. The inside was decorated in southwestern style. Beautiful designed throw rugs was scatter over the hardwood floors.

Polly told her that she had prepare the bedroom joining Chance's on the far side of the house, so she could see the stables from her window.

The bedroom was large, with a walk in closet, and closed in window seat on one side of the bedroom, and a baloney over looking the stable.

Kimberly had never seen anything like it.

"It is beautiful." Kimberly told Polly.

"We aim to please. Don't we, brother?" Polly asked Chance, as he came in behind them with Kimberly's bags and hangers of clothes.

Kimberly don't own luggage, what clothes couldn't go on hangers was put in either shopping, groceries, or garbage bags. She couldn't help but wonder what Chance would had done if they had to go through the luggage section of the airport with her bags. She couldn't help, but to smile at the thought.

Chance show her a huge bathroom, that had a shower to one side, and to one side there was a huge round bath tub. It had a rail going down in to it along the steps.

There color of the tub brought out the color in the tile floor, the color of the towels cabinets also brought out the color of the tile.

"It is beautiful." Kimberly told Chance.

"The damndest bathroom that Frankie and Jake had ever seen, huh?" Chance couldn't help but smile, as he leaned against the door, watching her.

"I would think that was safe to said." Kimberly chuckled.

"I thought that we eat a light supper, fed Frankie and Jake, then called it a night. You can try it out before you crawl into bed." He moved out of the door way, so she could go back into the bedroom. "Do you think that you will be so excited that you can't sleep, or so tried that you will sleep tonight and tomorrow?"

She looked up at him in surprise. "I don't know how I feel."

He grinned at her. "We have been going so hard that we haven't gave you to think about how you feel." He put his arm around her shoulders, and sit them down on the bed where he hadn't pile her bags and hangers of clothes. "Now, sit here for a minute, and think about how you feel."

She was quiet for a minute, trying to figure out how she felt. "I am excited, but I think that I can sleep, though probably not through tomorrow."

Even if the bed that they were sitting on, felt extremely comfortable. It was large, and it looked warm, and cozy.

"Although, the bed looks very inviting." She had to confessed.

He leaned down to her ear, and said. "You ought to see mine."

She was grinning, as she turned to looked up at him, she knew that he was teasing her.

150

But, his lips touched her lips, briefly, and softly. "But, that will come later." He told her, as he pushed himself off the bed pulling her along with him.

Polly was in the kitchen putting cold roast beef, and sand witch stuff on the table that sit in the middle of the modern kitchen.

There was tall chairs around the table for them to sit in, Polly had set three places for them.

Chance help Kimberly to the table, then said loud enough for his sister to hear. "Polly did the cooking, that why we are eating light." Then he wink at Kimberly.

Polly took a seat with them, and proudly began to take up for herself. "I will have you know that I can cook."

"Yea, that maybe, but somehow it doesn't turned out like when your jeans goes with your earrings, or when your boots goes with your purse." He teased her.

Polly raised her eyebrows, then admitted. "Well, most of the time it does. We will just wait until it is your turn to cook."

Kimberly held her stomach, and said. "Oh, no."

Polly giggled.

"I will have you know that my mother taught me to cook, just fine, thank you." He gave Kimberly a proud look.

Which she ignored, and looked to Polly. "Well?"

Polly wrinkled her nose, and said. "It won't kill you."

And that is all it took to cause Kimberly to burst out laughing, she didn't know if they caught on to what she thought was so funny.

Kimberly felt kind of bad about they not being able to have a cook and housekeeper during the time that she was there.

Chance said that it was because he wanted to used this time to just chill out, relaxed, and take it easy. It was their time to have fun, to spend time together.

Just him, Kimberly, Polly, and Brad, because after they arrival in Australia, Polly would had the operation, Chance would be busy running the station, Brad will handling the legal odds and ends for the station, and what he could for Sway and Company from there.

And of course, Kimberly Racks wouldn't be around, but what was said, was that she will be kept busy helping Chance and Polly.

It was also decided that when it was Brad's turn to cook they would either buy out, or have frozen dinners. It just seems like the thing to do to Chance and Polly.

Kimberly admitted that they would probably being that when it come her time to cook, too. They said that it would be handle.

Polly was left to clean off the table, while Chance and Kimberly went to give Frankie and Jake their grain.

Kimberly, Frankie, and Jake was introduced to the two riding horses that was stable with them.

One of the riding horses was General, he was a big, light, black kind hearted gelding.

The other one was Daffy, a smaller, dark brown, gentle mare with black mane and trail.

Chance told her that they were both well trained, gentle, riding horses.

He saddled them, so that he and Kimberly could took a moon light along the breach before they called a night.

Kimberly loved to ride, and it had been so long, since she had been on a gentle, well trained riding horse. It took the tire feelings right out of her, it made her feel alive, again.

The moon was full, and high in the sky, you could see its reflection in the gentle waves of the water, there was a breeze blowing.

It was a beautiful night, the horses was contented just to walk along, Kimberly felt like she was gently rolling along. They rode away from the cliff leading up to the house.

They had rode a short way from the stable, when Chance turned General toward the water, and stopped.

Kimberly pulled to a stop beside him, she said. "It is beautiful."

She didn't realized how close he was, until he turned in the saddle, leaned over to her, and before his lips met hers, he told her. "Yes, it is." He kissed her long and hard.

Kimberly felt his lips moving on hers, and she moved hers in what she hoped was the proper way.

Chance pulled his head away from hers, his eyes run over her face, he wanted the stressed out, tensed look to be gone.

And he never wanted to see it, again.

"I don't know how to kiss." She hated to admit that at her age she didn't know how to kiss, but in one way, it was just as well, that she didn't.

He smiled a smile that light up his dark, blue eyes. "That is okay, Kimberly. I would like to be the one who show you how. I would like to give you more than a game, a whole lot more than a game. That's if you want more than a game?"

Chapter Fourteen

K IMBERLY LOOKED UP AT HIM in absolutely amazement, she didn't think that anyone would want to ever give her more than a game, especially when it came to the romance department.

She knew that he wouldn't play games with her life, she know that he wasn't that kind of man, but she never thought that he would want to give her more.

"It isn't part of the deal, Kimberly. I know what you think of men." He sat up straight in the saddle, again. "You think that we are a bunch of whore chasing bastards that will unzipped ours pants for everything that rubbed against us. But, I am not like that, Kimberly, and I had never been like that. I was rear to have more respect for myself." He looked into her eyes, as he rode General around her and Daffy and stopped right beside her. They were facing each, when he leaned closer, and said. "I know that you don't believe me, but it is the truth. And I just wanted you to know that I want to give you more than a game, so much more." The tone of his voice said that he held passion for her, that his words just wasn't being said. "Think about, Kimberly."

Kimberly wanted to asked why he wanted to do that for her, but she didn't, maybe she just didn't want to know. She just knew that she wanted to know for herself that she could make love. She wanted to know what it would be like to have a man like Chance to hold her in his arms, to have him lay on top of her, kissing her naked body, rubbing his against her, feeling his hands all over her body.

When he took her in his arms to pull her close up against him, she told him. "I want more than a game." He pulled her all the way off of Daffy to sat her in front of him. "I can give you so much more." His kiss told her that he could.

She had rode back to the stable across General's back, in Chance's arms with her head leading on his chest. He held her like he was never going to let her go.

They had unsaddled the horses, and walked up to the house arm in arm. They didn't see Polly on the way up to Chance's bedroom.

"How about trying out that tub, now." He smiled as he pulled her close, he rub his cheek against her face.

"I will need to get a couple of things."

He chuckled. "Honey, you aren't going to need anything, but me." He pulled her along with him until his back was up against a door, he let go of one of her hands to open the door, then he turn the light on. She following him over to a cabinet, when he opened it, she could see that it full with towels, wash cloths, and bottles of liquid stuff in all kind of colors.

He grinned at her. "What kind of bubble bath would you like? Wild Musk?" He gave a few more choices that she didn't care for, then he thought. "I should have known, you like strawberry, don't you?"

Kimberly smile, and said. "I liked strawberries very much."

He still had her by one hand, when he took the bottle of bubble bath over to the tub, he pour a large amount of it in to the tub, and he turned the faucets on until he felt them were set at the right degree, then he sat her down on the edge of the tub, while he went over to the large window, and started to open the curtain.

"Chance, what are you doing?" She was kind of shock.

He smiled, and reassured her. "We can see out, but nobody can see in." He finished opening the curtain, they could see the moon shinning down on them.

He came back to her, and sit down on the edge of the tub beside her. He started kissing her face, then her lips, his hands went up to her shoulders, gently rubbing them, while pulling her closer to him.

Kimberly just had to tell him one thing before it went any farther. "I never meant to play games, I never did anything for a game, I really thought . . . ." She couldn't finished, she felt so stupid about what she had believed.

Chance pulled her to him, and hugged her close. "I put it to you all wrong, didn't I?" He thought for a minute. "It isn't that I want to give you more than a game. This isn't about a game. I want to do with you what they made you think they did, but didn't have the guts to.

There isn't a game involve in this, not between us, understand?"

She lifted her head to look at him. "It wasn't a matter of guts, they just didn't want to. He just didn't want to."

She smile up at him. "I understand that, I really do." She looked into his eyes. "And there aren't any games in between us?"

He shook his head hard. "Never between us. I promised you."

"Then why do you want to make love to me?" She had to know.

He reached down to turned the fraughts off even though the tub wasn't full. "I don't think that we will being needing this for awhile." He put his arm back around her to pull her on his lap. "Why?" He smiled. "I didn't take the time to tell you, how pretty you are, or how sexy that I think you are, did I?" He ignored the doubtful look on her face. "I didn't tell you, that all those emotions that show on her face, and all over body that you think is so awful that you can't control now, because of yours condition. I want to see and feel all of those emotions while you are in my arms making love. You don't know hard it was not to just made love to you awhile, ago." He took her chin in his hand, and gave a long, hard kiss. "Any more questions?"

She shook her head.

His hand left her chin, and started unbuttoning her blouse, he pulled it out from her jeans. His lips went from kissing her lips, to her neck, to her shoulder, small, light kisses. He unfasten her bra, his hand started feeling of her breast, then he held it in his hand, and kissing her nipple, then he took it into his mouth, and started sucking it. His hand pushed the bra out of the way of the other breast, and while his mouth never left her nipple, his hand started feeling the other breast, soon his lips followed, and he had the other nipple in his mouth, sucking it.

He brought his head back up. "You like that?"

All that she could do was nod, and say. "Very much."

"I thought so." He smiled. "I do, too."

His brought his arm out from behind her to pushed the blouse and the bra off of her. When they fell to the floor, he stood up with her in his arms, then he set her feet on the floor, he unfasten her jeans, when the zipper went all the way down, his hands pushed her jeans down over her buttocks, taking her panties with them. He brought his hands back up to her buttocks, he squeezed them, then he started caress them, bringing her closer to him, until her breasts were pressed against his chest with nothing between them, but his shirt.

Kimberly loved it when he started feeling and sucking her breasts, but being like this was just as good. He was feeling her rear like he did her breasts, he had made her feel like her breasts had swell with pride at his touch.

He bent his head down, so he could kissed her, this time his lips parted her lips, and his tongue went inside her mouth. Her arms went from being on his arms to being wrapped around his neck, bring him as close to her as she could.

He left his hands on her buttocks, and lifted her up off of the floor a couple of inches. When he set her back down, his mouth left hers to kiss her neck, down to kiss each breasts, then he kiss way down her stomach until his reach her hair between her legs.

Her hands were braced his shoulders, when his hands pushed her jeans and panty on down pass her knees.

She fought her desire to jump his bones, and told him.

"Chance, my legs ain't the best looking."

He came back up, his hands came slowly back up over her buttocks. "I don't care about your legs, Honey. I don't make love to legs."

Her arms went around his shoulders, when he put one arm around her back, and one arm behind her knees to lift her in his arms, then he laid her gently on a rug on the bathroom's floor. He went to her feet to pull her boots and socks off, he throw them out of the way.

In record time, he had his western shirt, jeans, and boots off. He had changed into them, again, before he went back on the plane. He throw them out of the way, too.

Then he laid down beside her with a smile on his face.

"You just don't how pretty you look lying there waiting for me to love you. And I will, Kimberly, I will."

He started kissing her, his hands starting feeling of her breasts, gently rubbing her nipple between his thumb and index finger, then he did the other.

She liked it so much, she moved closer, so he would kept doing it.

"Chance, what if I moved around too much." She asked, when his mouth left her on his way to her breasts.

When he looked at her, his eyes was even a darker blue than they usually were, they had a gleam in them, when he told her. "You just move around all you want to, I will tell you if it is too much." He had a grin on his face before his mouth starting sucking on her nipple.

She starting rubbing his arm up to his shoulder, to hang on to him, then she laid it on his back.

While his mouth went from nipple to nipple, and back again, his hand were on her hip, feeling of it, gently pinching it, then his hand went to in between legs. Gently moving his fingers up and down, until they went in her just enough to send her in to a wonderful world of feelings.

She felt nothing but pleasure, and she wanted to feel it over and over, again. And she did, she move her legs apart for more, so he could finally move between her legs.

He enter her, while she were having a tingle sensation over all over her body. She lift herself up to be closer to him, her legs were bent, so he could moved farther into her.

They went as high as a man and a woman could go in each other arms.

When he roll off of her, they both were ringing wet with sweat.

His arm went under her to bring her up close to him, and told her. "Damn, that is the best that I ever had." Then he thought to assured her. "Not that I have had that many women, Kimberly, because I really haven't. And I wouldn't be proud of it if I had, and I wouldn't want you to know about them if I had. I wouldn't hurt you that way for the world."

He starting feeling of her hair that was laying on her shoulder, and smile. "I knew that you would be good."

Her head was laying on his shoulder with his arm around her, she looked up in surprise. "Really? Why did you think that?"

He chuckled, and asked. "Are you kidding? You know how much passion and feelings that you used to put in your painting, I knew that you would put it in making love, with the right man, that is." His grin was crocked to one side. "And I am the right man for you."

He moved down so he was face to face with her, then he kissed her long and hard.

Her head was resting on his arm, when he raised his head, she asked. "Is that right?"

He nodded his head. "You are mine, now, and only you can ever change it."

His eyes went over naked body, she wonder what he thought it. She had never been face to face with a man seeing her without her clothes on, they have always been hiding behind two-way mirrors, and hidden cameras.

Chance was the only man that been there with her, and if what he said was true, it wouldn't ever change.

She didn't see repulsive in his eyes when he looked at her, but she had to asked. "What do you think?"

Chapter Fifteen

HIS GAZE WENT OVER HER again, and he grinned. "I think that you were right."

"About what?" She wanted to know.

"About us needing to do this before we took our bubble bath. The only thing is, we probably will need another bath shortly after we get out of this one." He left her to go check the water in the tub, he just turned the hot on, because the water needed warmer up.

"No, I meant what do you think about my body?"

He laid down beside her, holding himself up by lending on his arm. "Well, let me see." He had a look of muck thoughtfulness as he gaze went over her body, again. "I will show what I think." And then he bent down to start kissing her again.

When his lips left hers to start kissing his way down her neck to her shoulders, down to her breasts. She caught her breath long enough to asked. "What if the tub runs over, Chance?"

He chuckled. "We will catch it, Kimberly."

Then he stole her breath away, as he started sucking her breasts, she had a ache in the lower part of body, that only Chance could turn it in to a wonderful feeling, and he did.

They caught the tub before it ran over. He pick her up off of the floor in his arms, he stepped into the water. It was warm enough, but not too hot, when he set her down in it, there were plenty of bubbles.

They made her smile. "Do you take bubble baths often, Chance?"

He sit down beside her, facing her. "No, I think that it is Polly's stuff." He took a wash cloth from the edge of the tub, and starting gently cleaning off the dust and the dirt off of her.

He took a look at her face, and he couldn't believe what he saw, or maybe what he didn't see. The stressed out, tensed, and nervous was gone from her face, it was calm, relax, almost peaceable, now.

It made him smile, as he clean her face, her neck, down her arms, and her back, the roundness of her buttocks, he took his time washing her breasts. Taking them in his hands, squeezing the washed cloth over them, then he went down over her stomach, down between her legs to the tips of her toes.

Then she took a wash cloth from the edge of the tub, and told him. "Now, it's your turn."

He gave her a lazy smile, and said. "I can't wait, Kimberly. I can't wait."

Kimberly thought that she heard a teasing note in his voice. "You don't think that I will do it?"

He grinned down at her, and said. "I think that you are pretty shy, Kimberly."

Before he could say any more, she took the wash cloth in her left hand, the one that she had the most control of, and gentle started washing his lean handsome face, then down to his neck. She cleaned the back of his neck, down his strong arms, that could hold her so gentle, then she rubbed his shoulders, massaging them, she cleaned his back, and down over his buttocks.

Then she went to his chest, down over his stomach. His held out his legs where she could cleaned down to his toes.

When she started back up his leg to clean between his legs.

Before she had made that far, he grab her hands to stop her. In a low voice, he told her. "You have prove your point, Kimberly."

She looked up at him in surprise. "I wasn't trying to prove anything. I was just trying to do for you what you did for me."

He stand up, and pulled her close to him, he let go of her hands to put his arms around her, and held her close. "I know you were, and you

161

did very well, very well." He then swung her up in his arms and step out the tub, he set her feet on the floor. When he went to get a towel. "Why haven't you found a lover before." He started drying her off, then he told her. "Don't get me wrong, I am very happy that you didn't, but why? I mean before everything went wrong."

She smile, as she remember the time in her life before she had fell for the setup. "I wanted to wait for a good, nice cowboy, but I hadn't met one by a certain age, I was going to Las Vegas to look into a male hooker."

He jerked up to faced her, she couldn't tell whether he was shock or disgusted. "You mean that there wasn't any one that show any interested in you?"

"No, and then they fooled me. I can't believe that I actually thought that he was interested in me. After all of those years of being in the same town. All of those other women that he had been with." She shook her head so sadly. "I don't why I believe it."

"They were only interest in a game, not you." It finally dawn on him, how much she knew about the whole thing.

"Then he just had to show how many women that he had been with, while you spent all your time alone. He had been with all of your friends, and even some of yours family members.

All the time, he went on with his life, while they make a game of yours." Chance was talking in a very low voice, almost a whisper, as he held her close.

She realized why he was talking in such of a low voice, they shouldn't even be talking about this, so she answer him as quietly as she could. "It's a good thing that I never thought too much of any of them. And I was mostly happy being alone, I just should of found a way to make a living for myself. Painting, then Cricketts Rose, and being in the country were my whole life."

He could feel her warm tears running down her cheek against his chest, and it made him feel so bad. "I can't change the past, but I can make the future better, or I want to, Kimberly. I want to so much, Kimberly." He swept her up in to his arms, and carried her into his bedroom to laid her on his bed.

He spent the night loving the sadness and all of the hurt out of her. He told her over and over, again, how beautiful that she was, how he was going to spent the rest of his life making sure that she was happy.

When Kimberly opened her eyes, Chance wasn't there, and the sun was well into the sky. She looked at the clock, it was the middle of the morning, Frankie and Jake was going to kill her, when she finally got down to them, she felt sure.

She climb out of bed, and grab the first thing that she could put on, which was one of Chance's western shirt, snapped it closed, made it through the bathroom picking up her clothes from last night.

She smile as she remember the way that Chance had token them off, like they shouldn't even be there in the first place. She looked in the mirror before she went out of the bathroom, she couldn't believe what she saw, the tensed, stressed out look that made the muscles pulled up on the right side of her face was gone. The look that look like she could burst out in tears at any time was gone, too. She looked calm, almost happy.

Kimberly walked in to her bedroom to find all of the her stuff that Chance had pile on the bed had been moved. The hanging stuff was hung in the closet, neatly, all of the bags of stuff was setting around the room in the difference places.

Polly must had done it, while her and Chance were down at the stable. That was very nice of her, Kimberly just hope that Polly was out of here, before she and Chance made it to the bathroom.

Kimberly had started to find what clothes that she would need for the day, bra, panty, socks, jeans, and a light cotton blouse, when she thought to look out the window for Frankie and Jake. She decided that they must be under the shade of the stalls, because she couldn't see them.

She would shampoo her hair after she been to fed them, Chance had did a good job of bathing her, but he didn't do her hair.

She was remembering the way that he had held her, the way that he had touch her, when he started calling to her from his bedroom.

She snapped the snaps back closed that she had opened when he made his way through the bathroom.

"Kimberly, where the hell are you?" He called out rather loudly.

Loud enough for Kimberly to meet him at her bedroom's room leading to the bathroom, as she opened the door, she told him. "I am in here."

He smile as he came through the door, she had already made it back besides the bed. His eyes went over her standing there with his shirt on, it cover her down over her hips, but it didn't hide her shape, then he saw her clothes laying on the bed.

"What you are doing?" He went on into the room, he moved her clothes out of his way, so he could sat down on the bed beside where she were standing.

She looked down at him, he was leaning back on his hands looking up at her with his head crock to one side.

She had to catch her breath, before she could answer him, she had a feeling that he knew what she was doing.

"I am going to put my clothes on where I can go feed Frankie and Jake, before they get too upset with me."

"I had already fed Frankie and Jake, and I made sure that they understood that it was all my fault that you weren't there yourself. So, they wouldn't be upset with you, at all." Chance assured her.

She smile down at him, and said. "Thank you."

He sit up, and told her. "You are welcome. And there isn't any reason for you to put clothes on."

Before she knew it, he had pull the front of the shirt opened, had caught her by the waist, and he had lean back on the bed, holding her over him, so her breasts was over him.

He lower her down, so he could take her nipple into his mouth.

Gently sucking one, then he moved his mouth over to the other one. She had herself partly braced with her arms on the bed. He smile when she put one of her legs on each side of him, and settle on him close.

But, when she said. "Chance, I need you."

His mouth let go of her breast, to look in to her eyes, then he rolled her over on her back, he raised up off of her, and told her. "Pull my jeans down, Honey. And hurry."

While he kissed her, and kissed over, again, she pushed his tight jeans down. When his mouth left hers, she told him.

"For a minute there, I thought you were going to have to do it."

"That wouldn't have been a problem, trust me." He told her, as he settled back down in between her legs.

He didn't raise back up until she had felt the delightful tingle feeling that went through her body every time he made love to her.

He laid down beside her, he smile at the look of pure enjoyment, and satisfaction that was on her face. He was leading on one elbow, looking down at her. "I like hearing that you need me. Did I show you how much I like hearing it?"

He asked, as he caress her face with his hand.

They were both sweating from the excitement that they had shared together.

"You did a extremely good job of it, and you didn't even pulled your shirt off for it." Her eyes went over his shirt, that was clinging to his body.

"I didn't have the time, besides there wasn't a need to, was there?" When she shook her head in agreement, he moved his mouth down to her ear, and whisper. "I need to know that after all you have been thorough, how can you be happy here with me like this?"

"I don't know how, I just know that I am." She kept her voice down as low as she could. "It is like you had made all the hurt and pain go away, at least, for awhile."

Chapter Sixteen

CHANCE HAD TO SHOWER AND changed for a business luncheon, she had asked what he wanted her to do, while he was gone.

He had kind of look at her strangely, she had to remind him that she had went to work for him, and she needed to know what her job was.

He had a mischievous grin on his face, when he told her not to worry about it, they would figured it out when he got back later that afternoon.

For today, she would be free to whatever she wanted to do. So, after Chance left, she had shampoo her hair, took a quick shower, put her clothes on, and went down to the kitchen to find food, she was hunger.

Polly was there with the refrigerator door open, looking as though she was doing the same thing.

Polly smile, when she saw Kimberly standing in the door way with a surprise look on her face.

"I thought you would have went with Chance." Kimberly told her as she walked on in to the room.

Polly shook her head. "No, not this time. I usually go with him, but I thought that I would stay here with you."

"You didn't have to do that." Kimberly would feel bad if she have caused Polly to miss it.

But, Polly assured that she hadn't, and added. "Besides, we are coming to the end of business lunches and things like that, or maybe just this kind of business."

Kimberly was standing behind her looking to see what they could have. "You won't miss it?"

Polly shook her head. "No, I am more like Chance, I would rather be out in the country, not in the big business world." She shrugged her shoulders. "I don't know why we turn out this way, but we did." She turned to Kimberly. "How do you feel about breakfast for lunch, or dinner? Whatever you called?"

"I called dinner, and that sounds very good." Just about anything would sound good to Kimberly right now.

"Then that is what we will have." Polly started taking eggs, cheese, and sausages out of the refrigerator. "A omelet is okay with you?"

Kimberly nodded her head, asked. "What can I do?"

Polly put the stuff down on the counter beside the built in range. "You could put the biscuits on, if you wanted to."

Kimberly smiled. "I want to." While she found the can of biscuits, and was looking for a pan, she told Polly. "I wanted to thank you for cleaning off my bed, last night. That was very nice of you."

Polly was pulling a bowl out of the cabinet, and had started breaking the eggs in to it, while the sausages was cooking in a frying pan. "I was glad to do for you."

Kimberly had a feeling that Polly was trying hard not giggle, as Kimberly put the can of biscuits in the oven that she started preheating.

"Kimberly, I want you to know that you can trust me."

Polly looked up from cutting up the cheese. "I mean to fed Frankie and Jake, for stuff like that, you know what I mean, don't you?"

Kimberly nodded her head that she did. But, she was wondering what Polly thought about all of this. Chance and Brad must have told her everything, because she was going to bring a lot in to it, just knowing Kimberly Chandlers was a major part of it. And they must have told her not to talk about, either, because she looked like she had just give it away.

"I told Chance this morning that I could had fed them for you, but he said that he would. I went up to your room this morning, but you wasn't in there, and . . . ."

And the bed hadn't been slept in, Kimberly could had finished it for her, but she didn't, she just waited.

"and I know that you wouldn't even like me if I wasn't Chance's sister." She looked at Kimberly, who was gathering plates, knifes, and forks to set the table for them. "But, you just remember that I am Chance's sister, and there is stuff that I want to know."

Kimberly looked up at her, because Polly's tone of voice said that she meant business, in a fun sort of way, it made Kimberly smile, as she asked. "What kind of stuff?"

Polly took the sausages out of the pan, then she pour the eggs with the cheese into the pan, she was stirring it, when she said. "How well did you know my brother? Was you sweethearts, or what? Stuff like that, basely do you know anything that I could hang over his head?"

From the look on Polly's face, Kimberly knew that she was just teasing, but Kimberly pretended to give it some thought as she check on the biscuits, they would be ready just about the time that Polly would be ready.

"Well, I could out ride him, out roped him, and out shoot him. Is that the kind of stuff, you want to know?"

"Yea, that's exactly the kind of stuff that I want to know." Polly did giggle that time. "Could you really do those things?"

Kimberly starting setting table, and gave some thought before she answer Polly. "Yelp, and I was pretty good at, too, but I don't know if I was better than Chance. Although, I was just as good." She gave a honest answer.

"You just tell it like you were better?" Polly nodded her head, as if she understood completely.

Kimberly smile, as her and Polly put the biscuits and the omelet on the table, and she assured Polly. "He knows that I just meant it in teasing way."

"I know." Was all that Polly said, as they sat down at the table. She gave Kimberly time to take a couple of bites before she asked another question. "Were you sweethearts?"

Kimberly swallow the omelet that were in her mouth, and smile when she thought about it. She shook her head. "His mama," Then she thought. "your mama and my mama were good friends, so when Chance's father pass away. Your mama started doing other people's wash, and my mama helped her." Kimberly noticed that Polly's face soften at the mention of her mother. "I was surprised that he even remember me. It has been a long time, but I guessed that since y'all mother and mine kept in touch until she had pass way, that's probably how he remember me." Kimberly continued to stuff a biscuit in her mouth.

"You know my mama?" Polly wanted to know.

Kimberly's mouth was full, but she nodded, and finally got out. "Kind of."

Polly took a couple of thoughtful bites. "She was a pretty good business woman herself, wasn't she? I mean, she had to be to get her and Chance out here, and then make a living for her and Chance."

Kimberly smiled at Polly, and said. "She was a good, nice, fine lady, with a good head for business, Polly. You were wondering were Chance got his?" Kimberly asked before she went back to stuffing her mouth.

Polly swallowed what was in her mouth, and smile. "I had already figured it, but I was just wondering if you knew her. Chance says that is why I have a level head, and he thanks god for that." She looked at Kimberly with a guilty face. "We forgot drinks, Kimberly. What would you like? A diet cola?" She asked, as she started to get up.

Kimberly was surprised that she had made it this long without a diet cola, and she told Polly that.

"Here you go. Maybe now, you can wake up." Polly told her with she set a glass full of cola, caffeine down beside Kimberly.

"Thank you." Kimberly said, and when Polly sit back down, she asked. "You have a level head?"

"Yea, but we won't ever know what kind of teenager I would have been if the wreck haven't happen." She shook her head with the thought. "It happen before I was in my teens, I may have been so wild, that Chance would have token me to the Australia outback, and made me work. He has been wanting to move there for awhile."

Kimberly swallowed hard, and blink the tears from her eyes, and asked. "What kind of teenage were you, Polly?"

There were tears in her eyes, when she smile. "Quiet, oh, I had friends right up until the time I starting liking this boy." Her eyes became dreamily. "They had me believing that he wanted to go with me, but I found out that he was going with one of my girlfriends, and they was just making fun of me."

It was hard for Kimberly not to asked, if he didn't go with all of her girlfriends, and let her know just who all he went with instead of her, while he sat in front of her and talk about his wife that he never had, and how pretty other women were, but she didn't, because Polly wouldn't had been that stupid, nobody would had. But her.

"After that, I decided that I didn't need any friends, I mean close friends. I started spending most of my time alone, I did very well in school, because I decided that when I grew up, men wouldn't be like boys. Men would be more mature, they would look past my disability, look at who I am really am. But, they aren't any difference from silly boys, are they, Kimberly?"

Kimberly didn't answer her, she just let Polly talked.

"Nice men aren't suppose look and think about women with disability in that way, or is because they are suppose to be able to get one that is better looking, and sexier?"

Kimberly didn't know the answer to that one, either.

"Chance didn't like me spending my time alone, so he started taking me with him a lot. Brad took me to my High School prom."

It took everything that Kimberly had in her not to hallow "good for Brad", but she did asked. "Brad isn't as old as me and Chance are, is he?"

Polly had a beaming smile on her as she talked about Brad, it made her eyes bighted up, too. "No, he is in his very early thirties. He invested what his grandfather left him in Sway and Company, and he went to law school, too. I had been to business collage, but I can't decided what I wanted to do. I think that I am immature in that way. What do you think?"

Kimberly almost said that she could write a book on being immature, but thought about it, and said. "I could paint you a picture of immature, and it would be of me, or I used to could. So, I am the wrong one to asked about it."

Polly looked kind of shy when she said. "I do want to try sex soon, though. I mean, I have had offers. You know, they either wanted to go to bed with the Sinclear's name or the Sway and Company's money. I should have had tried it before, but I am one of those crazy people that thought my first time should mean something, so I waited. But, it don't mean anything to anybody any more, does it? They would do it with anybody at any time, won't they?"

Kimberly had a very sad feeling inside that Polly was right, that sex meant very little to people these days, one night stand was the rule now, not the excepted, and marriage meant nothing either. People cheated on their husbands and wives like it was just the thing to do, like there wasn't anything wrong with it.

Kimberly was about to tried to said something, and even if she didn't know what, when Polly's went pale.

"But, Chance isn't like that, Kimberly. I never meant that he was." Polly had worried look on her face. "Honest, Kimberly."

Kimberly had to smile. "It is alright, Polly. I waited a long time before I tried it. Even if Chance wasn't the kind of man that he is, I know what I was doing, and I know what I wanted."

Polly shook her head sadly. "There just isn't very many men like Chance, is there?"

Kimberly smile, and shook her head. "No, there isn't."

But, she wanted to asked, what about Brad.

"But, I want to tried it before we leave for Australia, though. I never wanted a one night stand with a man that I would see later on." She shook her head sadly. "I am just not made that way."

Kimberly was about to tell that she wasn't either, when Brad walked into the kitchen. Kimberly had thought that she heard something moving around, right before she and Polly had sit down at the table, but she had decided that she was wrong.

Brad set his cases down on the floor, and when he sat down at the table with them, he looked very tired, and upset.

And when he said. "Nice men aren't suppose to looked at women with disabilities in that way or is it because they are suppose to be able to get someone is sexier." He looked shock.

Chapter Seventeen

BRAD TOOK A DEEP BREATH, before he started. "Polly, people don't think like that anymore, they realized now that the disables are not to be look down on, or to be felt sorry for. They realized that the disables had normal desires and needs. Oh, there maybe a few small minded people left in the world that don't understand it, but it is very few. Isn't that right, Kimberly?"

Kimberly looked at him like he was crazy. "Boy, are you asking the wrong one."

"Oh, yea, I forgot." He give her a apologetic look. "And Polly, the men who can't see how sexy you are, those are the ones that you shouldn't want anything to do with." He smiled. "And believe or not, there are men that want to love and have a serious relationship." He grinned at Polly.

"And I think that you are very sexy, not the Sinclear's name and not the Sway and Company's money, but the woman Paulet Louise Sinclear is very sexy."

Polly looked at him like he was the world's greatest man, there was so much love in her eyes. "Really? Do you really think so?"

"I thought so, ever since that night I took you to the prom. Why do you think that I spend so much time with you? I want to be there for you, when you were ready to be love."

"But, you never said or did anything to let me know how you felt. I always thought that you thought of me as Chance's kid sister, nothing more." Polly was amazed.

"And I didn't realized how close I was to losing you."

He leaned toward Polly, but he noticed Kimberly, who was sitting there grinning from ear to ear.

When he looked at her, Kimberly started to get up, but he told her. "No, don't get up, Kimberly. We will take this some place else, but I just wanted to tell you that I got you off the disability payments."

Brad must had made the payments sound like a bad thing, because Polly said. "I thought the disability payments for the disable were a good thing."

Kimberly and Brad assured her that they were, that those payments were a like life saver for a lot of people.

"But, I feel like I crop out by getting on them. I feel like I should have went on to work, when I was younger, even if it was just part time, or finding something that I could had done at home to make a living. I feel like I took the easy way out, and now I don't like it." Kimberly shook so sadly. "But, I was so immature. I will always regret it."

"You are probably just being too hard on yourself." Brad told her.

But, Kimberly shook her head very sadly. "No, I am not.

And I am not sure whether it was because I don't want to leave the country, I do like being in the country. Or whether it was because I didn't feel like getting out and working, or whether it was because I was so immature, or what. But, I always regret not finding a way to make a living for myself, always."

Brad smile at her. "Well, any way, you are making a living for yourself, now. You are working. Congratulation Kimberly. We are very proud of you."

"Yea, we are. And we are glad that you are working with us." Polly told her, and raised her glass of cola for a toast.

Polly and Kimberly touch glasses, then Polly turned to Brad. "Would like a drink? Have you had lunch?"

He took her glass to toast with Kimberly, before his told Polly. "I ate on the plane."

Polly giggled, when he just took her glass from her.

"And now, if Kimberly won't mind, I think that we need to go to another room, and . . ." His eyes went over her. "talk."

Kimberly looked at him in surprise. "Me? Mind? I will say that it is about time."

Brad stood up and grinned at Kimberly. "Yea, I know, and I owe it all to you." At her and Polly questioning looks. "Meeting you and knowing about what . . ." He thought for a minute. "was going on, it made me realized how much I care for Polly. So, thank you, Kimberly Racks, very much."

He gave her a bow.

"You are more than welcome." Kimberly assured him.

"But, I never knew that this would mean that I wasn't a nice man." He grinned, and raised his eyebrows.

Polly stood up in frustration. "Oh, I didn't mean it like that, I was wondering if that is what men think that is how society sees it, that's all that I meant." That it dawn on her. "You were listening to ours conversation."

"I was just straighten up my brief case, before I came in, I just happen to be in ear shot." Brad was trying to look innocent about it.

But, Polly wasn't buying it. "Bradford Matters, I ought to . . . ."

Kimberly didn't even laughed, when Polly said Bradford, she had went back to munching on her omelet and biscuit, and was thankful that they haven't gotten too cold. She watched, as Brad pick Polly up over his shoulder, before Polly could finished what saying what she ought to do.

Kimberly then watched Brad go out of the kitchen with Polly over his shoulder, they was going somewhere to talk.

Yea, right, talk, Kimberly giggled.

Kimberly thought, as she finished her omelet and biscuits, that she would be making her own living from now, until the end of her life. Which wouldn't be too long, but that wasn't the point. The point, she decided as she finished her badly needed cola, was that she would be making her own living until the end.

She clean off the table, put the dirty dishes in the dish washer, figured out how to turn it on, before she found her sunglasses to wear out to spent time with Frankie and Jake. Brad and Polly wouldn't even know that she was gone, not that they would care, she smile as she closed the kitchen's door leading outside.

As she made her way down the cliff to the stable, she looked over the cliff leaving from the back of the house to the water. Chance was right, that side of the cliff was like a topical garden, trees, shrubs and plants was growing on almost every inch of it, it looked kind of like a jungle, you could make your way to the water without being seen. If there wasn't cameras around, she forgot to asked them about that.

When she made it to the stable, she was greeting by Frankie's whining, and Kimberly was almost sure that it wasn't "Hello, how are you", from Frankie's tone, it sounded more like "Where in the hell have you been and why in hell haven't you there sooner? And what in the hell happen that she wasn't?".

Yea, Kimberly felt sure that was more like what Frankie was saying, Jake wasn't saying much, but his look said it all. Frankie was fussy when you went to catch her, she would stand still for it, but she just had to nip at you, just to let you know that you wouldn't making her day by spending time with her, but it was alright that you would.

And that was the greeting, Kimberly got when she took the lead rope off of the stall's gate, and snapped in Frankie's halter. Kimberly petted her face softly, rubbed her neck, and apology profoundly for not being sooner, Frankie looked like she saying "Just don't let it happen, again," when Kimberly left her tried up in the cool breeze of the hall way to go for Jake.

Now, Jake wasn't as fussy as Frankie was when you went to catch him, it was just he wasn't sure that it was a good idea to be caught. He always looked like he was saying, "Either, do or don't.", but then he would stand quietly while Kimberly snapped a lead rope in his halter.

She petted his face softly, rubbed his neck, and again apology profoundly, and pleading for forgiveness for not being there sooner, as she tried him up in the hall way with Frankie.

When she left them to find a brush for the tack room, Jake looked like he saying, "I wasn't worry, I know you would be coming."

Kimberly came back to them with a brush and curry comb, Frankie and Jake was standing quietly. Well, actually, they had one of their back hoofs crocked back, their heads was held level with the rest of their bodies, and they looked like they hoped that Kimberly's brushing, combing their mane and trail, loving and petting on them, wouldn't keep them awake.

Kimberly thought all that time that she was feeling so bad about not spending with them, was what Frankie and Jake thought was something that they had to put up with to get their feed.

It made Kimberly smile to herself, as she started brushing Frankie, because it was alright, she enjoyed the time that she spent with them enough for all of them.

Kimberly had always thought that horses was better company than people, and when her brothers moved back home, and she moved out, she found out that she was right.

Kimberly had always knew that there was something going on, her nerves and her common senses would tell her, and some how, just somehow, she knew that he was part of it. Now, she knew that he was behind all of it.

She also knew that the only way the games would end, was if he would come to her, tell her why he had made such of game off of her life. But, that would mean the end of the game, and what would he do in between trips, and chasing whores, what would he do for fun. No, that could never happen.

As she brushed Frankie's legs down to her hoofs, she had stopped thinking about when that was going happen, and started wondering about how she was going to live her life.

She knew Chance was probably right, even before all of this had happen, she didn't knew if she could had work in a office with a brunch of people always around. It wasn't that she didn't like people, before all of this happen, she occasionally enjoyed meeting and being around people, when she used to feel good. But, not now, because now she knew that those people was part of a game, his game.

Getting a job now, would be a game to them that would be out of this world to them. It would make her a easy target. She wished that she didn't feel things like she did, she wished that she could hid her feelings better. She wished that she was as cold and unfeeling about her life, as they were.

But, her feelings was what made her a artist, and thank god that she couldn't painted any more. Because, she was sure that they would see it as her trying to play a game with him.

Living her life, and doing what she loved to do would be a game to them.

Chapter Eighteen

NO, IF KIMBERLY RACKS WAS going to live, she would have to be alone most of the time. She knew that they would still found a way to play with her, but she would just rather be alone to deal with what they did to her.

But, Kimberly Racks wouldn't have to live, she could bring a end to the games that they was playing with her life.

And Kimberly Chandlers could go on with her life, if she survive the operation. She too, would need to live a quiet life, but that wouldn't be a problem.

The end of the games, now that make Kimberly grin, as Frankie was brush to a shine.

She went over to Jake, and starting brushing him. The end to the games wouldn't be that good-looking cowboy coming to her, and telling her how much that he loved her, and how sorry he was that he caused all of the tests to see if she was good enough for him, while he went with all of her friends, members of her family, all of the whores that looked like Kimberly, and god only knows who else.

She figured that he wanted to tested her, because her condition, and his position in the county. She would always would regret being so silly and immature. Not because, of him, but because it would had been so better for her to act more mature.

The games wouldn't end with him coming to her, they would end on a much more final note, with her being killed.

She wonder if they would let it go at that, or whether Chance, Brad, and Polly would have to worried about them after she was killed. She hoped not, but they would have to wait and see.

Jake was brush until there was a shine on his coat, too.

Then she went to get a bottle of conditioner and water mixed, she pour it on a human hair brush, and started brushing into Frankie's and Jake's mane and trail. It made their mane and trail soft, silky, and easy to manage. But, she didn't tell Jake that, because it might sound sissy to him, and we couldn't have that. She smile to herself.

When she had Frankie and Jake looking like they normal gorgeous self, and when she had told them how gorgeous them were many times, she gave General, and Daffy a quick brush off. Then she could either, take General or Daffy for a ride.

Chance had told her last night that she could take either one of them out for a ride. He had told her, that it might be a good idea to take them to the riding pen, and ride them for a while before she just took off on her own. He said that it would gave her a chance to get her riding legs back under her, and she knew that he was right.

Or she could do what was right, and clean out the manure from the stalls, since it because of her that they couldn't have stable help. She thought that it would be better if she clean out the stalls. Maybe, she could go riding another time.

She found the shovel, a fine tooth rake, and a small enough wheel barrel that she could handle in the feed room.

Kimberly couldn't handle a large wheel barrel, because it would be too heavy for her, and too easy to tip over.

She had just gotten started good, when Frankie, Jake, Daffy, and General got so excited to see her working, that they just had to give her more to do. She grinned, and thank them for their help, of course. But, she also assured them that it really wasn't necessary.

She was getting to the point, where she was wishing for a wet band, and thinking that it would be a good idea to do this more often, so it wouldn't pile up, and take so long to clean up.

When Chance come up to the stable in the same truck that was at the airport last night. He got out and before he came to her, he pulled the coat off to his suit, and laid it back in the cab.

Chance walked up to her, as she was coming out one of the stalls. He wanted to know. "What are you doing?" His tone was part amused and part disapproving.

Kimberly looked up at him, that was the second time today, he asked that question, when she was sure that he knew what she was doing, but she answer him, anyway.

"I am cleaning out the stalls."

He promptly took the shovel, and the rake from her. "It wasn't necessary. Me and Brad are going to do it, every other day or two, so you don't have to worry about it, understand?"

Kimberly starting following him, when he took the shovel, and rake from her. She watched him put them back in the tack room.

"I thought you and Brad was going to be too busy with meeting and stuff like that." She grinned as she looked over his western cut suit, and his boots. "And I just couldn't see you cleaning out stalls in those boots."

She was leaning up against the door of the tack room.

Chance put the shovel and the rake up against the wall, and starting walking toward her. He had a lop sided grin on his face, and his eyes had a mischievous spark in them. When he came face to face with her, she didn't moved, before she knew it, he had pick her in his arms, and started carrying her out of the stable.

Frankie, Jake, General, and Daffy all watched with their heads held up and their ear perk up.

Chance sat down in a swing that was setting in the shade of the stable with her in his lap.

"Now, me and Brad are just about thorough with all of ours meetings, so we will take care of cleaning out the stalls. And just what is wrong with my boots?"

She had her arms around his neck, but she loosed her hold to looked down at his boots. She made a face, and told him. "They just don't look like the kind that you wear when you clean out stable. I don't why, but they just don't." She knew that they were a very high priced pair of rattlesnake boots.

He pulled her back close to him, and told her. "I will have to remember that before I clean them out."

His starting kissing her face, light, soft kisses, he had one arm holding her around her back, with the other hand, he took the chip from her hair, and let her hair down.

"Chance, I am dirty, and sweaty." She told him, as she move her head, where he could kissed her neck.

He raised his head, and grinned at her. "Well, it is a good thing that I am washable, and besides when I get through with you, you will be even dirtier, and more sweaty." He made it sound like a promise. "Did Brad made it in?"

"You haven't been to the house, yet?" She asked him, wondering how she was going to tell him.

"No, somehow, I just knew that you would down here.

Why, is there something wrong, Kimberly? Is he here?"

"Brad is here, and there isn't anything wrong. It is just . . ." How was she going to tell him that his little sister and probably his best friend was in the house, right now, making love. All of this was new to Kimberly, and she never did want to be put into this kind of world.

But, since it wasn't his wife or even his girlfriend that was doing it, it didn't seems too bad.

"It is just what, Kimberly?" He asked quietly, as his eyes search her face.

"Brad and Polly are together, now."

He grinned. "She got him to took her out to the airport to look at the paintings before they are moved, didn't she?"

Kimberly shook her head. "No." The last thing that was on Polly's mind was the paintings, but how she was going to tell Chance that. "They are together like we are."

It took a minute, then it looked like it had dawn on him, because he slump his back against the back of the swing.

He was still holding Kimberly, but loosely now.

Kimberly regretted putting it like that, he might think that she expected more of a serious relationship from him.

"I meant that they are in love, Chance, and there isn't anything wrong with that."

He nodded his head. "I know what you meant, Kimberly."

He crook his head to one side and look at her. "And that explained a lot. That's why he never brought a date around Polly, and he never talked about a another woman in front of her. And every time that she wanted to go anywhere or do anything, he always took her." Chance thought about for a minute. "I am not sure that he dated anyone else after he took her to the prom."

Kimberly grinned. "Well, if he treated her that good before, he will keep on treating her that good, don't you think, Chance?"

"You mean after the double wedding? Yea, Brad knows the value of a commitment. And like you said, if he always has treated her with so much thoughtfulness, he probably always will. Brad isn't the kind of man that worried about what other people thinks, he knows what he wants, he knows how he wants to live his life."

"After the what?" Kimberly didn't know what to say.

"After the double wedding." He sounded sure about it.

"You don't think that my best friend is going to make love to my little sister in ours house, and not married her before she has a operation that she might not survive, do you?"

She shook her head. "I don't know, Chance. They may not be thinking about getting married, right now. They may just want to enjoy finding each other for while, get used to being a couple, you know." She was trying to brace him for the possibility that they didn't want to get married right now, but for all that she knew, he could be right. Brad and Polly could want to be married right away.

Then she thought about what he had said, and repeated it as a question. "A double wedding?"

He nodded his head.

She smile. "Who else is getting marry?"

He looked at her in surprise. "I am."

Kimberly was shock to her bones, no one had say anything about him getting marry, not even Polly. She was out of his arms before he knew it.

She couldn't get her breath, her whole body was crying out in pain, she was so shock that the tears didn't come out of her eyes. She was sure that the tears would come later.

She couldn't believed that Chance had turned out to be this way. She had honestly believed that he was a good, kind, honest cowboy. He couldn't be like all of the rest of them, he just couldn't.

"When?" She barely got it out.

"Three days form tomorrow." He sounded very happy about it, since she wasn't in lap any more, he put his arms along the back of the swing, and looked up at her.

Oh, my god, she would have to be around for it. Why couldn't he wait until she went off the cliff. Why couldn't he wait? If he wanted to make it easier for her, he couldn't had found a better way. If she was to asked about last night, he would say that she needed him, and that he just wanted to be there for her, and both of them just got carried away.

"Who is she, Chance?" Kimberly was afraid that the shock was wearing off, and the tears would start coming down, but if his new wife was going to know about Kimberly Chandlers, she had to know about her.

Chapter Nineteen

"SHE IS KIMBERLY RACKS. DO you know her?"
She watched in disbelief as he pulled a ring out of his pants pocket.

He held it up for her to see, it was a blue stone cut in the shape of Texas with a roll of small diamonds all the way around it.

He got up and walk to her, he put the ring in her hand, and swung her up in his arms. He started toward the swing, then changed his mind, heading for the feed room, he stopped by the tack room to pick up a couple of saddle blankets.

Frankie, Jake, Daffy, and General watched with a mild curiosity, the looks on their faces clearly said that they was wondering what all of the fuss was about.

Kimberly looked from the ring to Chance. She was in shock, again, a happy kind of shock, but still shock.

When they reach the feed room, he spread the blankets down on the floor, and he laid her down on the blankets.

He didn't looked too happy, when Kimberly sat up with her legs under her, but he knew that they needed to talk, so he sat down beside her on the blankets.

184

He lean back on one elbow to face her. "Before anything else is said, the ring is to keep. I had it made for you as a gift. There is no strings attached to it." He bow his head for a moment, then he back up at her. "I just wanted you to remember that Texas isn't the cause of what has happen to you. While, it may not mean the same thing to us that it once did. It still had the spirit that it always did. It is a beautiful state, it should be proud of its history. Do you understand that, Kimberly?"

She looked from the ring to him, and nodded her head. "I know that, Chance. And it is a beautiful ring. But . . . ." But, she wasn't sure that she should accepted it. "you are doing so much for me, now."

He caught her chin in his hand, and asked. "Who did you think I was going to marry, if not you?"

She shook her head, while she told him the truth. "I didn't know." She shrugged her shoulders, her eyes was fill with uncertain pain.

"You thought that I was turning out to be just another whore chasing bastard, didn't you, Kimberly?"

She nodded her head. "I didn't know what else to think."

"And I just assumed that you would know that it was you that I was marrying. But, I guess, that I need to asked you first, uh? Is that how it works?" He was teasing her.

And he did made her grin, when she answer him. "I think that is how it is suppose to work?"

He took the ring from her, then moved himself, so he was bend down on one knee in front of her. "So, will you marry me, Kimberly Racks?" He smile at her in a questioning way.

There was beginning of tears in her eyes, when she asked. "Are you sure you don't want to tested me out, first?"

He knew that they had tested her out, because they thought that she would fall for anyone that paid the least bit attention to her. While he went with anything, everything that would spread her legs out for him. Those that he went with who wasn't Kimberly's friends, or used to be her friends, he would have them meet her in other ways. Either, had other men pretend that they were going with them, or have them meet in business.

And the worst and the saddest part of it was that Kimberly knew all of this, and she had to live the rest of her life knowing it.

Chance knew that Kimberly wasn't that easy for attention, if she had wanted it that bad, she would have got out more, and started to whoring around like the rest of them.

No, what Kimberly had wanted, and what she had wanted to be was a honest, loving, trustworthy mate. But, no one ever gave a chance to be that, or to have that kind of relationship. And now, Chance couldn't see how Kimberly would ever be the happy, outgoing, loving woman that she had once been, he didn't see how she could. But, maybe with him she could.

"No, Kimberly, I don't want to tested you. I just want to love you for the rest of my life."

She thought about it for a minute. "I will still want to sell my paintings, and put the money in the bank." Her voice and her eyes were questioning to be sure that he understood what she meant.

He nodded his head. "I understand that, Kimberly, and if you still want to do that after we are married. I will understand. But, you just might changed your mind. Just think about it." That is all he wanted her to do, all he could hoped for.

"Do you want me to sign a pre-nuptials agreement, so if I do change my mind about selling my paintings, you won't have to worried about me divorcing you, and then living on half of what you had?" Kimberly would understand if he wanted her to.

He looked kind of shock, but shook his head. "No, Kimberly, we won't ever be divorced." He sounded so sure of it. But, Kimberly wasn't, and she told him. "We would be if I ever caught you with another woman. That would be the end of ours marriage." And she meant it. "And I would probably take you for everything that I could."

He grinned, because he knew that she was telling him the truth that she would be that hurt and angry because he took another woman when he could had her.

"You won't ever catch me with another woman, I promised you that I won't ever hurt you that way. I promise you. I love you. So, will you marry me?"

"You better believe that I will." Kimberly didn't why any one wouldn't want to marry Chance.

He was a very honest, loving man, he wouldn't let any one used him, but he wouldn't used any one either.

Chance treated Kimberly like she was a real person, like she was capable of real feelings.

Sometimes, she thought that one, who had played the game with her, and those other people didn't think that she was capable of having any real feelings. She felt like him and those people had treat her no better than they would had a dog. And for a time, she had let them, then she got smart enough to realized that all she was to them was a game, and he was the one that was after every little bitch that came in heat.

But, Chance wouldn't treat her like that, she knew that for the next two weeks, he wanted to give her the way it was suppose to be between a man and woman. He wanted Kimberly Racks to be love and care for. A while after she had gone off of the cliff, he would had her declared as drown at sea, and go on with his life. And Kimberly Chandlers would go on her life in the Australia outback.

He put the ring on her finger, put his other knee down and then pulled her into his arms. She put her arms around his waist, and raised her head up to meet him in long, passionate kiss.

He was still holding her in his arms, when he told her.

"We will go first thing in the morning to file for a marriage license and to have blood tests." He pulled her closer and held her tighter. "It would give you a chance to look around to see where the closest shopping mall is, and then in three days, we will be married. I thought that, we would be married right here out in front of the stable, where Frankie and Jake could attend the ceremony."

When Kimberly raised her head from laying on his shoulder to look at him, there was so much love on her face, and laughter in her eyes.

He grinned down at her. "You like that idea?"

She couldn't help but to giggled with happiness. "I love that idea."

He nodded his head slightly, and said. "I kind of thought that you would, I don't know why, but I just kind of thought so. Going to be the damndest feeding time that Frankie and Jake ever seen, don't you think?" His voice was full of laughter.

"Oh, I would think so." She nodded her head. "Would it be breakfast or supper for them?"

"It will be a early supper for them, because once we are we married, it will be a long time before I get out of bed, and you won't be leaving it too soon, either." He sounded sure of it.

"Is that what you think?" There were a tiny bit of protest in her voice.

But, Chance kissed her long and hard, and his hands went to her buttocks to pulled her lower part of her body next to his. There was ache and longing left in the lower part of her body, when Chance ended the kiss.

She had to confess. "You are right, I wouldn't be leaving the bed too soon."

He smiled with satisfaction, as he continue to hold her close. "It will be a very small wedding. In fact, I thought Brad and Polly could stand up for us, if that is okay with you?"

She nodded her head.

"I would like to keep as quiet as possible. I didn't want to tell anyone or put a announcement out until after we leave for Australia. If that's okay with you?"

She nodded her head, again, and said. "Of course."

He kind of grinned. "That way, we have time to ourselves without being bother with a lot of calls and stuff like that, understand?"

She nodded her head. Kimberly knew that they wanted a very few people, if any, from theirs business's world to meet Kimberly Racks, that way, if any one met Kimberly Chandlers there would be less of a chance for any kind of suspicions.

And Kimberly was sure when his friends found that he was married, they would want to have parties, and stuff like that for him.

"Now, we can stand up for Brad and Polly, have a double wedding, what you think?"

Kimberly shook her head at the grin that was on his face. "Chance, in the first place, you don't know if they are planning on getting marry, and . . . ."

"Okay, if they don't mention getting marry in the first thirty minutes, after we see them, I will asked them about it." He would, too.

Kimberly raised her eyebrows, and gave him, a what I am going to do with you look, before she continued. "in the second place, you couldn't asked them to have that kind of wedding. They would want to have their friends and family there."

Chance shook his head sadly. "Polly hadn't have any close friends since the beginning of High School."

"Do you know why?" She asked.

He nodded his head. "Do you?"

"We talked at dinner, she told me." Kimberly said.

"Did you know that those same people came to me looking for jobs, because you understand, they were friends of Polly." Chance shook his head with disbelief.

"What did you do?" She asked.

Chapter Twenty

CHANCE'S EYES HAD A MISCHIEVOUS gleam in them. "Chance, what did you do?"

He lean his head to one side, grin, and assured her. "You really don't want to know, Kimberly. Trust me, you really don't want to know."

"Would it make me a partner in crime?"

He laughed, but he didn't say no. "Let just say that, when me and Brad got thorough with them, they had a whole new understanding of why you shouldn't hurt and play with a person's feelings like they did. But, it was good for Polly, too."

Kimberly looked at him like he had a mean streak in him.

"Now, wait a minute, Kimberly, think about for a minute. It taught her to be careful who she called her friends, it taught her that she could get hurt, and keep going. She didn't turned to be swallow and unfeeling. And it wasn't like what happen to you."

"I know that you are right, I guess, but I still wished that it wouldn't had happen to her."

"Me, neither." Chance had wanted to protect Polly from that kind of hurt from those kind of people, but he couldn't.

"What about Brad's family? Won't he want them there?" Kimberly asked.

Chance shook his head. "Brad's parents are snobby rich, they are from old money, if you know what I mean?"

"I think so. You mean, the castle, high society partying, we are too good for you kind?" She could almost see them in her mind.

"That is it. Just between you and me, I think that they are flaky."

Kimberly giggled.

Chance chuckled. "Brad is only child, and we are not sure how they pulled that one off." He rolled his eyes.

"Chance!"

"Well, any ways, Brad was rear by his grandparents on a ranch in Nevada, and my mother just adore his grandmother.

His grandparents had all of the money that his parents had, of course, but for some reason it went to his parent heads." Chance shook his head in amazement. "While his parents was traveling to, god only where, Brad was happy with his grandparents. They were good, solid, down to earth kind of people, but they had both pass-away. And he only sees his parents once every few years, if then. So, you see they will be happy with a quiet wedding, too."

"What about yours and Brad's friends? I bet y'all have a lot of friends." She didn't want to know about the women in his past, she wasn't the kind to be buddy—buddy with the women her husband been with. It just wasn't her style, maybe in that way, she was still immature. But, that was the reason that Kimberly Racks would never be married if she was going to live, but since she wasn't going to live for more than two weeks. Why not, be happily married? She still didn't want to know about the other woman, but she realized he and Brad would want their friends there.

"We know a lot of people in business, but they aren't ours friends, Kimberly. Oh, they would send gifts, cards, flowers, they would made the calls, and the arrangements for parties, and stuff like that. But, I would rather spend the time with you. What do you say to a quiet wedding, and spending time with me?"

She hugged him tight, and said. "That's how I would want it. But, I don't know about Brad and Polly, though."

He set her away from him. "We won't worry about them now, and I will took you riding over the ranch tomorrow, when we get back from town. Right now, I want to do what I brought you in here for."

191

He starting kissing her lips, then her face, while his hands went up her arms to her shoulders.

While he was kissing her face, she said. "I thought you brought me in here to ask me to marry you."

His grin was lop-sided, when he said. "I could had done that outside. And we could had done this outside, too. But, I thought that you would rather come in here." His hands went down to her breasts, he starting squeezing them, as his lips were kissing her neck.

Kimberly had to tell him, now, before she was lost in the moment. "Chance, I know why we need a quiet wedding, but are you sure that you would be happy with it?"

"I like quiet things, that is I am selling most of the company, and moving to Australia." He was smiling in between kisses.

When his hands went to the buttons on her blouse, she thought of the horses. "Chance, I need to go put the horses back in theirs stalls." She started to raise up.

Chance looked at her like she had lost her mind, then he shook his head. "No, I will."

He didn't looked too happy about it, but he stood up, and went off the door cussing under his breath.

Kimberly wasn't about to giggled out loud, but she did grin, as she pulled her boots off, then she stood up, unbuttoned her jeans, and pushed them with her panty down over her buttocks.

She sat back down on the blankets to pulled her feet out of the jeans and panty. She listen to Chance talk to the horses, as he put them in their stalls, while she unbuttoned her blouse, and laid it to the side, she was unfastening her bra, when Chance came back through the door.

He grinned, as he watched her pushed the bra off of her shoulders, when she looked up and saw him, she kind of got embarrass.

"Don't go getting self-conscious on me, Kimberly." He told her, as he closed the door behind him.

"I won't." Was all that she could say, and it came out very quietly.

He gave her a look that said he didn't believe her, as he sat down beside her on the blankets. His eyes took a long look over her nude body, he force his hands to pulled off his boots, while she started to unsnapping his shirt.

"Yea, but I had a feeling that if anyone else was around, you wouldn't even greet me with a hug."

She grinned, and confessed. "Yea, probably not. But, there isn't anyone else around, is there?" She wanted to know, as she pulled off his shirt, he had his arms held behind his back. "And we won't ever be around that many people, will we?"

When she had his shirt off and was laying it to the side, he turned to grab her, and laid her down on the blankets. He position himself by the side of her with one arm under her.

He grinned down at her. "You mean, we don't have to worry about it?"

She grinned up at him, and shook her head. "No."

He put pulled his arm out from under her, and then he leaned his head down to started kissing her lips. In between kisses, he said. "But, we do need to work on it."

His hand went to her breasts, softly rubbing them, squeezing them. He took nipple in between his fingers, and gently started pulling on them until his mouth went down to take a nipple, and gently started sucking it.

Kimberly felt a pleasure tingle feeling all over her body, she loved the feeling of his hands, of his lips, and of his body on her.

His hand went down over her stomach to her hip, grabbing it, squeezing, and pinching it gently, then his hand moved to the other hip, rubbing, squeezing, and pinching it gently.

When Kimberly felt his mouth leave her breast, and his hand leave her hip, and his body leave her side, she open her mouth to protect. But, then she saw that he was unbuttoning his pants with one hand, and his other hand was going between her legs.

She smiled, when she felt his hand start rubbing up and down the inside of her legs. His other hand was pushing his pants down, when he had them far enough down, he move on top of her.

She parted her legs for him, she bent her knees sightly to raise to him.

He smiled, as he felt her do it, he enter her quickly.

Spending pleasurable shock waves through her body, her whole body tingled, and sweated, she cling to him, getting as close to him as she could.

It was awhile later, when he rolled off of her. He was laying flat on his back on the blankets, he had one arm under Kimberly holding her close to his side.

She was laying on her side facing him, with her head on his shoulder, and her breasts against him. She had one arm under her, and the other one laying across his chest.

His hand was laying on the round part of her buttocks, rubbing it slightly. He had his other arm under his head.

"You really do enjoy making love, don't you, Kimberly?"

She raised her head to look at him.

He grinned at her. "I mean, a man would never have to worry about not getting enough, would he?"

She pushed herself up, and away from him slightly. She wasn't sure how to take it. "If it was the right man. No, I wouldn't leave him wanting more. But, it would had to be a man that I sure of, one that I was sure he wouldn't hurt me, or cheat on me."

He grinned at her. "Am I that man, Kimberly?"

She grinned at him. For the next two weeks, she with all her heart hoped that he wouldn't cheat on her. She was hoping that a man who would gave such a beautiful ring would think a enough of her to be a loving, faithful husband for just two weeks.

Couldn't a man be faithful for two weeks?

She looked from the ring on her finger to the man that was laying beside her. "Well, I certainly hope so. Because, if you aren't, we are going to have problems."

"I guess that makes me the man." He grinned at her, as he brought his hand from behind his head to lay it on her breast that was pointed at him. "I just want to be sure you w going to stay this loving."

She leaned her breast in to his hand, smiling as he started to squeezed it. "I will still this loving until you do something to cause me not to feel this loving toward you." She thought about for a minute." Do you understand what I mean?"

He moved her up and himself down until his mouth was level with her breasts, before he took the nipples in to his mouth, he told her. "Yea, I understand, and I won't do anything to cause you to lose the loving in you."

When he took her nipple into his mouth, she wanted to stay beside him for a long time, but it was getting late.

"Chance, it is getting late. It's feeding time, and I am afraid that maybe Brad and Polly may come looking for us.

But, maybe they won't, they did seems to had other things on their minds last time that I saw them." She smile as she remember.

Chance didn't say anything, he just fill her with a delightful feeling, as his mouth went from one breast to other one. She moved her body to give him easy asset to which ever breasts, he wanted, until he put his hand went to the lower part of her body, in between legs.

When his fingers started rubbing it, and making their way inside her just enough to sent tumors thorough her body, from the top of her head to the tip of toes, she just tingle.

Chance smile, as he moved his lips from her breast to put kisses on her neck, all over her face, and he pressed his face against her shoulder at the base of her neck. He held her for a minute, then he pulled away from her to sit up straight.

"You know, you could be right about Brad and Polly."

Chapter Twenty-One

KIMBERLY COULDN'T DO ANYTHING, BUT stare at him, as he pulled his pants up, they had found their way down to his ankles, almost off. They were both cover with sweat.

When he got his pants up, and fasten, he started pulling on his socks. Before he pulled his boots on, he turned to looked at her.

She was laying on her side leaning back on one elbow watching him. The tips of breasts was wet from his mouth had been on them, he looked on down to the roundness on her buttocks, even her toes was wet with sweat from their love making.

He smile at the confuse look on her face, his hands wanted to go to her beasts, to mold them, and shaped in his hands, to have his lips on her nipples, teasing them, and to feel the enjoyment that she was having from it, too.

"We will have all night in a bed, Kimberly. We won't had to worry about anyone coming in us." He grinned at her, before he pulled his boots on. "Right now, we need to find out if there is going to be a double wedding."

Kimberly rolled her eyes at him, before she turned over on her back, she watched him stand up. She giggled, as she asked. "And what are going to do if there isn't? Pull out your shotgun?"

He was pulling on his shirt, when he told her. "Why in the hell not? Polly would had held one on you for me, if you haven't agree to marry me." He was trying hard to not to grin.

But, Kimberly wasn't. "You mean, if I haven't agree to marry you, you would had Polly hold a shotgun on me?" She gave him hers most doubtful look.

"Oh, hell yea, Kimberly. Polly would had to make sure you made a honest man of me. Didn't you know that?" Despite his best efforts the chuckling sound came out, as he buttoned up his shirt. He knelt down beside her, as she sit up.

She put her arms around his neck, as his arms went around her. "I think that you are a easy man to love, Chance Kincaid Sway. But, I just can't see Polly doing that."

Chance liked the feeling her breasts pressed up against him, so he held her tighter. "What do you mean, easy to love? And Polly would had, if she needed."

She grinned up at him. "I just meant that you are the kind of man that is easy to love, and if you say that Polly would had held a shotgun to me, then I believe you."

He make a sound that said that he didn't believe her, as he set her away from him. "You put your clothes on, while I feed." He kissed her long and hard, while his hands found their way to her breasts, he squeezed them, then he gently pinched her nipples. He pulled his head back to watched them stand up.

When his eyes left her nipples to looked in her eyes.

She barely got out. "Tonight, a bed."

He just nodded, before he stand up, and found the feed buckets.

Kimberly started putting on her clothes, when she hear the feed hitting the bottom of the buckets, Frankie must had heard, too. Because, she went to nicking.

"I better hurry, or she will be fussing at me." Chance chuckled. "It is a good thing that they aren't spoil or anything like that."

Kimberly and Chance finished feeding, and drove to the house. They walked into the kitchen door just as Brad and Polly was about to walked out of the kitchen's door leading outside.

When Polly heard them, she turned around and ran to Chance. Her arms went around him, and she giggled up at him.

"Brother, I am glad to see you."

He tried not, but he grinned down at her. "Yea, Sis, it has just been a few hours since you saw me, so it kind of makes me wonder why you are glad to see me." He sounded skeptical about it, but he put one arm around Polly and the other one around Kimberly, and hugged both them to him. "So why you so happy to see me?"

There was so much happiness in Polly, that her eyes sparkled, and her face just beamed, when she told him. "We are getting marry!" She just couldn't hold it in any longer, even if she tried, which she didn't.

Chance gave her a muck look of surprise. "Really? I know who I am going to marry, but who in the world are you marrying?" Chance was trying hard to keep the look of surprise on his face.

Polly pulled away from Chance to walked over to Brad, who had his arms out waiting for her. She went in to his arms and turned to face Chance and Kimberly. "I am marrying Brad." She was so full of pride when she said it.

Chance looked Brad squarely in the eyes, and told him. "Do you know what you are getting yourself into? She will have you wrap around her little finger in no time."

Brad just grinned and said. "She always did had me wrap around her little finger." He just shrugged his shoulders like this wasn't going to change anything.

"Except now, he is getting something out of it."

Chance, Kimberly, and Brad all looked at her, and said.

"Polly!" At the same time. Their voices sounded shock, but Polly just laughed at them with a delighted look on her face.

The best wishes, congratulations, hugs, and kisses were out of the way, another round come for Chance and Kimberly.

When Chance told Brad and Polly that he and Kimberly were getting marry, they didn't seem a bit surprise. Happy, but not surprise.

"The only one that seems surprise by us getting marry was Kimberly. You should have seen her when I told her that I was getting marry, she looked like she was going to take my head off." Chance told Brad and Polly as they fixing a glass of cola for him and Kimberly.

Polly looked at him. "Don't tell me, you told her that you were getting marry before you asked her, to marry you?"

Polly couldn't believe it.

Chance looked innocent enough when he said. "Yea, you don't think it was a good idea?"

Polly just look at him, but Brad chuckled and said. "It is a wonder that she didn't knock the hell out of you."

Chance just shook his head. "I thought that she was."

Polly got her voice back, as she headed Kimberly her cola. "What didn't you, Kimberly?"

Kimberly grinned from Polly to Chance. "To be honest, I was just too shock to do it. I didn't know what to think."

All of the sadness came back to her face.

Chance leaned over to kiss her lightly on her lips. "I am so sorry if I hurt you, but I really thought you would know the only one that I would want to marry would be you."

When he said like that, who would be hurt? Not Kimberly, even Polly smiled at her brother, again.

"But, I should have asked you first, and I am truly very sorry that I didn't." Chance had to remember what all she had been thorough, he know that he couldn't just take away all the pain and the hurt that those people had cause her. And god help him, he couldn't forget it, either, or he would hurt her, not meaning to.

Kimberly looked at him, and smile, when she told him. "As long, as it was me that you are going to married, you are forgiven, but if it would have been someone else. You would have . . . ."

"the hell knock out of you." Polly finished it for her.

Chance gave Polly a disapproving look, and said. "I told Kimberly, that you would had held a shotgun on her at wedding, if she haven't agree to do the honorable thing by me." He shook his head discouragingly. "And here you are telling her that you would knock the hell of me. What kind of sister are you?"

Brad was chuckling.

Polly told her brother with a certain amount of assuredness. "You know, if she wouldn't agree to do the honorable thing by you that I would have been there with a shotgun, without a doubt." She wanted that to be understood. "You know, that I would had. But, if you would spent the night with her, and then told her that you was going to married someone else, then I would had knock the hell out of you for your own good." She didn't seem doubtful about it either.

Kimberly and Brad was chucking, as Chance raised his eyebrows at Polly. "For my own good?"

199

"Of course, you wouldn't want me to let you turned into one of those kind of men, would you?" Before he could answer her, she said. "No, of course not." She rubbed her hands together with excitement. "What kind of wedding are we having? Could we have a double wedding?" She look at Brad questioningly, he had sat down beside her at table.

Brad nodded his head.

But, Kimberly look at Chance, who was grinning, and she said.

"Maybe, you better tell them about our wedding first."

Chance gave her a nod. "It is going to be very small, me, and Kimberly, we wanted you to stand up for up, and a priest, and that is it. Beside, Frankie and Jake, of course, General and Draffy will be there. Because, it will be held down on the beach in front of the stable in three days. I thought that we would go in the first thing in the morning to get the license and blood tests." He looked at Brad questioningly. "We want to keep it quiet and out of the papers until we leave for Australia."

Brad nodded his head with a smile. "Let the offices handle all the calls, cards, and stuff. Sound good to me. We will keep it quiet."

"And Kimberly is afraid that y'all will want more for your wedding." Chance explained to them why Kimberly didn't think that they would want a double wedding.

Brad and Polly look at each other, then Polly started talking. "Let see, we will have Chance and Kimberly there."

"A beautiful day on the beach." Brad added. "Frankie and Jake will be there."

"And of course, General and Draffy will be there."

Polly said it like it was must.

"Of course." Brad agreed.

"We will hung wedding bells on the stables, put. What are your favorite flower, Kimberly?" Polly asked.

"Roses. I like roses." Kimberly smile.

"We will put roses in the horse's manes and trails, and we will have roses in ours bouquets there will be a stereo there to play "Here comes the Brides" along with other songs we pick out. Our gowns will be made of white lace, and white satin, we will wear white cowboy boots, and white felts cowboy hats with roses around the brims." Polly look from Brad to Chance. "These two will wear theirs black tuxedo, with black cowboy boots, and black cowboy felt hats."

"Without the roses on the brim." Chance and Brad said it together.

Polly look at them like they were being foolish. "No, of course, they will go on your tuxedos."

When Chance and Brad had just let out a sigh of relief, a gleam of mischief came in to Polly's eyes. "But, you know, since you have mention it, it doesn't . . . ."

Chance said. "No, no way in hell."

Brad started shaking his head. "No, no way in hell.

Certainly not."

Polly was about to start laughing, but she said. "Oh, but please.

It's ours wedding." She had a remarkable straight face.

Brad was still shaking his head, he said in all sincerely. "I know that is, but our wedding, too. And do you realized how stupid that we would look with roses on ours hats. Now, y'all will look gorgeous, but me and Chance would look stupid. Trust me."

But, Chance put his arm across the back of Kimberly's chair, and lean toward her. With a thoughtful look, he said.

"I don't know, Brad, one might not look too bad."

And at that time, Kimberly knew that Polly's bluff had been called. But poor Brad didn't, he looked shock.

Polly started giggling. "I was just teasing."

Brad's color starting coming back to his face, when he let the breath that he had been holding, when he said. "Thank god!"

"We will have chocolate cake with white chocolate icing, we will have bake and decorated at a bakery that don't know us." Chance irrupted Polly by asking. "So, it is a double wedding?"

Polly and Brad looked at each with questioning looks, then nodded, and said. "Yep." At the exacted same time.

Chance nodded his head, and told them. "I just wanted to make sure." And while Polly and Brad was discussing the details, he whispered in Kimberly's ear. "It didn't take thirty minutes."

Kimberly giggled and whisper in his ear. "Not even to plan the wedding."

Chapter Twenty-Two

"WHAT WAS THAT?" BRAD LOOK from Kimberly to Chance, Polly looked around at them, too.

Chance and Kimberly looked from each other to Brad and Polly with innocent looks, and said. "Oh, nothing. We just need to go and clean up." When Chance started moving to get up, Kimberly started moving, too.

Polly look at Chance, and wrinkle her nose, and said. "Yea, you do."

Chance's shirt trail was hanging down over his pants, he was still carrying the coat to his suit over his arm. He wrinkled his nose at her, and was about to say something, but Polly cut in, before he could by saying.

"You can go clean up, but Kimberly needs to stay here with me. We need to pick out what kind of dresses we want, so me and Brad can order them first thing in the morning."

When Chance and Brad started opening their mouths, Polly assured them. "I mean after the license and blood tests."

Chance and Brad nodded their heads with approval.

"Now, you go and get clean up," Polly pointed her finger at Chance, then she turned toward Brad. "and you start the bar-que for supper,"

Then she turn to Kimberly. "and you stay here, while I go to get the magazines, and stuff, so we can pick out ours dresses. Tonight will be like ours bridal shower, and their bachelor's party." She made faces at Brad and Chance. "Y'all do understand that this the only kind of bachelor's party, that you will ever have, don't you?" She asked them.

"Yes, mam." Brad said it like he wouldn't even want another kind.

There was laughter in Chance's eyes, when he said. "It would be for our own good."

"You better believe it." Polly nodded her head, as she told them about what her and Brad had plan. "Brad is going to bar-que outside, we have music for dancing after we eat."

Before Kimberly thought she asked. "Brad is going to cook?"

Brad was standing up to go start the bar-que, he put his hands on his hips, and asked her. "Did they tell you that I couldn't cook?"

Kimberly had to grin, when she looked from Polly to Chance.

Polly gave a firm shake of her head, and said. "No, he can't cook, not in a kitchen."

"But, you give him a grill and plenty of room, and he can almost cook steaks that are as good mine. Almost. They will melt in your mouth." Chance brag on him. "But, don't ever let him in a kitchen."

Kimberly bow her head to him, and apology to him. "I am very sorry, and I am looking forward to eating yours steaks."

Brad turned his nose up to her, and said huffy. "Even after saying what you did, I still want to pay for yours wedding dress." Brad tried not to, but he smile.

Kimberly didn't know what to say, she smile at his giving nature, but she had to tell him. "Thank you, but I couldn't let you do that. Besides," She looked at Chance, before she finished saying. "I am still going to sell my paintings."

Brad and Polly seem surprise to hear that, and when she added. "And I will be putting the money in the bank." They were shock and maybe just a little disappointed.

But, Brad just smile. "Well, in that case, if you let me pay for your dress, you will have more money to put in the bank, won't you?" At Kimberly's hesitation, he added. "I want it to be my gift to you. I don't have a sister, so I want to spend my money on my future sister in-law."

When Kimberly was still hesitated Chance told her. "You better let him, Kimberly, because once he married to Polly, he won't have any money."

Even Polly join with the laughter of Kimberly, Chance, and Brad, but she did tell them proudly. "I have money of my own."

"Yea, but his will spend better." Chance said still chuckling, and Polly didn't denial it.

But, Brad quickly assured them. "I am not worry about it, but I would like to pay for yours dress. My wedding present to you. What about it, Kimberly?"

"That's very kind of you." Kimberly told him.

Chance put his hand on Kimberly's shoulder, and bent down and said. "Yea, it is, and it won't happen very often, so you better took him up on it."

Kimberly nodded her head. "Thank you, very much, Brad."

"Now, that is settled, you go and get clean up." Polly motion for Chance to leave, then she motion for Brad to go. "You go and start supper."

"I am going, just don't let her go up before he come outside, or you won't have your party." Brad warned Polly, as he went out the door leading outside.

Polly just giggled, Chance looked like the idea appeal to him, but Polly just shake her head, and made a motion for him to leave.

Chance mumble something, as he was walking out the door.

Polly raised her eyebrows, and said. "You stay here, and I will go to the stuff." Then she was gone.

And Kimberly was left alone to wonder if this was really happening. If anyone would have told her two days ago, that she would be marrying a very, good-looking, kind, loving man like Chance, having quiet, beautiful wedding, and in less than two weeks, there would be a end to the game that man had played with her life. She wouldn't have believe it.

No, it couldn't be happening, because good, nice, and happy things don't happen to her, any more.

But, Polly come back in the kitchen with catalogs, and magazines.

Chance was order outside, when he come in after cleaning up and putting a clean white, western shirt, a pair of blue jeans, and a pair of black cowboy boots.

"These are mine dancing boots." Was all he had time to tell Kimberly, before Polly was pushing him out the door telling him. "You can't see her dress before the wedding."

When he was out of the door, Polly turned to Kimberly and asked. "Or is that just on the day of the wedding?" She gave a guilty looking grin.

Kimberly just shrugged her shoulders. "I don't know."

"Well, any ways, he need to be outside, while we do this."

They had pick out the dresses. Kimberly's was white satin, cover in white lace, the top was fitted, buttoned down the front with a sweetheart's neck, and a stand up collar in the back, and the skirt was full, and long.

Polly's dress was white satin covered in white lace the top was fitted with a stand up collar all the way around, and a zipped in the back, and the skirt was long, and full.

They had pick out the style of hats and boots that they wanted. Kimberly gave Polly her dress, hat, and boots sizes, Kimberly also told her that she needed a half of a inch lift put on her right boot.

Polly said that it wouldn't be a problem, everything would be ready in three days.

The style of cake that they wanted was pick out, it was a three layers fudge chocolate cake, with enough of room on the top for two brides, and two grooms. The icing would be white chocolate, and the roses that it would decorated with would be strawberry favor.

They decided not to tried the roses into the horses manes and trails, The roses would be put on ribbons, then the ribbons would be tried around the horses necks, and down their trails.

When everything was decided down what color of roses would go on what horse, Kimberly help Polly gather up the magazines, catalogs, and stuff off of the kitchen table, and take it to a part den and a part library room of the house.

While Polly put the French bread in the oven to get hot, and put forks, knifes, plates, more drinks and whatever else she thought that they might need in a picnic basket, Kimberly went up to clean up, and put on clean clothes.

Before she went up, she told Polly that it might take her awhile, so if she was ready before Kimberly came back down, she could go on without her.

Polly said that she would if she got tire of waiting for her.

Kimberly took just enough time in the shower to washed the dust and sweat off of her. She put her hair that she just shampoo once in a towel.

As she dried herself off, she decided if Polly wanted a party, she would dress more like she was going to a party.

Polly had changed from the jeans and blouse that she had on at dinner in to a skirt, and a pretty blouse.

While Kimberly hurriedly pull her thigh HI, panty, and bra, she thought about what she was going to wear.

She decided on a pretty, pink with flowers print sundress, it had lace, and ribbons trimming down the middle in the front of its fitted top, and the skirt was full, but not long as she would like it.

But, she pulled on her favorite pair of boots, which was a pair of light tan, knee high, cowboys boots.

Kimberly smile to herself, as she was putting a white, western, chop blouse, with a eyelet and ruffle yoke in the front. If she really wanted to matched the outfit, she would need a pair of white, cowboy boots. But, she couldn't afford too many pair of boots.

And because of her condition, Kimberly was too rough on them, she wore them out too fast. But, maybe Kimberly Chandlers wouldn't have that problem, or at least not for very long.

Polly said with a smile. "Now, you look like you are ready for a party." She was just taking the hot bread out of the oven, when Kimberly came back down in the kitchen.

Then they join Chance and Brad down on the deck.

The deck was made out of the same kind of wood that trimmed the house, it had a rail around it, but it wasn't too high off of the ground. It gave you a beautiful view of the ocean on one side, the house on another, the stables on another, and the green grass of cattle pasture on the other.

When Kimberly and Polly was walking up the steps to the deck, Chance and Brad wanted to know if everything was pick out and ready to be order, they was assured that it was.

The bar-que pit set in the middle of the deck, the steaks that Brad had grab from the refrigerator before he left the kitchen will melt in your mouth, the potatoes that Polly had put in Chance's arms before she pushed him out the door were hot and soft.

Kimberly and Polly started taking the stuff out of the picnic basket.

They sat around the deck talking about what they still had to do before they left for Australia. And they had decided that there wasn't much left to do. What was left of the business was pretty much running itself.

After they ate, they danced around the deck to country music.

"I will step on your toes." Kimberly gave Chance fair warning before they started.

He grinned down at her. "I change my boots. You see, you can take boot polished and cover up any marks you put on them." Then he pulled her in his arms.

After a dance or two, Kimberly told Chance. "I think that Brad had gotten my job."

"Yea." Chance crock his head to one side. "It is a good thing that I thought of that other position for you."

He took her hand in to his hand to look at the ring. "I think this one will better for you. And I am just glad that me and Brad are not nice men."

Kimberly giggled. "I am, too."

Chance chuckled. "Ain't you glad, too, Brad?"

Brad was looking at Polly in his arms, and he didn't seem to want to be bother. "Glad about what?" He asked still looking at Polly.

"That we aren't nice men."

Chapter Twenty-Three

"THAT ISN'T WHAT I MEANT!" Polly rolled her eyes at Chance, then she looked up accursedly at Brad. "You just had to tell him, didn't you?"

Brad shrugged his shoulders. "Well, yea, I thought that he should know what was going in that pretty little head of yours. I didn't know it was a secret. Honest."

"Yea, and I am glad to know that because I fell in love, made love, and plan to marry a disable woman, it makes me not a nice man." Chance pulled Kimberly closer, and crock his head to one side. "Not that I am going to worry about it, you understand." He grinned.

"It is just that sometimes, I think that society thinks that we (the disables) shouldn't have sex, or even think about it, or sometimes I think that they think that we are easy, and desperate for sex. Hell, there are times when I think that they don't think that we should have happy adult lives." Polly took it more seriously, than Chance did.

"Like I tried to tell you this afternoon, Polly. Most people don't think like that anymore. And when they aren't in love enough to see past a disability, they are probably not ready for a serious relationship."

"Maybe, that is it!" Polly exclaimed, as she looked up at Brad. "Maybe, they are afraid to date disable people, because they will feel bad if it doesn't work out."

Brad gave her a doubtful look, and said hesitantly. "That could be part of it."

Polly look at Kimberly and Chance with a questioning look.

"I don't know about that, Polly. I think that it is because they don't know what they are missing, and" He stepped back from Kimberly a step to pick her up in his arms.

"what I do know is I don't give a damn what society thinks." When Kimberly put her arms around his neck, he started walking toward the steps leading off of the dock, before he step off of it, he said to Polly and Brad. "If you will clean up tonight, I will cook breakfast in the morning?"

When they nodded their heads, he added. "Early in the morning, Polly."

Polly gave him a, oh please, look. "I know, and I will be ready." And before he left with Kimberly, Polly asked. "Could we take that dress to the dress maker's tomorrow for they to go by? It seems to fit you, just right." She smiled.

Kimberly nodded her head. "But, I would like the skirt longer."

Before Polly could said anything, Chance was off of the dock, and walking toward the house, asking Kimberly. "Did I tell you how much I like the dress?"

Kimberly grinned, but shook her head. "No, you didn't."

"I didn't?" He seems surprise. "I remember thinking how much I like the dress." He raised his eyebrows. "Of course, I like the tight blue jeans that you had on this afternoon, too. But, I didn't tell you that either, did I?"

Kimberly shook her head, again.

"Ah, but I do seem to remember showing you how much I like them." He had a mischievous gleam in his eyes.

"Is that what that was for? My tight jeans?" She asked.

He nodded his head. "And I bet that is what I was thinking tonight, that I would just show how much I like it." He put her down next to his bed, after he closed and locked the door.

She grinned up at him. "By all means, Chance, show me how much you like the dress." She held her arms open.

He took her in his arms for a long kiss, she opened her mouth, so his tongue could go in. His hands made their way up to her blouse, it was off of her, and flying thorough the air out of his way, before she knew it.

His hands went back down the curve of her back over her buttocks, he squeeze her buttocks for a minute, then his hands grab the skirt of her dress.

His mouth left her, and the dress and the slip landed not too far from the blouse.

She standing in front of him in her bra, panty, thigh hi, and boots.

His hands went up to her breasts, he pushed them together, then his lips went to the part that the bra didn't cover, he pushed her breasts together enough so her nipples would popped out of the bra.

His lips took a nipple in to his mouth, gently sucking one then the other, while his hands pushed them up and held together, until Kimberly felt a tingle aching feeling in the lower part of her body.

Her whole body ache with desire for him, for him to be with her as one. She felt him pull her arms off of his shoulders, she was barely aware of her arms being placed at her sides, so the bra would fall to the floor.

With his hands on her hips, he pulled her to him for a long kiss, while his hands pushed her panty down over her buttocks until them fell to the tops of boots. Then he sat her down on the edge of the bed.

As he started to took off her boots, he asked. "Did I tell you that I like the boots?"

She was leaning back on her elbows on the bed, watching him, she shook her head. "No, you didn't."

He grinned, as he set them to the side. "Well, I do."

Her panty fell to the floor, and Chance's hand went up the inside of her leg to pulled down her thigh hi's, one at a time.

When she was naked, he stood up straight and started pulling his shirt from out of his jeans.

She swung her legs on the bed, and pulled a pillow from against the headboard of the bed to lay her head on, while he sat down on the edge of the bed to get out of his boots, jeans, and socks.

She parted her legs for him, when he came on the bed where she was, it made him smile, as he slid in between them.

He kissed her lips, long and hard, he kissed her face, her neck, her shoulders, her arms, and her breasts. While his hands went all over her, squeezing, pinching, and rubbing her, until she raised her lower part of her up to meet him.

She was laying up against him on her side with one of her breasts pressed up against his side, and the other was laying on top of his stomach just below his chest. Her head was laying on his shoulder. She was happy, content, and felt very loved.

Chance was laying on his back with one arms around her, when he asked. "Kimberly, you never say what you think society feels about the disables and sex?"

She took a deep breath, and he felt her breast go up and down on his body, he bent his head to watched it.

She shrugged her shoulders. "I don't know what society thinks, but what I think is that, it would take a man that is very sure of himself to get involved with a disable woman. A man, who could handle the, Couldn't you find any one better?" She raised her eyebrows at him. "You know, that kind of stuff." She nodded her head.

"Yelp, it would take a very special kind of man."

"Couldn't you find any one better?" Chance repeated it thoughtfully. "Do you think that they would asked it out of hatefulness, or ignorance, or jealousy?"

Kimberly shook head sadly. "I don't know, but maybe all of the above." She shrugged her shoulders. "What do you think?"

He felt and watched her breast move up and down, again, and he smiled. "I think it is all of the above, too." He rolled on his side to face her. "Does this mean that me and Brad are very special men?"

"No, you and Brad are just very lucky that me and Polly put up with y'all. I was talking about all of the other men." She was trying hard not to grin.

He rolled her over on her back with him laying on top of her, right before his mouth met hers, he said. "Somehow, Kimberly, I just know that was how you would see it. Don't asked me how I knew, I just knew."

Kimberly's giggles was quieted by Chance's kisses, but she didn't seem to mind.

Chance was in the kitchen cooking breakfast, when Kimberly walked in. She had on a light blue, skirt with white lace trimmed around the bottom, her blouse was white with a trimmed yoke in the front. The shirt went down over the tops of her boots three or four inches, just the length the she liked.

Chance looked up from the pan on the burner, his eyes went up and down her. He gave a whistle, and said. "I do like those boots."

Everyone approved of Chance's breakfast. They had chicken fried steaks, hashed-brown potatoes, eggs, biscuits, and syrup.

Chance drove in to town with Kimberly snuggled up against him, and Brad with Polly following close behind them.

Chance motion to their right as they was going in to town. "That's the closest shopping mall."

Kimberly took a look at the collect of stores join together by a cover sidewalk.

"It isn't very big, but it should have everything that you would need, and if it don't just tell me. I will get for you."

Kimberly's eyes adored him, when she turned to look at him. "And there is a bank, too."

"Yea, there is a bank, too." His voice sounded sad.

But, when Kimberly gave him a questioning look, he put his arm around her to bring her even more closer to him, and asked in a teasing voice. "You won't rob it without me, will you?"

They went in and out of a door that was only known to a very few people, when they went to applied for their marriage license. They didn't see everyone, but a friend of Chance's and Brad's, and he assured them that he handled it every step of the way.

The blood tests was handled in the exact same way, a friend of theirs would handled it every step of the way. He would keep it to himself, and had them the results, as soon, as possible.

Chance and Brad assured Kimberly and Polly that everything would be legal, just kept quiet.

Chance and Kimberly left Brad and Polly in town, they was going shopping for what they needed for the wedding, and then they was going out to the airport to look at Kimberly's paintings, and sketches. A art dealer would be meeting them out there later in the day.

Chance told them that he was going to take Kimberly on a horseback ride over the ranch, he also told them not to come looking for him and her to very late.

Polly was giggling, when Chance and Kimberly drove away from her and Brad.

While Kimberly change in to jeans and another blouse, Chance fill a couple set of saddle bags with food and drinks.

Then they went to saddle General and Draffy, together.

Chance had fed before he had started breakfast, so he and Kimberly wasn't fuss at, when they saddled up.

Chance show her the large, cattle working pens, part of the pens was under a roof, so if they needed to doctor them in bad weather. There was another large horse stables for the working cow horses that they had kept, and or, breeding stocks. There was a smaller home on the ranch for the manger, it wasn't as fancy as the other home, but to Kimberly, it had a quiet charm to it.

They had a long ride over the beautiful cattle pastures, Kimberly loved to ride. And General was a calm, well trained riding horse with a smooth gait. Riding made Kimberly feel alive, excited, like life was good, and to her it was the most wonderful exercise that you could do.

Her and Chance ate dinner, and made love on the horse blankets in a hollow that was cover by shade trees, and brush.

Chapter Twenty-Four

"WE ARE GOING TO THE stables, and we are going to be marry. The stables of love." Polly sounded so happy signing it, that Kimberly started signing it, too.

They had the tack room, Chance and Brad had the feed room. Kimberly and Polly had tried on their dresses first thing yesterday morning to be sure the dresses fit, and so they would had enough time to be mended if they didn't. But, the only thing that those dresses needed was to be worn.

Everything fit, the hats, the boots, and more important than that anything else was, the brides fitted the grooms to a tee.

Yesterday, Kimberly and Polly had to make sure that they had something borrowed, something blue, something old, and something new.

They had decided the dresses was new, Chance and Brad had let them borrow a blue, bandana to wear around their legs under their dresses, for something old, Chance had found them two antique golden rings with roses painted on them.

There was a small refrigerator put in the tack room for Kimberly's and Polly's hat band of roses and theirs bouquets, there was a larger one in the hallway of the stables for the cake, Chance's and Brad's roses, and the roses for the horses who would be attending the wedding.

Kimberly and Polly had tried the roses with ribbons, last night, and they had shown Chance and Brad how to tried the ribbons around the horse's necks. So, the roses would lay on one side of the neck in their manes, while on the other side of the neck would be the ribbons tried in bows.

On their trails, there would be one big, bow at the tops of the trails, then a bow would be tried under each rose going down the trails.

Jake was going to love that, Kimberly was sure.

When Chance and Brad had went to pick up the cake, Kimberly and Polly had made, what seems to Kimberly several trips from the house to the tack room with what they needed to get ready. In their honest opinion, they should had used the truck.

But, somehow they could just hear Chance and Brad saying, "My God, y'all just getting ready for a wedding, not moving to the stable!" And they decided that they didn't want to listen to it.

Not after, the fuss that Chance and Brad had made about having to leave Kimberly and Polly to go down stairs at five minutes before midnight. So, the grooms wouldn't see the brides on their wedding day.

"It is bad luck, you know?" Chance and Brad was talking to each other, as they made their way down stairs.

Kimberly could hear they saying, "First, no bachelor's party, now this." They grumble, but she could hear theirs chuckles, and she knew that they was just fussing to be fussing.

At one point, Chance turned around to gave her a sexy grin, and a wink. Polly didn't see it, but she rolled her eyes, and said. "You would think that we was making them sleep in the feed room at the stable."

Kimberly didn't tell Polly this, but if you were with the right one, the feed room wasn't such a bad place to lay down in. There were a gleam in her eyes, though.

Kimberly had washed her hair, and put it on rollers, so it would be in soft, waves for the wedding, maybe. She folded up a bandana, tried around her neck, and then pulled it over her face under the rollers so her hair would stay dry, and not get wet from sweat, or when she took a bath.

Before, she and Polly put on their housecoats to go down to the stable to get dressed.

The tack room had been divided off with a full length mirror on each side of the divider, so Kimberly and Polly could had privacy getting dressed.

But, now they stood in front of one mirror in theirs dresses of white satin cover in white lace. The dresses was were difference in styles, but equal in beauty. As were the brides.

Kimberly and Polly had just put their hats on, and with their bouquets in their hands, they were ready.

They had heard the Revered Moloney's car awhile ago, so it wouldn't be long now.

Kimberly had been told that the Revered Moloney was a old friend of Chance's and Polly's mother, and he was also about to leave for a foreign country to help the people. With a major donations from Sway and Company as well as others.

And Kimberly was sure that after today, the Sway and Company's donation would get larger.

Polly looked at Kimberly's reflection in the mirror, and asked. "Shouldn't we be nervous or scare or something, besides just happy?"

"We are marrying Chance Kincaid Sway and Bradford Matters, why would we be anything, but happy?" Kimberly grinned at Polly's question.

Polly nodded her head. "Good point. But, what if they back out on us? Shouldn't we be worry about that?"

Kimberly shook her head. "They are not that kind of men or we wouldn't be marrying them, would we?"

Polly nodded her head with more confident. "Another good point, and if they were to do us like that, we would be better off without them, right?"

Kimberly smile and nodded her head. "I would think that we would."

Polly said very quietly. "Sometimes being alone is for the best, it isn't disgrace." Then she grin, and added. "But, we are very lucky to had found Chance and Brad."

Kimberly nodded her head in agreement, before she could said anything, there was a voice at the door.

A voice that Kimberly didn't recognize was saying. "Polly, Kimberly?" He said Kimberly like it was new to him.

"We are ready whenever y'all are." It was a statement in a questioning voice.

Polly giggled as she went to the door. "Revered Moloney, we are ready."

There was a chuckle from the other side of the door, then there was. "We will start the music then."

"Revered Moloney?" Polly asked quickly, before he could walk away from the door.

"Yes?"

"Do they look like they are ready to run?" Polly wanted to know.

"Mm," He started in a voice that sound like he was thinking about it. "its look to me like they are more ready to come in there to get y'all."

"In that case, Revered. Start the music!"

They heard a "Right away", then they heard his foot steps leaving the stables.

In a few minutes, they heard the wedding march begin.

Polly opened the door, and she walked out with Kimberly not too far behind.

It was a beautiful day, not too hot, and not too cool for Kimberly's fluffy short sleeves, or Polly's high collar.

They walked under the bells hanging over the stables entrance, they walked pass Frankie and Jake on one side of them, and General and Draffy on the other.

The horses was tried to old fashioned hitching posts that Chance and Brad had built for them. And they did looked very beautiful with the roses hanging in theirs manes and trails, and the bows were tried just right. Their coats shinning, their heads was held up, and their eyes were bright, as they quietly took it all in.

Chance looked extremely handsome in his tuxedo, and his black cowboy hat, his tan made his dark blue eyes stand out even more. And his grin was sexy without him trying. He would make your heart slip a beat without even trying to.

But, what Kimberly love the most about him was that he was calm and sure of himself. Not conceited, just sure of himself, and he was calm until he had to be other wises.

He was a man that you couldn't took advantage of, but not one that you have to fear other wises. He was a man of honor, and pride. He was a man that knew what he wanted, and wasn't afraid to go for it. He wouldn't play games to get what he wanted. He was a straightforward, kind man.

And from the look on Polly's face as she took her place beside Brad, she felt the same way about him.

When Kimberly took her place beside Chance, and they had join hands, the Revered began the ceremony.

Revered Moloney looked to Kimberly to be in his sixties, a kind hearted, man that took things in stride.

He started with. "Ladies and Gentlemen, we are gather," Then he stopped, raised his eyebrows at Frankie, Jake, Draffy, and General, and started again with. "Dearly Beloved, we are gather here today to join these men and these women in the holly state of matrimony. This is a state, which is not to be took lightly. Do we understand this?"

Chance, Kimberly, Brad, and Polly, all nodded their heads, and said. "Yes." At the same time.

"Do you, Chance Kincaid Sway take Kimberly Blanche Racks to be yours lawful, wedded wife? To have and to hold from this day forward, in sickness and in health, for richer or poorer, until death do you part?" Revered Moloney grinned at Chance.

Chance answer him without hesitation. "I do."

"Do you, Kimberly Blanche Racks take Chance Kincaid Sway to be yours lawful, wedded husband? To have and to hold from this day forward, in sickness and in health, for richer or poorer, until death do you part?" Revered Moloney grinned at Kimberly.

Kimberly also said. "I do." Without hesitation.

After he had said the vows two more times, Kimberly would have liked to make a donation to his cause.

When Polly had said her "I do", Revered Moloney turned to face all of them, and asked. "Is there any one here that can show a reason why these men and these women shouldn't be join together. Let them speak now, or forever hold their peace."

They look at Frankie, Jake, Draffy, and General, when all they got were "it's alright with us and what do we care" looks.

The Revered Moloney shrugged his shoulders. "Then by the power vested in me, I pronounced you Husbands and Wives.

Gentlemen, you may kiss yours brides."

And they most certainly did, long, passionate kisses to start what would be finished later, after the Revered Moloney had left for home, and the couples had went their separated ways.

The cake were brought out with strawberry daiquiris to drink, the cake were cut after a feed bucket of feed where place in front of each of the horses.

The Brides and Grooms had a dance together, then the Revered had a dance with both brides, before they sat around in chairs that brought out earlier in the day.

They listen to the Revered talk about the work that he would be doing for the people. He was hoping to improved theirs and his life a great deal.

From what Kimberly had come to understand, the Revered had lost his wife not too long ago, and it really didn't sound like he was planning on coming back to the U.S.A. soon, if ever.

Chance, Kimberly, Brad, and Polly walked him to his car, before he left, he told them. "You don't know how much it meant to me to see Chance, Polly, and Brad married before I leave." It was quiet obvious how fond of them, he was. Then he turned to Kimberly. "And Mrs. Chance Sway, I just know that you will be happy for the rest your life."

Chapter Twenty-Five

REVERED MOLONEY HAD BEEN RIGHT, for the last several days Mrs. Kimberly Racks Sway had been very happy.

She had been horseback riding every day, it was a proud moment in Kimberly's life, the day that she had saddled up General, put him in the riding pen, and had went riding by herself. Chance, Brad, and Polly had been gone to business meetings, so it was the right time for Kimberly to try it.

She felt very happy that she could do it, again.

She also enjoy the long rides with Chance. For the last few days of her life, she had found out that she could live with, loved, and more importantly be loved by a man, despite her condition.

She had spent time Frankie and Jake, she had watched Chance, Brad, and Polly go scuba-diving. She had watched carefully, but not obviously how they wore theirs gear. And she refused theirs offers to join them, saying that she would just rather watched them.

This morning, they had the house gone over for bugs and more importantly cameras. She didn't know what they did with what they had found.

Nobody seem upset by what they had found, it was just one of those things that Sway and Company had been going through for years.

And it would just give them enough time to get everything in place, before Brad came back with the money.

Kimberly's paintings and sketches had brought a small fortune. Even the ones that had already been stole, and redone by another artists had brought a lot of money.

She couldn't believe it, there was enough to give Kimberly Chandlers a good life after the operation. Kimberly Chandlers had been saving all of the money that Chance had been paying her, she didn't go anywhere to spent it, she didn't need but a very few clothes.

Kimberly Chandlers was going to be a very wealthy woman, if Kimberly Racks Sway wasn't killed going off of the cliff.

Brad had to get the money in cash without the numbers on the bills being on record everywhere. He had brought it out to the house in small bills, a case full of small bills, just to show Kimberly what it looked like.

Then he and Chance had decided that it will be easy for her to handle several large bills. The series numbers on these bills wasn't wrote down, even when Chance had gotten them. It was part of the business being moved.

The several large bills were now in a plastic bag taped to Kimberly's body under the wet suit, which was under a long blue jean skirt, with a long, blue jean blouse hanging down over the waist of the skirt. She wore a conch belt around her waist, and the bandana that she had wore on her wedding day was now around her neck.

She was cover from her neck down, you couldn't tell a thing, when she got in to her pickup. Chance and Brad had it brought out a couple of days after their arrival.

It was the first time that she had drove her pickup in California, and it would be the last time that she would ever drive it. She hated that part, too. Because, it was a beautiful pickup, royal blue with silver trim, but it couldn't be help, this way it would be paid for.

She pulled her rings off, and laid them on the seat before she back out of the garage. She slowed down as she went pass the stables, she took a long, loving look over Frankie and Jake.

If everything went okay, she would see them again in two weeks, when they left for Australia, if it didn't go okay, she would never see them again. But, ever if she didn't do this, Frankie and Jake could be kill at any time for a game.

Knowing that made going on with this easier. She had to be going at just the right speed as she rounded the curve to carrying her off of the cliff safely.

When she went around the curve, there was a pickup coming up the road. Oh, my God, it was him.

He was slumped down behind the wheel, trying to hide his tall, lanky cowboy frame, he had his elbow resting door's arm rest with his hand covering part of his face, and there was a whore snuggle up against him.

But this time, Kimberly didn't start crying out on a public road. She almost slowed down to make sure that was him, but with one look she just know it was him.

She hit the speed pedal hard, the pickup shot forward, she made a turn at the steeling wheel, but the pickup went over the cliff, she didn't turned hard enough or quick enough. Of course not, she hadn't intent to.

She didn't remember taking the seat belt off, she didn't remember getting on the floor board, and trying to protected herself from being hurt. Especially from being knock out, a bump on the head or everything like that.

When the pickup hit the bottom of the ocean, she was still alive. As she got out of her clothes, she wasn't worry about him trying to save her, he wasn't that kind of man, but they would call someone else. He may have his whore there where it happen, or maybe one his whore look alike would be there, Pretending to be crying and putting on a good show for everyone. Kimberly could see now.

She was out of her clothes, and had on the head gear, when Chance and Brad found her.

They motion for her to try the window, and it went down, they pulled her, her clothes, and the air tank out. The clothes was let go, the tank was put on Kimberly's back.

She didn't know how to tell them that they had to hurry, but somehow she thought that they knew. Because, in just a few minutes, they were swimming away pulling her along with them. She remember thinking as she went off of the cliff, this will be the end of the games, he see me being killed, it have to be the end.

Chance and Brad pulled off theirs wet suits, and Kimberly wasn't sure how, but theirs jeans and theirs western shirts were nice and dry underneath.

They pulled on their boots as soon as they crawl inside the outside door going to Chance's office.

Polly didn't even look down at Kimberly crawling on the floor, when Chance opened his office's door. He and Brad went back to the desk to get theirs brief cases to give Kimberly time to crawl out of the door.

Polly wanted to know if Brad was still going by Kimberly Chandler's apartment, and if he was, she had a pile of clothes that she wanted him to took to Kimberly Chandlers to try on. Polly told him to tell Kimberly, what she didn't want or couldn't wear, they would give away before they left for Australia. She would try to make it to see her before they left.

Chance had went back in to the office to answer the message that Polly had took down while they was going over stuff, and couldn't be disturb. Brad was walking through the house with one arm around Polly, and the other arm was carrying blue jeans, blouses, a couple of dresses, and skirts. They were brand new, and would fit Kimberly, but it couldn't be said.

Kimberly was crawling far enough ahead of them, so they wouldn't have to worried about stepping on her. When Kimberly got to the door leading in to the garage, she stopped making sure that Polly had closed the door behind when she left in her pickup. Polly had.

Kimberly crawled to Brad's car, Polly had left the passenger door opened, she crawled in to the floor broad. She was very thankfully that Brad was almost as tall as Chance, it gave her enough room to sink in between in the dash and the seat.

Brad cover her with the clothes. You couldn't tell that she was there.

"Will you be able to join us the restaurant when you are finished with Kimberly?" Polly gave him a thoughtful look as he closed the door, and went to open the garage door, Polly followed him. "What are we going to called them?"

"Who?"

"The Kimberlys." Polly answer him giving it more thought.

When Brad had the door up, he gave her his full attention. "We called them a part of Australia."

Polly gave him a playful push backwards, he backed to the driver's side of the car, pretending to be afraid of her.

"Not those Kimberlys. Ours Kimberlys!" Polly gave him another playful pushed.

Brad was leading back against the car. "Well, I didn't know that." He put his arms around her.

Polly didn't object to it, but her look clearly said that she didn't believe him. "We will call them, Kimberly S and Kimberly C. What do you think?"

He pulled her closer, and grinned. "I like it, and I will be with Kimberly C a good while, so I won't plan on meeting y'all at restaurant. We have a lot of stuff to go over." He kissed her before he let her go. "And I need to get going, because I told her that I would be there tonight." He opened the car's door, started the motor, and put his brief case behind the seat.

Brad and Polly both knew that there wouldn't be a need for Kimberly S and Kimberly C, but just in case anyone was listening. They had decided not to talk about Kimberly C very much, just let Kimberly became the person that she want to.

Anything that they would had said about Kimberly C, Kimberly would to live up or down to. This way she could start with a clean slate.

As he drove along, he wanted to move the clothes off of her, and make sure that she was okay, but he didn't. And it was a good thing, too.

Because, when he rounded the curve, the road was cover with Sheriff Department cars. Now, why wasn't he surprise?

He had a urge to beat the steeling wheel, but instead his fingers tighten around it, like it was some body's throat.

There was also Highway Troopers cars, Ambulances, Fire trucks, wreckers, sub-divers, he could see boats in water, and there was a helicopter in the air.

It was all a good show, but it was too late for Kimberly, he wonder why they was doing it. And he decided it was to make themselves feel better, or hell, maybe they was just amusing themselves, again.

Brad stopped his car, rolled down the window, when a office came over to him. "What has happen, Office?" Brad was polite and calm as usually.

Kimberly was listening as the office told Brad.

"We had a call that a pickup went off of the cliff awhile ago, and we are looking for it, now."

A call? You meant he didn't had one of his whores there, crying and putting on a good show? Kimberly wonder why not, these boys always needed a good whore around them.

"What kind of pickup?" Brad had just the right amount of surprise, and urgency in his voice.

These boys had met one of their matches, and the other would here shortly.

"It was a royal blue, with silver trim, long bed, half- ton Ford pickup, Sir. Do you know the pickup?"

Brad thought it was a awful good depiction of a pickup you just saw going of off a cliff. But, he didn't said it. "Yea, I know that pickup, it is my sister in-law's pickup."

"She was married?" The office looked like he could go into shock.

Brad almost told him, that yes, she had married the man she deserves, and they couldn't treat her like that anymore, but he didn't. "Yes, she was married to Chance K. Sway. I am married to his sister, Polly. We had a double wedding just several days, ago." Brad smile as he remember it, then he looked like he was going into shock. And he really was.

How did they know so fast? He and Chance had the house, the garage, the cars, and the pickups gone over this morning.

He bound to had someone watching them.

"I don't remember seeing anything about in the paper."

The office had a questioning look on his face.

It took Brad a minute to pulled his eyes away from the flashing lights that was going on front of him. "We were going to keep quiet until we left for Australia." Brad shrugged his shoulders. "We wanted to enjoyed the peace and quiet, have time to ourselves."

The office nodded his head.

"I need to call Chance, so he can be here." Brad took another look around. "Y'all must not think there is a possibility that it was a crank call."

"Oh, no Sir, there isn't a possibility that it was a crank call." The officer sounded sure of it.

"Oh, really? Who called?" Brad wanted to know.

Chapter Twenty-Six

THE OFFICER'S FACE WENT BLANK, just for a minute, he had forgot what he was suppose to say, then it came to him. "It was lady, who called, she was crying and pretty upset about what had happen."

Brad wanted to chuckled, if she had anything to do with this, she was anything but a lady. "Did she leave her name, or she did wait here for you?"

The officer started shaking his head. "No Sir, she didn't leave her name, and she didn't wait for us. Like I said, she was pretty upset about what had happen."

Brad had a feeling at any time, they was going to hear Kimberly saying, Ah, the poor, little bitch! But, they didn't. "What did happen?"

"From what we understand, yours sister in-law was going too fast, meeting this lady, she pulled over too far off of the road and couldn't get it back to go around the curve."

Brad nodded his head sadly, as he reach for his portable phone that was thankfully laying on the seat beside him. "My brother in-law will want to talk to the one who saw his wife before she went off the cliff."

The officer left Brad to make his call, he caught Chance coming in from feeding the horses.

Chance wanted to know, what in the hell had happen, and Brad knew that the only one who could tell them was hiding in the floor board of his car with a pile of clothes over her, the Sheriff Department all around her, and she wasn't making a move, and he had no idea how she was doing it.

Brad didn't get out of his car, until Chance and Polly got there, his back was to the car, Chance stood facing the car.

Brad left after they found the pickup with nobody in it.

He drove the speed limit, even though, he wanted to drive like a bat out of hell to get Kimberly to the apartment building, where Kimberly had been living for the past few weeks.

Sway and Company own the building, there was a privacy garage with a elevator going up to the apartment. Brad pulled in to the garage, the outside garage door closed behind him, he stopped the car before he pulled in front of the elevator with the security camera in it.

He kept out of the view of the camera, until he got it turned off, then he hurry to pull to the car up, and got Kimberly out.

She had been clamped in the floor board for too long, the feeling had gone out of her legs. She was barely able to make to the elevator. The feeling in her legs started to come back, it felt like hundreds of needles barely poking her.

When they got in the apartment, Brad put a new lap top computer down on a dining room table. And he wrote.

"There is clothes in the bedroom for you to change in to, while I go change the tape in the camera. Are you okay?"

When she nodded, he went in to the living room of the apartment, he turned the T.V., the news was on.

The news reporters was getting to the cliff as he drove away. Kimberly Racks Sway's picture would be all over the news, just in case, she was able to hang on to something that could had floated to shore. But, in two weeks, she would be forgotten about, old news.

As he set the tape that they had made with this date to a few minute before they got there, he wondering if Kimberly knew about the news reporters, especially the blonde whore that used to be on. He decided that she probably did, but he find out soon enough, any ways.

He went back down, put the tape in the camera, change the clock on the camera, turned the camera back on, kept out of it view, as he went the car that he had back up, while Kimberly made it to the elevator.

He got in the car, started it, pulled it up to the elevator, got his brief case, walked around the car, got the clothes, put them over the time on his watch, and went up to the apartment.

He put the clothes on the couch in the living room, took the tape out of his brief case, put in the video recorder for Kimberly to watch the next day, they had to know if there was everything on it.

He found Kimberly in the kitchen, gulping a glass of cold water. She gave him a apologizing look, she knew that Frankie and Jake didn't even make that much noise.

But, Brad just shrugged his shoulders, make a motion that it was okay, and got a glass for himself. He promised himself, when he was finished with this, he was going to had one good stiff drink. Just one, but stiff, and maybe, he would fix Kimberly a strawberry daiquiri before he left. She was going to need it.

He motion her to the dining room table, where the computer was.

Kimberly had put a pair of blue jeans, and a comfortable blouse, she was very glad to be out of the wet suit. She took a seat in front of the computer, Brad took one next to her.

He wrote. "What happen?"

"He was there meeting me with one of his little whore snuggle up against him. I speeded up, and move off of the road, made it looked like I tried to get the pickup back on the road, and couldn't." She put it on the computer.

Brad nodded his head, and wrote. "There must had been a boat on the water, or maybe, someone watching us at the ranch, then they let him know that you were leaving. You do know he is the one that took trips, did all the things that you wanted to, and if he had really wanted to take you, he would have?"

Kimberly nodded, and wrote. "I know." She didn't why, but she had a feeling that he was about tell her something very bad, because he look like she really had been killed.

Brad took a long hard look at her, he had no idea how much she had figured out on her own. "Kimberly, you know that I would never say anything just to hurt you?"

She smile, and nodded.

He shake his head like he didn't know where to start, so he wrote. "I am going to start at the beginning, okay?"

She nodded.

"They thought that you were molested as a child."

Before he could finished writing it, she went to shaking her head. "No, that was a part of one of his games, he had two of his whore's mother, which she was probably one of his whore, too. But, any ways, it was a game to embarrass and hurt me, while I was in job training. Daddy were involved in it, that is how he abused me." She remember the hurt that it had cause her, when she had figured it out, but like she had told Chance, she wouldn't had expected anything else from her father.

Brad nodded his head, and wrote. "We know about that, we are talking about when you were a child."

Again, she went to shaking her head. "Daddy has a bad temper, he used to get rough with Mama, when he couldn't get by with that any more, he would tell her to take the girls and to get the hell of there, when he knew that she couldn't, not when she was taking care of her mama, too. He probably cheated on her, too." She didn't look up at him. "And he got a good time out of the games that the man was playing with me, talking about the whores that he was fucking at the time. Daddy enjoyed that, but as far as molested me, it just didn't happen."

Brad shake his head, and wrote. "No, not your daddy.

The rumor started after you started school, you were so friendly, smart, pretty, and yours talent started showing, that people started talking about you, and one of the rumor was that you were molested, it got back to your mama and daddy, they got scare that you had or would talked about it.

So, they started doping you to make you feel bad, so you wouldn't go to school. The school didn't want you, because they were afraid of what you might do or say. They didn't want you with their upper class kids, and you were too smart for the abused kids, so they just let you stay at home to be what they believed to abused and molested more. Charming bunch of people, wasn't they?"

She grinned and nodded. "That is why they treated me so funny? I knew that they didn't want me there."

Brad nodded. "And when you don't feel good, you can only take it for so long, and when you couldn't take any more, you started hating school, the school didn't want you with theirs upper class kids, and your parents didn't want you out and about, to talk about what happen."

She wrote. "And the upper class kids became the whores."

Brad grinned. "We thought you would like that part."

"I thought that I just felt bad when I was a kid, and mama and daddy couldn't afford the doctors and the medicine to make me feel better." She had really thought that.

He shake his head. "Remember? After it was too late to go to school, you felt better? You were a happy kid? They couldn't believe that you were happy, it was just wrong for you to be happy."

"What happen, Brad?" She didn't want to believe this, but Brad wouldn't lie, and it would explained a lot of stuff.

He looked so sad. "The rumor was that you molested by your dad's uncle."

"Why did they think that?" She wanted to know.

Brad shook his head. "We don't know, whether it a cruel joke, like the cop said, or innocent misunderstanding, we honestly don't know. But, they started doping you, because your mother was afraid that they would take you away from them." His face soften, as he wrote. "She didn't want to lose you. But by the time the cop decided it has been a cruel joke, it was too late, you hated school. They didn't want you to like cops, they thought you might you go to them for help, so," It was all that Kimberly could do to kept from laughing out laud.

"they told you that the cops was going to put your mommy and daddy in jail, because you didn't go to school. You felt like you should hide from people, cutting off a chance that you might tell someone. When they took you out, you doped to feel bad. No one would think anything about you not going to school, understand?"

She nodded, and wrote. "I am afraid so."

Brad gave a sad smile. "Then the state said that Kimberly Racks had to go to school. You bounce into the last year of Jr. High, and bounce of out a honor student.

Couldn't have that, in High School, you were doped, again."

She took over. "I wouldn't have make it out of High School without my sister help, they don't think that I deserve my diploma. The boys didn't asked me out, because I might would turned into a whore at any time."

He smile a sad smile. "They were waiting, but you didn't. You was on way to becoming a great artist, but by that time, he knew about you, about the dope, and about your grandmother, Kimberly. He set up the wreck, your friend wasn't killed, she just move away, he has a way with the whores, doesn't him?" Brad didn't wait for a answer. "Your art career was over, but then they had a chance of you becoming a whore. You started riding a group that was known to be rowdy?"

"Yea, it was a way for me to ride. They got the use of a truck and trailer, I got to ride. But, I was silly and immature, starting thinking that one of the guys like me. I talked about him, too much, for the life of me, now I don't know why. He was a set up, too, that other guy was fucking his sisters. But, my whoring behavioral started, like when I got too excited about going on a trail ride, went out of the house in a night grown that was too thin, I just wasn't thinking. I rode double with this guy one time in a parade, the saddle didn't have a back girth, it bounce against me, busied the insides of my legs. My sister saw them, and I don't want to know what horrible things got started, because it didn't happen. The guy got married, the other guy is still fucking his sisters. I stayed at home, couldn't have a riding horse, because it was a part of a game. Besides, being silly and immature, the only whoring behavioral I had, is trying to figure out why my breasts wasn't very big at all. That's why he had to tell anyone was to hurt and embarrass me, or was I suppose to run scare?

But, any ways, he wouldn't have known if they had cameras around me. I was just making sure that I was like everyone."

Chapter Twenty-Seven

BRAD SMILE. "YOU DIDN'T DO anything wrong, if he hadn't had the cameras on you, nobody would had ever knew. That is why they have to get you out, to see how you would behave.

They didn't know if you were going be a whore or if you were afraid of men. You didn't go to town much, then later, they thought that you were afraid of him. Were you ever afraid of him?"

Kimberly shake her head. "No, I was never afraid of him. To be honest, I was beginning wonder if he used the whores or whether the whores used him? He was hiding behind cameras. He was behind my mama losing those places, he wanted them for him, and his whore to have a place to have a roping arena, and for hunting and fishing. I didn't lie on the witness stand, it was a set up deal, we couldn't win, we wasn't suppose. As far as my grandmother being abused and neglected, it depend on how you want to look at it. I am pretty sure that my mother was afraid of putting my grandmother in a nursing home, I am pretty sure that my mama was afraid that her brother would get to her, and maybe killed her, that is why she was with my mother in first place. I will be honest with you, I know that my grandmother should had been put in a nursing home sooner, but I also know in my heart that my mama believed that she was doing what was right."

Brad wrote. "Like doping you?"

"What if they would have token me away, what if they put some place where I was really had been molested, it would have destroyed me."

"But, what if they did it to protect your dad's uncle and not you?" Brad knew that it sounded mean, but what if.

She shrugged her shoulders. "I didn't have to go to school."

He shake his head. "This isn't funny, Kimberly. What if the uncle told them that just to ruin you?"

"The uncle didn't ruin me, Brad, the people who would had believed it and let that ruin the rest of my life, ruin me. You know my nerves used to stand up on end when I went to town, and that was why, not because of my condition, right?"

Brad nodded. "He was behind that, the people acting like they couldn't understand you, making you feel funny about your condition, he didn't want you in town, he was afraid that you would found out about his whores, the ones that wasn't married to who that they was suppose to be, or that wasn't married at all. The people that didn't go with the right name. Then when you started going out, he had to get you down on yourself as he could, so you would fall for the man at job training center for the disable. That would mean that Red and Cricketts Rose would have be kill, your fault, of course."

"I watched the live go out of Cricketts Rose while one of his whores had a baby shower." She remember it like it was yesterday.

Brad nodded. "Yes. He has ways to dope the horses, he can make them high, hard to handled, he can make them bite, kick, ran over you, make the life go right out of them in front of you. The way he does you."

"I don't know my horses, do I?"

"No, it is just another way to hurt you. Well, any ways, he wanted you to fall for this other man, that would bring you down to his level. He wanted to show the county that he could get you to fall for him, when he did, he would start showing you all the whores that he had been with to hurt you, so you couldn't keep a job, you wouldn't be able to sale your pickup, wanted to keep you broke, or you would have turn it back in and ruin your credit, that would keep you feeling bad, then you would stay at home, then he wanted show you that he had sold one your idea to your favorite artist, that your favorite author was one of his

233

whore. He wanted to show you that he could and would ruin everything in your life. He even sold one of your sketches for a lot of money, and if that wasn't enough, they was about to let you know that everyone knew about you being molested as a child. That was his ace in the hole, and if that still didn't just destroyed you, then they would keeping doping you to keep you feeling bad."

"Aces don't count, when you are not playing with a full deck." She watched him swallow a chuckle. "But, that's why they thought that I would be kissing a negro by my mild twenties?" He nodded his head. "That is why that I always felt like I was in a prison? I thought that I was just being wimpy about my condition."

He nodded. "You was put in a prison. The government checks was another to stop you from doing any good. You don't have P.M.S., low blood pressure, allergies, sinus problems, or low self-esteem. He has drugs to make you feel any way he wants you to feel. And Kimberly, your condition can be correct very quickly and very easily. But, your paintings were about to start selling, they couldn't keep blocking them, you had to be stop. The wreck caused the condition, and the condition stopped the painting." He smile at her. "And Kimberly Chandlers will have the operation, and probably will able to paint again. Would you like to hear about Kimberly Chandlers now?" When she nodded, he wrote. "Just one more thing, if everything had happen to Kimberly Racks as a child, it wasn't your fault, you were just a child. You wouldn't have known it was wrong. Now, is there anything you want to tell me?"

She smile, and wrote. "No, I had a hot temper and a bad mouth, if there would have been anything to talk about I would have. I guess, that's why they thought that I had been molested." Brad nodded. "And I thought it was because of my great artist ability." She put her hand behind her head and did her best Mae West's impersonation.

Brad smile. "May I asked you something?" She nodded.

"Why did you want to be a boy?"

"Because, I didn't have dates all thorough High School, so I didn't think that there any hope for me after the wreck.

And if you are a boy and end up alone, it is because you never asked, but if you are a girl, and end up alone, it is because you were never was asked. Understand?" He nodded. "It wasn't because I was gay. That's when you are a girl, and you want another girl for more than a girl friend, isn't it?"

Brad shrugged his shoulders. "I don't know."

"What does Chance think about me being molested?"

"He thinks that it was a cruel joke. Now, do you want to hear about Kimberly Chandlers?" She nodded, and Brad continued. "She was born in a very small town in Nevada, her parents was killed in the auto wreck that gave her condition, she has no living family, she was sent to a institution. A while after she was sent away, the city hall was burn down to the ground. All the town's records was destroyed. The institution where she spent most of life was closed."

Kimberly gave him a, ah really, look.

Brad smile. "Yes, it was very tragic, you understand."

She gave him a, why of course, look.

"That is how she meet Chance and Polly, they was about to start running tests on her to see what they could do with her. Chance hire her, put her to work for him before they started theirs tests. She been doing personal stuff for him, stuff that Chance has been doing himself. It is either typed stuff that was put in note books, or work put on computer disks. We have all the work that she had been doing for him in boxes here. For the next two weeks, you need to thorough it all just to see what she has been doing for him. There are also books and magazines for you to read. That is how you will know about horses, and the country. I will need you to change the way you sign your name. It can't look like the way that Kimberly Racks Sway signed her name, understand?" She nodded. "If Kimberly Racks Sway wanted to take them to court we still could."

But, she shook her head. "No."

"You know how much money it would mean, you say so yourself, before you moved, remember?"

She nodded. "I said a lot of things before I lost Red and Cricketts Rose, and I would have done just about anything to get them out of there, before I lost them. But, I couldn't, and now it is too late for them."

Brad couldn't believe that they was going to get away with it. "But, they was going to literally ruin the rest of your life, if you would got a job, they would have made impossible for you to keep it. If you would have tried a business, they would had ruin it. Anything that you would have enjoyed doing, they would have ruin for you."

"They just couldn't live, and let live?"

Brad shook his head. "They would have went on with their lives, but they would have ruin yours."

"It is a good thing that Kimberly Racks Sway was killed, isn't it?"

Brad smile. "Maybe. I will be back in two days for you to sign some papers. We can tell by then how long the food supply will last, we have the photos copies made. We are getting the books together. You still want that lady books?"

She nodded. "Yes. He would have made the perfect hero for her."

Brad couldn't believe this. "Kimberly, I don't understand. I thought heroes was suppose to do what was right, and never hurt the woman that he loved."

"I said that he would have made the perfect for her books. He is a tall, good-looking cowboy, and because of his position with the county, you would think that he was made of what heroes was made of. I didn't say that he was the perfect hero, besides I think that I have been reading about him and his whores." Brad made a face. "And it is like when I see my work redone by another artist. It hurt like hell, but you go on with your life. That is all I could do without you, and Chance to help me. But, Kimberly Chandlers won't had to, she can go on to live a healthy and happy life."

Brad smile and nodded. "She wouldn't used the new phones or sign language, because she just know this operation would happen one day. That is what she has been living for, or that is what we think."

She nodded her head. "Yea, that's what she had been living for."

Brad nodded. "And she just won't go out, this operation is the only reason that she is going out now. Sway and Company had been furnishing the apartment, me, Chance, and Polly had buying her anything that she needed or wanted.

Because, she refused to go out in public. I will take the money and put in my bank account."

She wrote. "What?"

He grinned. "No, I wouldn't do that. Chance has been investing her paid for her, she would be a very wealthy woman. I will take the money funneling into difference investments, then I will funneling them out into a account for Kimberly Chandlers. Kimberly, I need to be going, my sister in-law was in wreck, and I need to be with my wife, and brother in-law, you understand?" She nodded. "But, before I go, I am going to fix me a drink, and you a strawberry daiquiri, if you want one?" She nodded. "While, I do that, you need to think of any questions you might have, okay?"

Chapter Twenty-Eight

KIMBERLY NODDED HER HEAD, AND while Brad was in the kitchen fixing him a vodka and coke, and her strawberry daiquiri, she thought about it.

"What about my tan? And what do I with my hair?"

Brad came back to the table, put her drink down for her, sat down again, and wrote. "There is a closed in patio with the apartment in Nevada, we can get by with saying that Chance took out to the ranch to ride when no one else was around. Yea, we can do that." He seem to be thinking to himself. "And I think that it would be better to color your hair. I wouldn't think that it would be a good idea to start off in Australia in a wig. We lost Kimberly Racks Sway's dental's records in her moved to California."

She grinned.

He did too, but he kept writing. "Kimberly Chandlers medical records won't look anything like Kimberly Racks Sway's. You are already started feeling better, haven't you?" When she nodded, he added. "In two weeks, you will feel like a new person, literally. What's wrong, Kimberly?"

"I think that he had been trying to tell me about me supposedly being molested, because the daughter of my dad's uncle's whore used to worked at a place where I used to go to shop a lot, I guess the daughter was one of his whore. And I had met difference people through the years that make it a point to mention that they was molested." She gave him a self conscious grin. "And I didn't know why."

He shook his head sadly. "They was going to used it against you, instead of helping you."

She smile and shook her head. "I wouldn't have expected anything else from them. I just wished that I would have left home after High School. If I couldn't have painted, and wouldn't have my condition, I would have went to the Australia outback and been a Jillabroo for awhile. I will always wonder what kind of person I would have grow to be, instead of always being so silly and immature."

"It was the dope, that is why you didn't go to work."

Brad gave her a apologetic look. "I need to be going, now.

You have ours beepers numbers, if you need us, call and we will get to you. The apartment's staff is like the ones in Nevada, they wouldn't came in without giving us notice. I will be back in two days with papers to sign. Watch the tape for us. And the place is all yours, there isn't any bugs, or hidden cameras. Push the Delete button, when you are ready.

Are you going to be okay, Kimberly?"

She nodded, as she watched him pick the money up off of the table.

He put his glass in the kitchen, put the money in his brief case, as he was walking out of the door, he wonder what it felt like for her to have her privacy back.

Before, Kimberly pushed the Delete button, she thought about the part that said; he wanted to bring you down to his level, show the county that you would fall for him, then he would show you all the women that he went with instead of you. Just to hurt you. You whole life was a game, when you found about it, from then on any joy you got out of life would be ruin.

Kimberly pushed the delete button, then she pushed the capital letter button, and typed. HERE IS TO KIMBERLY CHANDLERS, MAY HER LIFE BE HEALTHY, AND HAPPY. AND MAY HER LIFE MEAN MORE THAN A GAME.

Then she turned the computer off, and finished her drink.

Kimberly Racks Sway's purse with her driver's license, and credit cards was found in her pickup.

Chance was asked to identified three rings, a blue stone cut in to the shape of Texas with diamonds around it, a antiquated golden ring with a rose painted on it, and a simple golden wedding ring.

Yes, those was her, why did she take them off? She wanted to get them clean and polished while she shop, and stuff. Was there anything else gone? Just a lot of money that must have just floated away.

Chance was on the phone at the ranch making arrangements for his own crew of drivers, boats, and a helicopter, when Mrs. Holt came by.

She was his neighbor from up the road, they had knew each other since him and his mother had moved to California.

Chance, Mrs. Holt, and Polly was sitting at the table in the kitchen, when Brad walked in, and leaned against the kitchen counter. Polly went in to his arms, and they listen.

"Chance, I am very sorry about your wife. I heard about it on the news." She gave him a sad smile. "I saw who called in your wife's wreck."

"You did?" Chance asked.

"Yes, I was going in to town, when they turned off on your road in front of me."

"They? I thought it was a lady." Chance said.

Mrs. Holt snorted. "A lady! She was sitting so close to him, you would have thought any minute she was going to be in his lap, so they could . . ." Mrs. Holt blushed as any proper lady in her early sixties would. "well, you know. He was a tall, good-looking cowboy, but he was slumped down in the seat. That's why I thought that they had turned off of the road, so they could . . . ." She blushed, again. "well, you know."

Chance nodded.

"When I went around them, I got a good look at him, he was on T.V. just the other night."

"You mean, that he is a actor?" Chance was surprise.

He didn't know any actors, well not personally.

"No, no, not a actor, he was one of those missing persons shows, he is a law man from Texas."

Chance's face fill with silent rage, but kept it out of his voice for Mrs. Holt's sake. "A law man from Texas? Are you sure, Mrs. Holt?"

She smile a sad smile. "I am sure, Chance. A tall, good -looking, cowboy, law man from Texas, it makes quiet a impression. If you know, what I mean?"

Chance gave a sad smile, and nodded.

"I mean, we would like to think that there are people left in this world with principles and morals. But, I am not sure any more." She started shaking her head. "But, I am sure that was him, like I said it made a impression."

Chance didn't tell Mrs. Holt this, but that missing person probably wasn't really missing, or killed, or whatever it was suppose to be. It was probably just a prank of some kind for whatever propose it would served at the time.

The good-looking cowboy, law man from Texas was good at those things. But, Chance didn't tell Mrs. Holt that, or she would really be in the state of shock.

"Mrs. Holt, have you told anyone else this?" Chance wanted to know.

She shook her head. "No, I haven't told anyone else. I just wanted you to know."

"Would you do me a favor, and don't? Because, I am pretty sure that I know the man, you are talking about. He is married, and I am pretty that wasn't his wife." Chance know that he didn't have a wife. "It may be too late for my wife, but . . . You can understand, can't you, Mrs. Holt?"

She smile at the man that she had watched grow from a boy, with adoring eyes. She was so proud of the way the he had turned out. "Why, of course, I understand. And I won't say a word. I wouldn't bothering you now, but I just wanted to tell you."

"And I am so glad, Mrs. Holt. I am so glad that you did." Chance told her, and gave her a hug before Polly show her out.

Brad walked over to the table. "Just remember, he saw her go off of the cliff. Just remember that."

Chance nodded.

Chapter Twenty-Nine

"LADIES AND GENTLEMEN, WE ARE gather here today to celibate the life of my wife, Kimberly Racks Sway. Not to mourn her death." *You wouldn't have the decent to mourn her death.*

The only thing you mourning is the fact you couldn't cause it sooner.

"She wouldn't want you to mourn her death." *She wouldn't want you any where around her, not even her dead body.*

For over week, Chance had headed a in the water, on the water, on land, and in the air search for Kimberly, they didn't found anything of her, but a couple pieces of her clothes.

While, that was going on, Brad and Kimberly had made Kimberly Chandlers come to life. She had anything that she would need for a new life, even credit cards. After the operation, she could go shopping for whole a new person.

All that they had to do was get through this Memorial Services here in Kimberly Racks Sway's home town, and tomorrow, they would be on a plane going o Australia.

"All you have to do is to get through this." Brad said a silent pray for Chance.

Polly had been helping Brad with the company, anything was ready for them to leave tomorrow. Polly had felt sorry for Kimberly's father and sister, until Brad and Chance had told her that Kimberly's father and sister used do stuff to keep her upset, so she wouldn't find out that it was all just a game.

And that is all that Kimberly's life was to them, a game. For awhile, they had token the pride out of Kimberly, making her believed that if she played, she could had a happy ending, or whatever. But, Kimberly had gotten smart, and she had gotten her pride back again, before she went off of the cliff. And even if, she hadn't went off of the cliff, she wouldn't had let them took it away from her, again. Never.

But, Polly still didn't understand why he did it to her, and why they had helped him. Even the disable had a right to dream.

"I just don't understand why." Polly said it out loud.

Brad put his arm around her, and they listen to Chance.

"My wife wasn't a easy person to get to know." *Not even with all of your hidden cameras and wire taps, you still didn't know my wife.* "She would tell you that she felt bad most of the time, she was better off being alone." *And she was better off, than being with you low life, sorry, thieving people.* "She loved the country, horses and cattle." *They have more love and feelings in them, than you ever would. Or even know was possible.*

Chance believed that the man had started the rumor about he molested her, because in his mind it would had meant that he had got to her first, and ruin her, so no other man would want her. Chance believed that there was men like that, and he also knew that there wasn't a better man there, now.

Kimberly had told Brad, that she could remember her father's uncle telling her mother that they shouldn't had gave her that medicine.

They wouldn't ever know if it was done to keep Kimberly or to protect the uncle. Not that it matter, the only thing that matter now, was that they believed that she was gone.

So, Kimberly Chandlers could live a quiet life.

"My wife would tell you, that she had always been too silly and immature. But, I had been in the business world for a long time, and I have dealt with some cold calculating people." *And he knew that he was looking at most cold calculating people there ever was right now.* "I kind of like that part of my wife that she thought was silly and immature.

I think it was the part of her that made her such a great artist. And she was a great artist." *She didn't even have steal, either.* "I asked her one time, where she got the ideas for all of her paintings." *Face to face, you wouldn't understand.* "She looked at me kind of funny, and said, I made them up, she said that occasionally she would used her painting to help her deal with a problem." *He couldn't wait to see the first one after the operation.* "But, she said that she didn't do often, that most of the time that she started with something real, then built a pretty painting around it. She said that she tried to paint a picture that would make people smile, that way they would want to buy the painting. She wasn't all silly and immature, she had a pretty good head for business. She said that if she could, she would have made her living painting and brought her a cattle ranch.

If she could have." He bowed his head, then raised it back up with a sad smile on his face. "My wife believe in recreation, if you live out one life, you will get to came back and live another one. I don't know about that, but I would like to think that for a while that Kimberly would be in god's country with her horses. I know that I was a very lucky man to have gotten to know and to had spent time as I did with my wife. A very lucky man. I could talk about my wife all day, but I won't. I would like to thank you for coming today."

He couldn't believed the people that was here, but Kimberly had told Brad that with Chance's money and looks, that they would be there for him.

"I can't tell you what my wife would say if she was here." He shook his head sadly. "I just can't tell you."

I would love to tell you what she would say.

Chance stepped back for the minister to take his place, he was going to say prays for Kimberly's soul. Chance hoped that he said one for the whole crappy town.

Chance took a seat with the family, and read the head stone that would be placed in the cemetery with her mother, later. It read.

TO MY LOVING WIFE
KIMBERLY RACKS SWAY
IT WAS A MATTER OF PRIDE

Below that was her date of birth and the date that she was killed. And on one side of that was a picture of Red with his date of birth and death, and on the other was a picture of Cricketts Rose with her date of birth and death.

Chance thought that is how Kimberly would want Kimberly Racks Sway to be remember, with Cricketts Rose and Red.

Brad and Polly dealt with most of the mourners, because if one of those crying whores threw themselves in to Chance's arms, and told him, we feel yours lost. It might be more than he could take, and if he lost his temper, and said something.

It would cause them to watched him, Brad, Polly, and Kimberly Chandlers more closely, and they didn't want that.

Chance dealt with Kimberly's father, who didn't want him to take Frankie and Jake to Australia with him tomorrow.

Chance told her father that was okay if he wanted to fight the will, but the money wouldn't be released to him and her sister until they agreed to let him have Frankie and Jake.

Her father agreed to let Chance have Frankie and Jake then. Her father didn't know that Chance had increased the insurance money, and that Sway and Company was putting the bill, not the insurance company. But, he didn't know and he didn't need to know.

Chance remember Kimberly telling Brad about the that man saying right in front of her, "Wait until she find out that we wasn't afraid of her father, and wait until she find out that it was me that went all of those whores."

Yea, and Chance knew just how long and how hard that they would have to push her before she lost it, and it wouldn't be like before she lost Cricketts Rose and Red, it wouldn't be just talking the talk, it would be walking the walk. Which would have been more dangerous to them, and for her.

And as he looked over the gutless town, he knew that he, Brad, and Polly had done the right thing for Kimberly Racks Sway, because that gutless man would have kept on picking at her. Anything to hurt her.

Brad and Polly was glad to get on the plane back to California.

Chance walked through the door of the apartment, this would be the first time that he ever saw Kimberly Chandlers.

Kimberly went running to the door, she knew it would be him, because Brad said that he would be coming after they got back from the Memorial Services in Texas.

She went in to his arms, and he held her tight for awhile, then he set her away from him. He looked her up and down.

She had on a light blue, western blue blouse with a white ruffle yoke in the front and back, she had it tried at the waist, and she had on a pair of tight blue jeans that he like. She wished that she would had put on a sexy night grown, but she was afraid that Brad and Polly would have come up with him. They must have went on to the ranch, because it was just him.

And he was just looking at her hair. She was a golden blonde, now. She wasn't sure how she had gotten it just right like she did, but she did it. Her hair wasn't a *bleached* looking blonde, she didn't like that kind. Hers was a darker blonde. But, she know that she probably couldn't do it, again.

Chance just look at her. She held out her arms on both sides, then she twirl around, he still just looked at her. She put one hand behind her head, and one on her hip, then she gave her body a sexy twist as she could. That got him to grin.

But, he still didn't said anything, then she thought, he couldn't talk, either. She ran to the lap top computer that was setting on the dining room table, but before she could get it turn on. Chance swept her up in to his arms, and carried her to the bedroom, he gave her a long, hard kiss, as he set her feet on the floor. He kissed her face, and down her neck, as his hands open her blouse, then her bra.

But, Kimberly wanted to know what he thought about her hair, but as his hands cover her breasts, she decided that it maybe one of those times where he was going to show her. And it was.

They make love without saying a word.

Chance was in the kitchen, when Kimberly came out of the bedroom wearing his shirt. She had been going barefoot or in socks for the last two weeks, so when she put on the boots with the braces on them, it would be new to her. And she would walk difference.

Chance motion for her to fallow him to the dining room, where he put a plate of sausages, eggs, and biscuits on each side of the computer.

Kimberly sat down in the chair that he had pulled out for her, he kissed the top of her head, as he turned the computer on. When he was seated, he wrote.

"How are you?"

She smile with a mouth full of eggs. "I am okay. How do you like my hair?"

He grinned. "We have got our own Kimberly Racks Sway look alike, don't we?" She nodded, and he wrote. "Has the shock worn off, yet?"

"Pretty much. I mean, I believed what Brad was telling me. It just took awhile for it to sink it."

Chance could eat with one hand, and type with the other.

He wrote. "We thought that it would, that is why we waited until you could be alone for a while. I was planning on being able to be with you sooner, but you know why that I couldn't, don't you?" She nodded. "Brad said that you still didn't want to do anything about it." She shook her head. "Can you live with what they did to you?"

She smile. "I feel so much better now, Chance, and that makes a world of difference to me. I want Kimberly Chandlers to have a chance at a life that Kimberly Racks Sway would never have had. But, can you live with it? Do believe that I was molested?"

"I can live with it, if it is what you want. And I don't believed that you were molested, but you were a child, Kimberly. It wouldn't had been your fault, they should had help you."

Kimberly just shook her head. "You are forgetting who we are talking about. But, is there anything that you want to know about?"

He grinned. "What was it about a dream that you had about one of yours friend being gay?"

She had to think for a minute. "She isn't a friend of mine, she is one of his whores. And the dream was that we was at a rodeo, and she was there roping with her gay, whatever, and we were told that she had turned out to be gay, it broke up her marriage, and her father had disown her. But, it was that man that broke up her marriage, if she was ever really married. What kind of dope did they have me on?"

"You do know that is why you could had never gotten a job there, don't you? Because, people didn't go with the husbands, wives, or even the right name? Everything were made up?" She nodded. "And there was different drugs to make you feel different ways. Is there anything you want to know about yours funeral?"

She nodded. "Did you make me sound good?"

He nodded his head sadly. "Hell, Kimberly, I am even going to miss you." She grinned. "Hello, Kimberly Chandlers."

"Hello, Chance. I am sorry about your wife."

He pulled her on his lap, and wrote. "I need my shirt."

 He got his shirt, after a while.

Chapter Thirty

CHANCE HAD WENT BY THE ranch to pick up Frankie and Jake, he were unloading them, when Brad, Polly, and Kimberly Chandlers made it to the airport.

"I know it is the damndest trailer that you had ever seen. But, it got you were you was going before, and it will get to where you are going this time, too, and I will promised you that you will be well taken care of and loved, when we get there. All you have to do is get in that damndest looking trailer, one more time." Chance told them, as Brad got to them to took Frankie's lead rope.

Chance took Jake by the lead rope, and starting toward the ramp, Brad was fallowing with Frankie.

Chance and Brad were doing their best to tell them that everything was going to be okay.

But, Kimberly could tell that Frankie and Jake had serious doubts that it really was. She also knew that she couldn't just start talking to them, and tell them it was going to be okay.

What she could do was, to go around them, came to the front of them, where they could see her first. She went to Jake first, he looked at her like he was saying, what in the Hell happen to you?

Kimberly had on a western blouse, and a blue jean skirt that was short enough to show the braces that were on the boots. The braces made her limp barely noticeable when she walked, and they kept her legs from leaning in at the knees when she was standing still. And with her long blonde hair and large sunglasses covering most of her face. No one would ever think that it was Kimberly Racks Sway standing there with Frankie and Jake.

But, Jake took another look at her, and when he started smelling of her face and her hair. She started rubbing her face against his face, and petting his neck. When she left him to go to Frankie, Jake looked like he was saying, where in the hell have you been?

Frankie must have already guess that something was going on. Because, her eyes were fill with curiosity, and she starting smelling of Kimberly just the second that she was close enough. Kimberly rubbed her face against Frankie's, and petted her neck.

When Kimberly started walking away from them toward the ramp, Frankie let out a whinny, and Kimberly knew that whinny. It was Frankie's "Where in the hell have you been?". And it made Kimberly grinned.

Chance knew it was time to start leading Jake toward the ramp. He also knew that if Frankie and Jake could talk, he, Brad, and Polly would be doing some fast talking right now.

He was very grateful that they couldn't.

Kimberly walked up the ramp, and stood to the side as Chance and Brad tried Frankie and Jake in a stall.

Frankie and Jake may had been there before, but they were still excited about it.

"We are going to get the clothes, and other stuff now, Kimberly." Chance told her.

Before he could turn and leave the plane, she started unzipping the carrying case to the lap top computer. When she got it opened, she wrote. "Do you want me to help?"

"No!" Chance knew that he had said it too fast, but he didn't want her out too much. "We wouldn't want to be seen too much, now would we?"

She gave him a dirty look, and wrote. "But, this is difference, I am about to have the operation. I will do everything to get there, remember?"

He nodded his head. "I know, but we will hurry. You just stay here with Frankie and Jake, they were my wife's horses, Kimberly. You can keep them company."

"Where are the other two horses?" She wrote.

"They will shipped over there in a few days." He told her, he turned to go out the door, but then he turned back to her. "You can keep them company, but just one thing you should know," He tried not to grin. "they won't be able to read your computer."

Kimberly don't even bother to write down a reply, she just turned her nose up to him, and started looking for a bush to bush Frankie and Jake with.

Chance went out the door chuckling.

By the time Chance, Brad, Polly, and a pilot had everything on the plane, and ready to take off, Kimberly, Jake, and Frankie were back on speaking terms. Well, they own kind of speaking terms. Frankie and Jake knew who she was, and that is all that really counted to Kimberly.

Brad told Chance that it was nice of him to let Gus off of this flight, and Kimberly had to agree, it was nice of him with a grin.

When they had taken off, and after she made sure that Frankie and Jake was okay. Kimberly sat down in the chair next to Chance, when she had her lap top computer settled on her lap, she wrote. "What do I put in the files for Frankie and Jake?"

That is what Kimberly Chandlers did for Chance, or one of the things that she did for him. She keep a file on every horse and every head of cattle that Sway and Company own.

Every place had its own set of records, but Chance had his own set of records on every animals on every place. What kind of breeding they had, what they was good at, if they was breeding stock, what was they bred to, what kind of foal or calf had, what color, what kind of built that it had, and what price did it bought when it was sold.

If it was show, racing, cutting stock, or working cow horses, the breeding back ground was kept, along with what they had won, when, where, and how much that they had won, who was working with them at the time, what they was fed, what kind of health problems had they had, what kind of bridle, blanket, and saddle was used on them. You could even find out what kind of attitude, Chance thought that they had.

251

He looked at her for a minute, then he decided that she was right. He had a file on every animal that he own, if any one would happen to start nosing around, it definitely wouldn't be a good time for changes in his personal's business.

"Jake is a fourteen year old, dark chestnut stallion with a tin white blaze down his face. He is fifteen hands high, with a lean built. He is halter broke. A pretty quiet attitude. He is out of cutting blood. I acquired him from Kimberly Racks Sway. The price was a life."

Kimberly looked up when he said that, but for the first time, she wasn't even tempted to say anything. These were his records.

"Frankie is a thirteen year old, sorrel mare with a wide, white blaze down her face. She is fifteen hands high.

She has two white stockings back legs. She is slightly, heavy built. She is out of racing blood. She is broke to ride, but hadn't been very much at all. She is a little excitable, but very sweet. She has kind of a nonchalant attitude. She and Jake lost their first baby a few months ago. She is pageant again, though. I acquired her from Kimberly Racks Sway. The price was a life."

Kimberly was writing it down, and he did pretty good, too, but there was just one or two things he had forgot.

She wrote. "Health problem?"

Chance looked at her, and shook his head. "Frankie has had a colic problem, we think we know what was causing it, now, but maybe you better put it in there, any ways."

She was right about him making Frankie colic. He has dope to make them feel any way that he want them to.

"You can also put down that they were pamper and spoilt." Chance grinned.

She gave a dirty look, and wrote. "What do you means was? Aren't you going to keep it up?"

"Me? The only things that I ever spoil and pamper were you and Polly." He tried not to smile. "If you want them spoil and pamper, you will have to do yourself."

She turned her nose up to him, and wrote. "I will. What kind of feed do they get? And how much?" She tried to looked huffy, puffy about the whole thing.

Chance told her, what and how much to feed them. She put it down in their files, then she wrote. "Will this hurt theirs baby?"

He shook his head, and said. "It shouldn't."

It was a long flight to Sydney, Australia, when they landed Chance, Kimberly, Brad, and Polly was almost excited as Frankie and Jake were to go down the ramp.

Chance had a small place outside of Sydney rented, it had a house, a small stable for Frankie and Jake, and a enough room for them to moved around in.

The house was large enough from all of them, but small enough to had a charm about it. It looked like a ranch house, the ground around it was cover with trees. Kimberly wasn't sure what kind of trees they were, but they was pretty.

The whole place was pretty, it looked quiet and very peaceable.

They unloaded Frankie and Jake into a small stable, then after a few minutes, Kimberly turned them out from under their barn to where they could have room to play. And they did. They run up one side of their place and down the other.

Kimberly and Chance was standing there watching them, when Chance said. "It's the damndest part of Texas that Frankie and Jake had ever seen, wouldn't you think, Kimberly?"

She just grinned, nodded her head, and put the lap top computer in the crock of one arm, and wrote. "Yea, from what I seen of Texas on T.V., this would be the damndest part of it that I have ever seen, too."

"Well, I will just have to take you there one of these day, now that you are out and about." Chance told her.

She thought to herself, Yea, not bloody likely you will, but she just grinned. She knew that when they went back to the states, it would be to Nevada, she knew that they need to back for so many days a year to retain their citizenship.

They watched Frankie and Jake look the place over, before they went into the house. This time they would have a housekeeper, and a garden, handyman. They were husband and wife, Mr. and Mrs. Slam, they were in their late fifties. Both seems to be very good nature, happy people.

This is where Chance, Kimberly, Brad, and Polly was going to stay while Kimberly went in for tests, and then the operation. Polly didn't need the tests, she had already been though all of that. But, they had decided to have Polly wait for the operation, so that way it would be easier on Chance.

He wouldn't have to go through it, twice.

Kimberly fed Frankie and Jake that night before they ate supper, she wanted to made sure that they settled in. Frankie and Jake seems to like Australia. They had everything that Kimberly thought that they would need for awhile, after she had the operation, she and them was moving out to the ranch.

After they had ate supper, the Slam's asked if any of them would be needing anything else that night. The Slam's was assured that they would okay. Before they retired, the Slam's told Chance, how sorry that they were about his wife.

Kimberly knew that it made him feel uncomfortable, when that happen, but people would think that was because he was still missing his wife. It was only natural.

There were three bedrooms upstairs, each one had its own bath. Brad and Polly had the largest bedroom, and the other two were about the same size. Kimberly took the bedroom that the windows facing the barn.

She had taken a shower, and where about to climb into a very, comfortable looking, double bed, when she thought to turned on the computer on.

She brought up the file on Frankie, and added part of one white front stocking leg. She didn't know how she and Chance could had forgotten it.

After she had turned the computer off, she pulled off her housecoat to reveal that there she had nothing on under it. She turned out the light, and crawl in between the covers on the bed.

As her head hit the pillow, she heard her door opened and closed. She knew it was Chance, even before she turned over.

He pulled off the bottom of his pajamas before he crawl in to the bed beside her. His lips gave her a long, hard kiss, while his hands went down her body making sure she had nothing on.

He smile, when he found that she didn't. His hands went to her breasts, pushing them up, and together, then he started kissing the tips of her nipples.

Her legs started to bent, and spread apart for him. She loved what he could do for her, the feelings that he could made her feel.

Kimberly had waited along time to know what making love was about. Maybe, it was because of her disability, or maybe it was because most people thought that she was retarded, and wouldn't know how it was suppose to be between a man and a woman with a mutual attraction.

But, she did, and thank god, she had waited for a man like Chance.

Chapter Thirty-One

KIMBERLY WOKE UP THE NEXT morning on her side with her breasts pointed and almost touching Chance's lips, but he was still asleep.

He was so handsome, that she couldn't hardly believe it.

She took the tip of her breast and moved over his lips, when he woke up, he took it in to his mouth.

As he pulled her closer, they heard Mrs. Slam's voice from the door, asking. "Kimberly, do you need any help?"

Chance rolled over Kimberly on to the floor on the other side of the bed. Kimberly went off his side of the bed, pulling her housecoat on and feeling very grateful that Chance had lock the door, last night.

She made sure that Chance pulled his pajama's bottom off of the bed when he went off. He had.

She opened the door, and gave Mrs. Slam a smile.

"Good morning, Kimberly. I wasn't told and I didn't think to ask. Do you need help getting dressed or in other way?" Mrs. Slam's smile said that she wasn't sure that she should be asking.

Kimberly shook her head.

"Mr. Sway would had probably told me, if you did, wouldn't he?" Mrs. Slam looked as if she should have known he would.

Kimberly gave her a probably look, and nodded her head.

"I am sorry that I bother you, but if you need anything, you just write it down for me, okay?"

Kimberly nodded her head that she would, and waited to see that Mrs. Slam made her way downstairs, then she closed and locked the bedroom's door, again.

She turned around to find Chance at the computer, she went over to read what he had wrote. It said.

"Yea, do you need any help with your clothes?" She swallow a giggled, as Chance opened her housecoat, and lead her to the edge of the bed with him. When he sat down on the bed, she put one leg on each side of him, and he held her close. He could make her feel things that she never thought it was possible for her to feel, sexy, desirable, loved, and most of all, wanted.

Kimberly fed Frankie and Jake, who seems to be happy and settling down in Australia, okay. They probably did think that it was the damndest part of Texas that they had ever seen.

After they had have breakfast, Chance took Kimberly to the hospital, where they just talked to one doctor. It was the doctor that would be doing the operation.

She got the idea that the doctor didn't quiet know what to think about any one that would want to stay alone all of the time.

Kimberly knew that she had to convinced him that she had normal intelligences, and that she was a reasonable happy, person, she just didn't go out.

The doctor wanted to know about brain damaged after the wreck. No, she didn't have any brain damaged from the wreck, they had just pulled her out wrong. The limp and the damaged to the nerves in her hands and arms would be gone after this simple operation.

They had gave her drugs to made her looked mentally retarded, especially before she went to the beauty shop, she would had to sit and watched herself for a long time. They could and did give her drugs that would made her mouth looked deformed.

They gave her drugs to make her speech impairment sound worse, they gave her drugs to make her seems silly and crazy about every man that she met, or that is the way it would appear.

They put drugs in her food, her drinks, and even her shampoos, conditions. She couldn't used mousses, hair spays, and stuff like that. For whatever reason, he didn't want her hair to look pretty.

Brad told her, when you are older, and start showing your age, he was going to had a field day with you. He couldn't let you be happy, or feel good about yourself, you do understand? That why you used to cry for hours at a time, it wasn't allergies like you thought. They just wanted you to feel that bad.

And to think that it all started when she was a kid, she could remember her sister telling her, we thought you were going to be a whore, and there was another time when she told Kimberly, mama was right, we could have let you went everywhere. Even the man that had set her up at the job training place told her, we can't believed you got over what that man did to you.

Maybe, that is why they thought that they could treat her that way, because they believed that she was molested as a child. Was that why?

"I don't understand why."

That had to be it. Her family had thought that her life was ruin, anyway, so they just starting doping her. Whether it was to keep her or to protect the uncle, she didn't know, and would never know.

And by the time, she was old enough to start thinking about starting to work and leaving home. What did Chance say, Mrs. Holt had called him, that good-looking, cowboy, law man from Texas must had found out about it, and the doping started again, where she wouldn't feel good again, then the wreck happen. Taking away her chance to make a living for herself, then let's keep making her feel bad, so she wouldn't be able to have even a part time job. Let's take away her privacy, lets hoped that she is smart enough that her nerves pick up on it, making her do things that she probably would had never done, this would take away her pride. Let's take away any chance that she might have for a healthy rational ship with a man. We won't ever have to worry about giving her anything for we take away.

Yea, her life is ruin anyway, we will make a game out of it to amused ourselves, and what not? Who is going to stop us?

"Miss Chandlers?" The doctor said it, again. "I don't understand why."

Kimberly had to grinned at him. Kimberly Racks Sway could tell him that was the only way she could live now, alone most of the time.

But, Kimberly Chandlers couldn't tell him anything like that. She thought about for a minute.

Then she wrote. "It was probably just a easy way out.

When I was young, I stay by myself a lot, I did my school work, no one paid me must attention. When that place closed, and Chance was good enough to give me a job. They left it up to me, whether I went out or not. And I was happy alone. I like to read, watch T.V., listening to music, and doing the work that I do for Chance. I like keeping the records on all of animals on the different places. I am a loner, but I always knew that this operation would happen. I just knew that one day I would be able to live on a ranch, ride a horse, and be able body again. I will, won't I?"

"As far as I can tell, there isn't a reason that you couldn't have this operation. Yours medicals tests had said that this will work for you. All, but for the fact, you haven't been wearing yours braces like you should had." He raised his eyebrows in a disapproving way. "But, I guess, being alone must of the time, it was easy not to make the effort?"

She nodded her head, and wrote. "Yelp, besides, I can do a mean fast dance even without them."

The doctor chuckled, and Chance just shook his head.

"Is that how you got your exercise?" The doctor asked.

Kimberly nodded, and wrote. "One of the ways, I also had a exercise bike, a small stairs master, and sometimes, Chance would take out to his ranch to go riding."

"You didn't want to live on the ranch?" The doctor asked, then it look like he had a awful thought. "Or maybe, it wasn't a choice for you to make?"

Chance started to say something, but she wrote. "Yea, but there was other people on the ranch, but in my apartment it was just me."

Chance shrugged his shoulders.

The doctor grinned like he had a idea of what he had been going thorough. "But, you had been making a living for yourself?"

She wrote. "Yes." But, she thought, yea, you ought to see the living that I had been making for that whore chasing bastard. He had sat there and told them, you just wait until she find out that I am the one that made all of her money. He meant that he was the one who had stole her ideas from the paintings, and he was the one that had the connections to sale them.

259

Her sister had even told her that they had already stole all of her ideas. And Kimberly had very foolish wrote down ideas for future paintings, and those ideas were stolen now, too.

She smile to herself, only theirs paintings wasn't quiet just like what she had in her mind, but still close enough for her to know her idea. At first, she thought it was the people that she was trying to sell her paintings to, but after she found out what was going on. She knew that it was him having them redone, then selling them.

While, she was living on disability payments, mediciad, and even food stamps, that bastard was having a ball on her money. Chasing all of the whores, taking them on trips, and or meeting whores at the places he was going.

She just wonder how many whores had moved to Texas fallowing that tall, good-looking, cowboy, law man, or how many had moved to the places that he visited a lot.

"Miss Chandlers, you hadn't been foolish with your money, had you?" The doctor wanted to know.

She shook her head. "Chance has been investing it for me. He had made me a lot of money." She wrote with a grin.

"Let me guess, you are going shopping after the operation?" The doctor asked.

She nodded her head enthusiastically, and wrote. "Look out Sydney!"

Chance rolled his eyes, and said. "I second that, you better look out Sydney!"

The doctor laughed. "There is just one thing that I would very much like for you to do for me. Could you say something for me?" She started shaking her head, he added.

"Anything? You can even tell me to go to hell, if you want to?"

She grinned, and wrote. "Do I need to?"

"No, but I think that is what you having telling the world most of your life, isn't it?"

She just shook her head, but she thought, no Doctor, you have it all wrong, that is where they put me most of my life, and that is where they had meant to keep me.

Kimberly couldn't and didn't say a word for the doctor.

There could never be a tape of what Kimberly Chandlers's voice sounded like before the operation. The doctor didn't know that, but Chance and Kimberly did.

The doctor had agree to do the operation on Kimberly, in spite of being a little worried about the way that she had choose to live her life. He said that she seems to be healthy and happy mental wise with normal intelligences.

The operation will be perform on her the first in the morning of the day after tomorrow. She and Polly would check in to the hospital late tomorrow's afternoon.

They thought if her and Polly had it on the same day, it would make it earlier on Chance and Brad, but Kimberly didn't think everything was going to make it easy for Chance and Brad.

While, the operation itself was simple, the time it took that could cause problems. But, to Kimberly and Polly it was well worth it.

Especially, after Kimberly had watch all of the cute and pretty nurses tell Chance, how sorry that they was about his wife, and if there was everything that they could do, just let they know, they would be glad to do it. Kimberly was thinking, I just bet that you would.

But, that wasn't why she was doing it. She was doing it for herself. Even if after she watched the other women walk, and seeing the way that they could fix their hair, left Kimberly feeling old and disable. That still wasn't why she was doing it.

Besides, Chance didn't paid them any attention. And she appreciated that.

When they got back to the house, Kimberly went to spend time with Frankie and Jake.

That night when Chance came into Kimberly's room, there was enough light shinning thorough the window for him to find the lap top computer.

He took it over to the bed to where Kimberly were. She sat up with her back against the headboard, and the cover pull up over her breasts.

Chance sat down beside her, and wrote. "You know, you don't have to do this, you are just right the way that you are. You do know that, don't you?"

She wrote. "I want to do this."

She knew that there wasn't any way Chance could understand what this would mean to her.

Chapter Thirty-Two

THE OPERATIONS WENT WELL, FIRST Kimberly's then Polly's.

Chance had spent the nights in Kimberly's room at hospital.

They said that Kimberly hadn't been out before, she would feel so much better if he was there with her.

Actually, they was afraid that Kimberly would be woke up during the night, forget and say something. But she didn't, not even during the operation, she didn't forget.

Chance was there with in the operation room with her, she didn't asked how he had pull that one off. He just had and she knew why.

After the operation, it wouldn't matter, because she would be sleeping at home before she could talk.

Kimberly and Polly had been home for a couple of days, when one day they was all sitting around the dining room table eating dinner, when Chance just started looking at Kimberly. He was just looking at her and he started to smiling.

When everyone noticed it, too. Kimberly had enough, she wrote. "What?"

"I was just thinking that after all of these years of not talking, what it is going to be like you do start talking." Chance rolled his eyes.

Brad took a deep breath, and said. "You know, you are right, I never thought of it before. But, she will go non stop for days, don't you think?" He was trying not to smile.

"That's what I was thinking, or it could be weeks before she wear down." Chance chuckled, his eyes had a teasing sparkler in them.

Mrs. and Mr. Slam ate with them, and they was chuckling, too. "Maybe, you shouldn't teased her too much, Mr. Sway."

They advised him.

Chance shook his head. "You just don't know, she has always been bad enough with a keyboard or a pen, but God help us when she gets a mouth."

"Had she been able to let you what know was what?" Mr.

Slam asked with a grin.

"And where I could put it." Chance nodded his head.

"Maybe, she should had been a writer." Mrs. Slam was thinking about all of the time that she like to spend alone.

Kimberly shook head, and wrote. "Can't spell."

"Yes, that's right, Mrs. Slam, she spent most of the time working for me with a dictionary in her hands." He tried not grin.

"Don't the computers had spelling checkers on them these days?"

Chance and Brad said it as Kimberly wrote it. "But, you have got to get close."

"She means that you have to get close to the right spelling for it to be able to correct it." Chance grinned.

Brad gave them the most serious face, that he could when he leaned toward Chance and asked. "What are we going to do with her?"

He looked like he was giving it some thought, before he said. "The only thing that we can do with her. Take her to the outback, and leave her with the kangaroos, koalas, and dingoes, and just let her talk it out with them. Take her food and water every few days, until she wear down." He shrugged his shoulders. "That is about all we can do with her."

While everyone else was trying not to laugh, Brad said very seriously. "And we wouldn't have to worry about the aboriginals."

Chance shook his head. "They wouldn't know what in the hell to do with her."

"You are just too cute, you know that?" Kimberly wrote.

He narrowed his eyes at her, and asked. "Who is trying to be cute? What did you think that I was going to do with you?"

"I thought now that I am out and about, that I would go with you for awhile, I have a lot of questions." This time it was her that had the teasing sparkles in her eyes.

Chance shook his head. "I was afraid of that."

When the doctor gave the okay for Kimberly to start talking, she told him. "Go to hell." In such of a clear voice that it even threw him.

She was told that she could do her own therapy, and was told what to do, and for how long to it. And she would need to came in every few weeks for they to see how she was doing.

They was getting ready to move out to the station, and Kimberly knew that it was time to go shopping. The boots that Chance had bought for her was okay to wear back and forth to and from the hospital, and even to spend time with Frankie and Jake.

Not she could do very much with Frankie and Jake, because the doctor didn't want her to be bump around too much. But, the few days that he said to wait was over.

And Kimberly Chandlers was ready to live, after she did some serious shopping, of course. She was going for boots, more jeans, blouses, the basic bras, panties, socks, and maybe even a dress or two, or maybe more.

When Chance told her right before she left, to buy plenty of dresses, and skirts, because they would be dressing for supper. It didn't matter if it was just going to be him and her.

Brad and Polly had decided to buy the house that they were living in, and stay in Sydney. Brad was going to rent a office for Sway and Company, and maybe start a small law practice of his own, and Polly was going to open a clothing shop in Sydney.

Kimberly was about to asked him, if he thought that was really necessary, when Mrs. Slam said, that was a good idea, because it would be so easy to forget your social skills living on a outback station. Kimberly almost told her, that she didn't have any social skills to forget, but she didn't.

She had the idea that Mrs. Slam still believe in a time when a lady should look like and act like a lady. So, Kimberly promised them that she would, and off she went.

She had found a couple of pairs of dress boots, they both were knee high, one was a lighter color for the spring and summer, and the other one was a darker color for the fall and winter.

The jeans was brought, and she had on a new pushed up bra under a beautiful, white sundress, with a fitted top, and a full skirt. It was a very romantic dress to Kimberly. Of course, she was too old for all of the romantic stuff.

Those years in her life that she could had romance, or just the dreams of romance was gone. Taking away from her with dope, because they thought that she had been molested as a child. A innocent child.

He had one of well endow whore, actually tell her and her sister, we know that she had been molested. She had said in a game way, and after Kimberly had caught on to the game, she understand what that well endow whore was saying. And now Kimberly would have to tell her, you don't know anything of the kind, in less, you were one that did it, or if you were there. And if you were either one, I would keep my little, whoring mouth shut, if I were you.

But, ever since Brad had told her what they had believed. Kimberly had went back thorough her life to try and figured out what had went wrong.

She remember one of her father's friend telling her that her, that her father had poison them against her, another time he asked her father, how would you like to had been the one who had walked in her being molesting.

She also remember, that uncle telling her mother about a little girl running out and telling him that she was naked.

He was rubbing in her mother's face what he had said that had done to her little girl.

It was before she had started school, she was maybe four, of five year old, when one morning her dad's two uncles came by before her mother and sisters had gotten theirs clothes on, they had sent her out in her pajamas to talked to the uncles. Her pajamas had a tear in them, so she run past him, and got into a bed that was kept in the dining room and cover herself up with the covers.

The uncle told her that he wanted to see, and was about to pull the covers off, when the other uncle walked in. Was he about molested her? Did he tell them that he had molested her to ruin her, because he did ruin her. Did her mother and sisters feel guilt over sending her out? Or was them like the men thought that she had brought it on herself.

She was too happy and too loving of a child. She remember a time when she was in teens, she had been out sun bathing in a halter top, that was too big for her. God, she shouldn't had been wearing it, but nobody was going to see her, until her mother and sister wanted to go to the land fill in a small town. Kimberly wanted to change, but they wouldn't give her time. Is that why they did it? Was that why they did it, they was saying see what a whore she is.

In her last year of high school, one of the whores, who mama had said that her father was molesting her, came up with a picture of Kimberly at the whore's birthday party in her cowboy outfit.

Kimberly was a tom boy, thorough and thorough, Chance said it was to start the gay up.

Kimberly smile at the pretty, white sundress, she had grown up to like pretty dresses, they had grown up to be whores like theirs mama.

She had to chuckled, she hoped that they wasn't afraid that she was interested in any man that they was, because any man that would be interest in them, just wasn't Kimberly's kind of man. Any man that couldn't see what they were wasn't too bright in Kimberly's was of thinking.

Besides, that party was when they were just kids, she couldn't remember how old they were, though. She guess, that they didn't know that she about to became a disable, and they didn't have to start such a ugly rumor about her. Or they probably did know about the upcoming wreck, and wanted to get another rumor started about her.

She often wonder why people were so mean, she had thought that people said bad things like that about other people to make themselves looked better.

She knew that there were a lot that she wished she hadn't said. She could only hope that she was like that because she felt so bad, and she just didn't understand what was going on.

She liked the way the skirt of the dress swirl around of her legs. Her legs didn't bend together at the knees, any more, she couldn't believed that she was able to wear a pair of high heels, sanders with the dress. She didn't had a balance problem like she had always thought, they had a dope that cause it.

Talk about your mean people, he had baby calves that theirs front legs would go together like her did, they had a cow that her mouth pulled to one side like Kimberly's did at times. She could guess that he wanted her to see what she looked like, she could have told him that she had always knew what she had looked like, and that she would never forget what he looked like, either.

She liked the way that the top of the dress fitted her, it was low in the back, but not too low in the front. She had a problem with wearing stuff that was too low in the front.

It started, because her back would stink, her sister said that she smell like a little man. The odor was cause by dope, but she didn't know that, and she started trying to wear stuff that was low in the back. But, that usually meant that it was low in the front, too.

And Kimberly didn't had too much in that department, she had thought about breasts implants, but had decided against it. She had just found out about pushed up bras, they still didn't made her, well endow, but they made the most of what she had. And that's all she really ever wanted to do.

She liked the way that the bras made her look, but they had to take away that feeling away from her, too. God only what they would had done, if she would had the implants.

But, Chance had give the good feeling back to her about the way that she look. She whirl around in front of the mirror, one more time, when she notice that there were a lot more people now, then when she had come in the first thing this morning.

Younger women, that was still in theirs romantic years.

That made of think of Chance, she wonder if as he got older, he would want a younger woman.

She thought that men usually do that, because as most women grew older, they came to stand on their own. While, younger women would dote on and hero worshipped a older man.

Kimberly hated to admitted it, but she would dote on Chance for a long time, if he treated her right, and that probably wasn't a good thing.

She had gotten enough dresses, and even a couple of pairs of shoes, but a few pairs of thigh hi's and that was it. She had to spend her money on Kimberly Chandlers's future.

Chapter Thirty-Three

"**Y**OU DID WHAT?" CHANCE ASKED Kimberly, while they sat at the super table one night after they had been out at the station a few weeks.

Everything had settle down to a quiet routine, most days. Kimberly spend most mornings doing book work, and computer work for Chance, and the station. And the afternoon, she spend with Frankie and Jake.

When she had been able to break Jake, it was a awesome feeling, one that she had thought she could never had, again.

She had put a lot of riding with Chance, before she started breaking Jake. She had went with him, when he had going thorough his herd of cattle, deciding which ones that he wanted to keep, and which ones would go to the sale with the calves that had reach market size.

The branding and the vaccinations of the younger calves was done at this time, too. She had help penned and worked the cattle, when she thought that Jake was ready, she had rode him out with them. She had enjoyed every minute.

As matter of fact, Kimberly could live the rest of her life like this, especially with Chance coming into her bedroom at night, making love to her, or just holding her in his arms. While, they slept. It was too soon after Chance's wife had been killed for him to marry again.

And Kimberly had learn the hard way that it was better to look out for yourself. Not to be too happy or to count on what you thought other people could do for you. Not even Kimberly Chandlers could do that.

"I bought the Silver Blue Sky Station." Kimberly told him, again, but the shock look was still on his face.

"But, I have been trying to buy that place, ever since I bought this one, and they wouldn't sell it to me."

"I don't think that they like you too much. You are a rich, American, city boy." Kimberly tried not to laugh at the way, the older couple had talked about him. The older couple had live on their station all of their married life, but now, they had felt like it was their time to spend with relatives in the city, and visited other parts of Australia.

And they just to afraid that Chance was just too modern, and too American to appreciated the quiet charm of their modest station.

He narrowed his eyes at her. "Well, did you tell them that you have been living in a apartment in the middle of a big, American city?" He smile at her.

She smile, and nodded her head. "I tell them that. They said, that if I like being alone, I could really appreciated the station."

"Have you sign a agreement yet?"

"Just a hand written one, between me and them. I wanted to talked to you before I talked to Brad."

"That was nice of you." He wasn't happy about this at all. "Just what in the hell, are you going to do with it?

Quit me, and start your own station?"

Kimberly watched him take a deep breath to hold his temper. "No, actually I would rent you the land for Frankie and Jake, a place to keep them here, plus a few mares to go with Jake." She watched the anger go out of him.

"Frankie and Jake were my wife's horses, I can't part with them, Kimberly, and you know it."

"Even if I put in writing that I won't ever sale to any one, but you?" Kimberly wouldn't believe that he wouldn't do this for her.

Chance look like he was debating it in head, when Sparkler, the housekeeper was just about finished cleaning off the table.

"Your wife is gone, Mr. Sway. She won't be needing those horses any more, and Miss Kimberly is the one, who loved and care for them now. She is the one that should have the horses, and you know it."

Kimberly wanted to pat Sparkler on the back for that.

Sparkler had been helping run the house, making sure the meals were cook and on the table, and helping to keep the house clean and in order. Sparker was in charge of the help that she would need.

"Isn't any one afraid of being fire, anymore?"

Chance asked, as if he was really afraid of losing the upper hand.

"Oh, Mr. Sway, you know that the only reason that we would be afraid of you, is if we were to do you wrong. And we know you aren't going to give us any reason to want to do you wrong." Sparkler shook her head at him, like she wasn't sure what to do with him.

Chance smile, in spite, of himself. "I will agree to it, if you will tell me two things, why did you do it, and how did you do it?" Chance told Kimberly.

But, before Kimberly could say anything, Sparkler said.

"I can tell you why she did it." Chance raised his eyebrows, and she said. "Miss Kimberly isn't getting any younger, and what if you took leave of yours senses, and married a snooty, little, young thing, or worse yet, you started bring them in here, one after the other. Me and Miss Kimberly would need a place to go. She needs to be sure that she had a future."

Chance looked absolutely amazed.

"Sparkler is right." Kimberly told him. "But, I couldn't pay you as much as Chance does, though." She told Sparkler with a apologetic smile.

"Oh, that's okay, Miss Kimberly, you wouldn't need me to do as much work as Mr. Sway does, either. We could work it out."

Chance looked from one to the other, but didn't say any thing.

Sparkler pick up her tray of dirty dishes off of the table, but before she turned to take them to the kitchen, she said. "But, I should would like to know how you did it, too."

"Why don't you bring yourself out a cup of coffee and piece of that chocolate pie, and have it with us, Sparkler?" He invited the fifty-something house keeper to join them. He smile at her. "We will bring it out of her with a piece of yours chocolate pie."

"I think that I will, Mr. Sway. But, you know, Miss Kimberly, it may take two pieces to get it out of her. She does like sweets, you know, Mr. Sway?"

"Oh, don't I know it." He and Kimberly just kind of look at each other, while Sparkler brought out the pie, a pot of coffee, and a cup of hot chocolate for Kimberly.

The pie were so good that would melt in your mouth.

Kimberly wished that she could cook better, but either she just didn't have the talent, or the patience that it would take to learn.

Maybe, Kimberly just like to spend time on her painting, and horses. But, as much as she like sweets, she should really learn how to cook better. She thought to herself.

Kimberly told Sparkler and Chance, that she was out practicing her driving today, when she saw a sign that said, The Silver Blue Sky Station, and it was such a pretty sounding name, she went by to see it.

"I told the couple, who I was, what I was doing, and why I came by. It seems to please them a great deal, they show me around, and we had a cola and cookies, and got talking, one thing lead another. And I brought the place, Chance, you know it is a pretty place."

He nodded his head, as he took a slip of his coffee. "I know it is a pretty place, Kimberly, but are you sure that is what you want to do with yours savings?"

She grinned. "Yelp, I was going to start looking for a place in a week, or two. but I never thought that I could have the place next to yours."

"Are you sure that you didn't take out so many fences, that it was just cheaper for them to sell it to you?"

Sparkler started chuckling, and Kimberly just rolled her eyes at him.

Sparkler took her leave, saying that she needed to be getting home to her husband. Kimberly didn't have any idea where she live. She just show up to cook their breakfast, and left after supper in the evening. She had asked her, and all Sparkler would say was that she live on the station. But, Kimberly knew that she didn't live in the living quarters where most of the hire hands and theirs family live. She guess that Sparkler and her family wanted more privacy, and she should respect it.

Kimberly told Chance about the deal that she had made on the place, and he told her, that she had made a pretty good deal. She had been listen to him and Brad talked about what land was selling for, and about what that place should be would worth.

271

She hadn't used all of the money that her paintings had brought, with what she had left, and with her paid that Chance would be paying her, she should be able to save some, after she had bought a truck of some kind. She didn't need a fancy one, just a good reliable one.

Kimberly Chandlers had never learn to drive, so Chance had took her out in one of his ranch trucks, and turn her a loose in the middle of a cattle pasture.

It was the first time driving for Kimberly Chandlers to drive, and the first time, in a very long time, that Kimberly Racks could drive a standard. After her wreck, they had put a restriction that she could drive only trucks with automatic transmissions.

But, now she could drive anything that she wanted, and it was a great feeling.

When they thought that she was ready, they had gotten what she need to drive in Australia, and they had found a good deal on a reliable truck. They also told her, that they would say a pray for all of the Australians, as well, as themselves. Kimberly assured them, that she wasn't amused.

Kimberly wasn't planning on doing a lot of driving, she just wanted to be sure that she could, if she had to.

Chance had his pilot's license, and when they needed to go to Sydney, he could fly them in a few hours, where driving it would take a few days. He had bought two small planes, he had told her, what kind they were. But, she didn't know enough about planes to understand. He told her, that she would learn more about planes, when he taught her how to fly.

And Kimberly wasn't sure that he was teasing, either.

Oh, well, she thought to herself, she would deal it when and if it happen. The place had bought and paid for, Chance had bought the cattle that with the place. They had went thorough like they had the other herds, and kept what he wanted, and sold what he didn't. He had put a foreman on the place.

The Silver Blue Shy Station wasn't as big as Chance's, but it was well tended to, and had made a profit. There wouldn't be any major changes done to the station without her approval, and she didn't see a need for any changes.

They was picking out fillies and mares for Jake to bred next spring. Kimberly was planning on training his foals, and seeing if she could make a living doing it. His foals wouldn't be high price register stock, just good common horses, the kind that Kimberly knew the most about.

Like Sparkler said, just in case, Chance took leave of his senses, she had a good start on a future alone.

Right now, Kimberly was sitting in the middle of a cattle pasture, painting. She had started taking Jake and Frankie out in the afternoon, she would ride one of them out one day, and the other out the next day. She would paint for two or three hours a day, then she would bushed them off, and tell them, how gorgeous they were. Before, she cleaned up for supper.

Chapter Thirty-Four

KIMBERLY PAINTING, AGAIN. NOW THAT was something. She had a favorite place on the station. It was a clear water pond that was fed by a underground stream, and it was surrounded by trees and brushes of all kind. It was a beautiful place.

And Kimberly didn't know why, but there was a feeling about the place. She was sure that there were something special about this place, like it was in another world.

They had told her, that the outback was a wonderful place, and she had to agree with them. Because, she was painting, again.

The painting that she was doing now, wouldn't be quiet as big as her favorite, that he had stolen form her, and this one didn't had the same feel to it. It seems to had a lot more sadness to it. It was almost done, but there seems to be something missing in it, she wasn't sure what, though.

While, she waited for the paint to dry, she took a swim in the pond. She worn a two pieces bathing suit under her blouse and jeans.

She loved the cool, clear water of the pond. She wasn't sure how much longer she could keep doing this, it was the beginning of fall. And Kimberly didn't know much longer the warm weather would last, so she knew that she had better enjoyed it while she could.

She looked up, when Jake whinny to see Chance riding up on Frankie. She grinned, as she watched him dismount, and tried her up beside Jake. As usually, Jake and Frankie was happy to see each other.

"What are you doing here?" She asked him, as she watched him untried a blanket from behind his saddle.

"I wanted to come see where you go, and what you were doing out here." He looked from the painting that was turned away from him to watch her come out of the water toward him.

"You are painting . . ." He almost said again, but stopped.

She pick up a towel that she had brought with her, and started drying herself off, as she sat down beside him on the blanket, while he was lying on one side popped up on his elbow.

He took the towel away from her, and started drying her off. He told her quietly. "You know, this is the first time that I had seen naked you in day light."

She was about to tell him that she wasn't naked, when she felt him taking her top off. As she felt his lips on her breast, she told him. "Chance, I thought about having breasts implants when I was younger, would you like it?"

She remember, one of his whore saying at the beauty shop, one time, that they were right, she don't have any breasts. It was said in a game way, like everything was said.

Chance grinned at her. "No, everything is just right."

His lips went to her other breast, while his hands took off the bottom of her swim suit. When he started pulling off his clothes, he said. "Oh, I forgot, will you marry me?" He pulled out a blue stone ring cut in the shape of Australia surrounded by a row of diamonds on a band made of silver.

He put the ring on her finger, before she answer him, when she raised her eyebrows, he said. "Well, you got to marry to me, because if you don't, I might take leave of my senses." He grinned at her. "And we wouldn't want that."

He had his clothes off, and took her in his arms, again.

"Chance, will my painting bother you? You won't worry about what is in them, or who might look like someone in my painting, or if they do what my painting is about, will you?"

"Painting is what you do. I won't worry about anything but you being happy."

Her arms went around him, and she held him tight, then she thought. "I thought that you want to wait longer, before you got married, again? So, it wouldn't looked too bad to the people in Australia?

He stopped kissing her face, to tell her. "I decided that they could go to hell, Kimberly. You will marry me?"

She nodded her head. "Of course, I will marry you. And Chance, painting isn't the only thing that I do." She grinned, as she laid back on the blanket.

He grinned, and said. "Don't I know it."

His hands and lips cover every part of Kimberly's body, by the time that they put their clothes back on, her painting was more than dry enough.

Chance wanted to know if he would see it, but she like to wait until the painting was finished, before anyone would look at it. He understood, and promised to wait.

They was riding Jake back to the house and leading Frankie. Kimberly was sitting in front of Chance, leaning up against him.

When a older man appear out of the bush along the path that they was fallowing. Kimberly's heart sunk, the man, who had set up her at job training place had told her, that she would start seeing things that wasn't there. It was said in a game way.

She had, too. It was part of his plan, to keep her alone, and from driving. They wanted her to said something about it, to make her look mental ill.

But, this man seems to be real, he started cracking the whip that he was carrying, speaking to Chance in a friendly tone.

"Kimberly, this Owl, he is one of the best bushmen in All of Australia." Chance told her, as he petted Jake to calm him.

"Hello, it is very nice to meet you." Kimberly smile. "One of the best, that's quiet honor."

"Your husband lie to you, Mam. I am not one of the best, I am the best." He brow his head.

"Yea, he does get things mess up some times, but he isn't my husband, yet. We just got engage." She show him the ring.

Chance smile at her. "Owl, this Kimberly Chandlers, I. thought you knew my wife was kill right before we got to move down here." Chance had a questioning look on his face.

"We know you wouldn't do that either one of the Kimberlys like that, and we found out what and who was after her. We know why you paint out here, where no one can see you." Owl said with raise eyebrows. "We really didn't know that America had became that bad. And I know some of ours took part in it. But, we want you to know, they are not ours, no more, those Americans are yours."

Kimberly look at Chance, but neither one know what to do. Here, was a man, who knew their pain and heart break, and they couldn't say anything, but as if by some salient agreement, they didn't have to lie either.

"And to know that there is a operation that could gave your life back to you, all you have to do is take a chance on dying."

Owl shook his head, like he didn't even think about people that bad, much less how to deal with them.

Kimberly said a salient pray to God, that he never have to try to deal with them.

"But, I guess there is some lives that is worth fighting for, especially when you got right on your side and the law went bad on you." He kind of laughed, like he didn't know what else to do. "Well, anyways, we would like you two to join us for a outdoors meal, dance, and I will marry you when the full moon is raising." Owl grinned and said. "If you like."

Kimberly starting grinning.

"You're just trying to rush me in to it." Chance started grinning.

Owl starting shaking his head. "Oh, no, Mr. Sway, it is up to you. It is a tradition with us, suppose to bring good luck."

"In that case, count us in." Chance grinned, he bent his head to kiss her lips, when they looked back around Owl was gone.

"You do know where we are suppose to go tonight, don't you?" Kimberly asked him, as he started Jake moving again.

He shook his head. "No, idea, but I think that I know who will."

They put Frankie and Jake up, and went to tell Sparkler that they wouldn't be there for supper. They found her in the kitchen putting together a picnic basket together.

She looked at them, and said. "Oh, good, you are here.

I have Miss Kimberly, a bath ready, and we need to pick out, what she will wear." She told them, as she started to lead the way upstairs to Kimberly's room. "What do you think, Mr.

Sway, the white, fancy sundress, that you like so well? And the knee high boots, you do like them, don't you?"

His eyes sparkled with laughter, as he open the door to Kimberly's room, walked in to her closet, pick out the dress, lay on the bed, and the boots besides the bed. "Yea, wear this." He told her.

She was leaning against the door, with her arms across her front, she grinned. "You forgot bra, panty, a slip, and thigh-hi's." Before she knew he was at her dresser, going thorough the draws. He had good taste, too, anything he pick out was trimmed with lace.

Before, he went out the door, he pulled her close, and gave her a long kiss. "I will be downstairs when you ready."

She washed and rolled her hair first, then she took a warm strawberry bubble bath, then dressed, took her hair down, and was downstairs, as fast, as she could.

Chance and Sparkler was waiting by the front door. He had shower and was wearing a white, western shirt, a pair of blue jeans, a pair of black, dressed western boots, and a black felt western hat. "I thought that I was going to have to come get you." He meet her at the bottom of the stairs, to put his hands on her waist, and lift her to the floor. "But, Sparkler said that she would if you wasn't ready in time."

"That's right, Miss Kimberly. Because, if he would went up there, we would never had made it on time." Sparkler shook her head like she didn't know what she was going to him. "My people have made this for you, Miss Kimberly." She unfolded a beautiful white wrap with hand embroidery horses running wild, and around the edge, it cover with roses.

"It is very beautiful, Sparkler. Like your dress."

Kimberly couldn't do anything, but admired the details that went into every horse, and every rose that was on her wrap.

And Sparkler's dress was cover with hand embroidery animals, birds, and flowers that native to Australia. The colors were bright and beautifully correlated.

Sparkler's face beam with pride. "Why thank you, Miss Kimberly, it was my wedding dress made by my family."

"Sparkler has agree to tell us the story of her family on our way out to where we are going." Chance told her, as he put the wrap around her.

When Kimberly stepped out of the front door, there was a carriage with a top on it and two beautiful white horses to pull it. The horses had roses and ribbons in their manes and trails, and the carriage was trimmed with roses and ribbons.

"It is beautiful." Kimberly loved it.

"Yea, I thought that you would like it, and beside that it will get us to where we are going." He made it sound like it nothing as he lifted Kimberly in to the carriage and then give Sparkler a hand up.

Kimberly and Sparker gave each other knowing looks.

"Where to Sparkler?" Chance asked with a grin, as he climbed in the carriage on the other side of Kimberly.

"Just go a mile or two pass the pond, and we will be there." When the carriage started moving, she asked. "Would you like to hear the story of my family?"

"Very much." They both told her.

"Well, we can named the babies for their personalities the minute that they are born."

Kimberly grinned.

"But, there are people, who believed that we don't even exist, that the gift that had been pass down thorough the years is not real, that we are just a part of the Never, Never."

Kimberly's grin was ever wider, now.

"You like the part about the Never, Never?" Chance asked Kimberly in a teasing voice, and when she nodded eagerly, he said. "I thought that you would." He shook his head.

"Mr. Sway, don't you think it would be a better world, if there was more romance, and not so much sex and violence." Sparkler smile at him.

"I can't argue with you." They had made it well pass the pond. "How do we find them, Sparkler?" Chance asked.

"Just a little more, then take a left."

And they come to a stop in front of two-story home, hidden by trees, bushes, and flowering plants.

There was a group of people, who had came in for a celebration, there would be more coming later. Kimberly didn't asked, how they was going to know, they just would.

Kimberly and Chance stood in front of Owl, Sparkler's husband. Their family were gather around them.

Owl wanted to know if they were ready?

Kimberly asked, sweetly and every so innocently. "Can I think about it?"

Chance told her. "Just nod your head."

And when she did, Owl started speaking, he said. "May the stars in the sky at night be the only diamonds that you will ever need to feel rich, may your love keep burning as hot as the outback's sun, may the need to love another remain a big of a mystery as the outback, and may the trust that you have put in each other flow as clear and clean, as a spring of water."

It was a beautiful wedding, as beautiful as Owl's words.

They stay to dance a dance or two, but when came to fast and newer songs.

Chance whisper in her ear. "It is the damndest two-steps, that I had ever seen." As they sat on a rug that Sparkler had provided for them.

Chance and Kimberly thank Owl, and his family for the wedding. They stopped by the pond on their way back to the station.

Chance laid out two bed rolls for they to lay on, while she found a part of a fudge chocolate cake with white chocolate icing, a container of hot chocolate and one fill with coffee.

Chance told her what a beautiful bride she was, and how much he loved her, as he let down the top of her sundress and pulled off her panty. They made love by the light of the full moon that was raising as they were married.

Chapter Thirty-Five

IT WAS A FEW DAYS later, they had been legally in Australia, Chance said that they would do again when they were in the states, just to be sure it takes.

Kimberly was putting the finishing touches on her first painting after the operation. She was painting on the patio of Chance's office, while he was going over stuff for the station.

She went in the door, and when he look up, she said. "You can see it, now. But, just remember, it is my first try." She almost said, after the operation, but she caught it in time.

Chance put down what he was doing to walk out on the patio. His breath caught in his throat, as he looked at the painting.

In the middle of it, there was a beautiful, quarter horse filly, full of life, her head was held at attention, her ears pert, listening, and her beautiful body looked as if it could spring in to action any minute. Beside her there was a older gelding, just as beautifully, and just as full of life, maybe he was more calmer about it, though.

They was standing on their own graves. To one side at the bottom, was a healthy, happy little girl, beside that was the same little girl looking sad and feeling bad, above that was were two cars wreck, all around were a town full of people talking.

Above that, there were two couples being married, with horses as the only guests that they needed. Then that was a pickup going off of a cliff in to the ocean, beside that there was a tombstone.

Then was horses with riders gathering cattle in country that was so beautiful country, you could feel its beauty.

And at the bottom on the other was a couple standing in the middle of a happy outback family, as the moon was raising. You could feel that there was so much love between them, that there would never be a need for a game in theirs life together.

Chance put his arms around her, and pulled her back against him. He wanted to say, so this how you deal being doped as a child, being doped to protect the man, who said that he had molested, being doped in High School with the help of the whores who you thought were friends, so you couldn't get out to collage, being in a wreck that took away your talent, your way to make a living for yourself. Watching your only other hope to make a living for yourself being took away from you, not to mention it being a pet. Watching the land that your mama had left you being took away from you for a fancy whore with a title. Watching two of the most beautiful, loving horses that you had tried to kept out of pain, spend the last days of their lives in nothing, but pain.

All so the man that should had help you the most could have a game, and show you all the whores that he had went with. So, this is how you deal with it, he thought.

"Well, what do you think? Would you think it would be worth my time to keep painting, or not?" She turned her face up to him.

"It is a start." He smile.

Kimberly knew that if Kimberly Racks had live, they could had never let her live. They had doped since she was a child, they had believed the man, who said that he had molested her, when he had told them that she was trying to be sexy, and lead him on. A full grown man saying such a thing about a four or five year old child. Or at least, that is what she believed he did, that is why they treated her like that, and protected him.

It would had impossible for her to live, they couldn't have let her. She would always wonder why that tall, good looking, cowboy, law man from Texas hated her, so much, but she knew that he did.

But, it was worst than just him hating her, far more worst.

Chance and Brad had to go back, and get it clear up, of course, Kimberly and Polly was going to help.

They had found out that her mother and father didn't know what was going on, they had been victims themselves, and all of the law, and Government would say, it has just been on too long to do anything about it.

But, they knew it was just cult's law and government, that would say that. They was going back to do what was right. They had to, Chance and Brad couldn't let them get by with it, and neither could Kimberly. She just wanted the operation first.

Then Kimberly Racks Sway would spend the rest of her life in the Never, Never.

THE END

In side this novel, there is autobiography of me, Patti Lou Witter, and my life with Cerebral Palsy, a cult of Nazis and Narcos after me, and everything that they can steal. We will call it, "MY LIFE WITHOUT A CHANCE".

And then there the romance fiction of "WHEN THE GAMES HAD ENDED, HER ONLY CHANCE HAD JUST BEGAN", which is written by me. You will meet Kimberly, who was left disabled by a automobile accident, just as her art career had started, and with a dangerous cult after her, when she hears of a new operation that can give her back the ability to paint, will she take the Chance?